The Intruder

Greg Krehbiel

Crowhill Publishing

Laurel, Maryland

http://www.crowhill.net

Copyright © 2012 Greg Krehbiel

All rights reserved.

ISBN: 0615746950
ISBN-13: 978-0615746951

Crowhill Publishing
http://www.crowhill.net

Crowhill Publishing is the imprint for books by Greg Krehbiel.

CONTENTS

1	The Implant	9
2	Newbie	25
3	No Way Back	37
4	Hanna	49
5	The Study of Ghosts	65
6	Implant Psychosis	79
7	MacKenzie	93
8	Captured	101
9	Inside	109
10	The Network	119
11	Duncan	131
12	The Dragon Lady	143
13	Choosing Sides	153
14	On Watch	165
15	Lenzke	181
16	The Underground	195
17	Hijacked	207
18	Global Trouble	217
19	In The Wilderness	229
20	Alliances	239
21	Endings	247

Author's Note

This book was originally written back in the early 1990s. I tried to get it published by a traditional publishing house, but it was a frustrating process and I let it drop. I had other things to do, like raise a family. These days it's trivially easy to publish a book, so I've been going through my old files to see if any of it's still worth a read. In going through *The Intruder* I was surprised how little I had to update to make it relevant in 2012. The essence of a book shouldn't be the technology, after all, but the story, and this story still resonates. Only time will tell if my technological predictions come true.

Greg Krehbiel

Chapter 1 – The Implant

His whole body tensed when he heard the noise of someone approaching on the forest path. He turned his head to listen. It was only one person. So the target was alone, just as planned.

He waited until the footsteps approached the bend, 20 yards ahead, and then he walked confidently toward his victim. His chest felt constricted. He fought the urge to quicken his pace by concentrating on a steady rhythm of strides against the dirt path. His heart raced, confusing his count. Only a few seconds and the two men would pass. His right hand twitched, eager to reach for his knife, but he resisted the temptation.

It was definitely the right man. He walked casually, suspecting nothing.

Weatherstone was a tall man, and trim, but not muscular or fit. The man with the knife looked down and took a deep, calming breath. It would be all too easy. A part of him wanted to cry out and make it a fair fight. But Weatherstone didn't deserve it.

His mouth went dry.

He glanced up and noticed that Weatherstone was watching the path. The man with the knife grew grim. Few people looked into his eyes these days.

Five steps, maybe less.

"Hi Jeremy," Weatherstone said. His words were more jarring than a gun shot.

Three steps. Don't speak to me.

"I'm so sorry about what happened to Amy."

The attacker's lip curled into a smile. Perfect last words.

One step.

He grabbed his hunting knife. Before Weatherstone could react he thrust his left fist into the man's windpipe, preventing a scream. As the right arm coiled for a strike the left slipped around Weatherstone's neck, grabbed his shoulder and twisted his body, making a clean target of his lower lung.

A sharp thrust buried the five-inch blade. Weatherstone's body tensed and was motionless in shock, then struggled vainly against Jeremy's powerful arms.

It was eerily quiet and death took longer than expected. The slight sound of air escaping through a constricted throat, the shuffle of feet against dirt, the gurgle of air rushing past the knife blade into a pierced lung hardly disturbed the peaceful woods.

Weatherstone continued to struggle, but an iron grip fastened around his mouth. The killer looked into frightened eyes, which seemed to fill all his vision, and then the collage of images began again, just as it always did: the gavel came down in the council courtroom. A mother cried at the verdict. A rush of sights and sensations filled his head. The knife, the bloody body of Weatherstone, the sticky, warm feeling on his hand, the bubbly sound as air rushed into the punctured lung, the dead body in the field, Weatherstone's twitching eye, the knife as he wiped it clean on Weatherstone's pants, another man's eye, twitching, Amy, the knife.

Jeremy sat up suddenly in the train, accidentally bumping the person in the seat next to him. It was a long moment before he realized where he was. The dreams were too real.

"I'm sorry," Jeremy said. "I must have dozed off."

"I'd stay awake, now," the man said. "We're pulling into Washington in a few minutes."

"Thanks," Jeremy said.

He sat up and gazed out of the plate-glass window at the unfamiliar skyline of Washington, D.C. The Advocate had insisted that he come here to see Dr. Berry. She was, he said, the best in the business, and it was important for someone of Jeremy's age to have a skilled physician install the implant.

The train slowed to a stop. As the other passengers got ready to leave, Jeremy slipped his wedding band off and put it on the third finger of his right hand, and as he did he wondered if that meant the same thing in Society as it did back home.

It wasn't the kind of question you asked a stranger on a train.

*   *   *

Jeremy almost gawked at the physician's office. Nothing in the Community had looked like this. The walls were of carved, rich, dark wood, decorated with a kind of living art. They were small pieces, usually nestled in an alcove, or a small recess built into the wall, and each was alive with color and motion. One seemed to be an impressionist representation of a ballerina, performing her dance in a fantastic landscape out of some fairy tale. If he watched it for more than a moment, he could hear the symphony she was enacting. But if he looked away, the sound was gone.

The corner of a book shelf held a miniature string quartet, playing a tune Jeremy vaguely recognized, while the base of a world-shaped lamp seemed to be supported by a comical representation of Atlas, who struggled under his burden. But these were only the ones he liked. Most of art seemed to be a three-dimensional, moving version of what they called "non-representational art" back in school. There were swirling, rippling daggers of green, orange and brown, that resembled nothing more than autumn maple leaves caught in a tornado. And then there was the blue-green, viscous goo, that lapped its slimy waves against a jagged collection of amber crystals.

Everywhere he looked there were new wonders. And yet, the art was normal and home-like compared to the people. They looked normal enough at first glance, until he noticed the eyes. Everyone in the room looked preoccupied, and as he discreetly studied them, he noticed that they shared a blank, dumb stare. They seemed to look off into nowhere with their right eye, while their left twitched and moved rapidly, following some invisible target.

What are they seeing?

Jeremy's few interactions with people from Society had so far reinforced his impression that they weren't all there. Back in the Community, people gave you their whole attention. They looked at you when you spoke, and you could tell that they were listening. The people in Society seemed in a constant state of distraction.

"Jeremy Mitchell?" a man asked. Jeremy looked up and signaled with his hand.

"Come this way, please," the smiling man said, and gestured for him to go through the door.

The contrast between the waiting room and the office area couldn't have been sharper. Everything in the corridor that wasn't gleaming metal was perfectly, brilliantly white. He wondered how they kept the room so immaculate, but then he noticed a small machine slowly working its way across the ceiling.

A cleaning robot, he thought. He had already seen some of the Society robots. They had none in the Community, but when he visited the Advocate to discuss his plans to transfer his citizenship, he had to take a ride in a robotic shuttle.

"Go in this room, take off all your clothes and put on this gown," the young man said, handing Jeremy a green, neatly folded garment. Jeremy assumed the man was a nurse. "I'll be back in a minute to give you a basic physical exam before the doctor arrives."

The examination room was the same brilliant white as the hallway. Jeremy took off the clothes he had purchased from the Advocate the day before and set them on a table in the center of the room. They made a surprisingly small heap -- less than his favorite wool shirt would have, back home. Like almost everything else, Society's fabric technology was way ahead of the simple Community manufacture. His new shirt and pants, tan and blue, respectively, felt more like a swim suit than clothes, but they had managed to keep him warm in the chilly morning air.

The green gown the nurse had given him was likewise thin and insubstantial, as if it had been woven of spider's web, but when he tried to tear a corner, his strong fingers could do no harm.

Something like jealousy welled up in his soul. They couldn't do everything right, after all. There had to be a hidden weakness in this inhuman, technological beehive.

In the corner of the examination room he saw a narrow, unremarkable stall. He wouldn't have recognized it except that a similar compartment in his hotel room had the same style of control panel. It was a shower, and he wondered whether he was supposed to use it before the nurse returned to examine him.

Why not, it only takes a minute, he thought, and stepped in. He closed his eyes while the stall filled with a thick, moist vapor that seemed to seep into his skin.

When his entire body felt dripping wet and deliciously warm, a sudden cool blast of some misty substance came down from above, followed by another blast of warm water, which slowly washed his body clear of the cleansing agent. The liquids were followed by a stream of warm, dry air that dried him more thoroughly than he could have done with a towel.

He had only just wrapped himself in the fairy-threaded gown when the nurse reappeared. He pointed to Jeremy's clothes.

"You can run those through the launderer if you want," he said, opening a door under the table as he spoke.

He'd only worn them for a day. Did they really need to be cleaned so soon?

"I just toss them in?" Jeremy asked. "What about the ..." he paused. He was going to ask about the things in his pocket, but he realized there was nothing there. The Advocate had taken his thumb print, which served for identification until he was registered with an implant. With that provisional account he had set him up with the monetary exchange. Jeremy had insisted on some pocket change -- a few brightly colored coins -- but they weren't necessary, and he had left them in the hotel room. Pocket knives, a necessity for his agricultural life in the Community, were considered uncouth in Society so he had left that in the hotel room as well.

He realized that he had nothing. Just these ephemeral clothes. So he shrugged and tossed them, along with the slight, light-weight shoes, into the launderer.

The nurse asked Jeremy to stand behind a six-foot tall, transparent screen. Jeremy could see through it just as if he was looking out a window, but as the man looked at Jeremy, he seemed to be seeing more than the green gown.

"What is that thing?" Jeremy asked.

"It's a scanner," the young man explained as he worked, adjusting a few knobs on the edges of the screen as he looked up and down, focusing mostly on Jeremy's stomach. "It allows me to see your bones and internal organs, measure your vital signs, check your muscular development and the efficiency of your nervous system."

"So does this mean I won't have to turn my head and cough?" Jeremy asked with a smile.

The man looked confused for a moment, and then laughed.

"Oh, yes," he said, looking straight down at Jeremy's pelvic region, "we don't do it that way anymore. You're perfectly healthy," he said, pushing the screen away and pointing to a chair. Jeremy sat down.

"The doctor will be with you in a moment. You can get dressed as soon as your clothes are done. They should only be a minute." He turned to leave, but just then there was a voice from under the central table.

The clothes are clean. Would like them pressed?

The nurse shook his head.

"No," Jeremy said, and the door to the launderer suddenly fell open, revealing a neatly folded shirt and pants, and a clean pair of shoes.

I've got a lot to get used to, he thought as he dressed.

*   *   *

"Hi, Jeremy, I'm doctor Berry," said a tall, attractive woman in her early forties who breezed into the room as if she owned the place. "Dr. Jenkins' report says you're in perfect health, except for a small amount of sun damage to your skin, but we can fix that very easily," she said with a reassuring smile.

So he was a doctor, not a nurse, Jeremy thought.

"I did a lot of work outside in the Community. We wore sun protection, but I guess it wasn't enough."

"You'll be fine," she said, with a doctor's down-to-business air. "You also have a slight enlargement in the occipital region of your brain. There's nothing wrong with that," she quickly added, "it's just unusual."

"And since you have a clean bill of health, we can install the implant today and start you out with the basic audio function," Dr. Berry continued, taking a large, shiny, hand-held instrument from a drawer in the central table. "This is the basic communications implant," she said as she dropped a pea-sized ball into the steel instrument in her hand. "In Society, a child is fitted with this at the age of one."

Jeremy reflexively raised a hand, signaling her to slow down.

"Can I ask a few questions about the implant, doctor?" he asked.

"Absolutely," Dr. Berry said, lowering the threatening instrument into her lap. "What do you want to know?"

"These implants," he began, "they connect to my brain, right?"

"That's right."

"And there is some kind of interface that allows them to send thoughts into my brain, and it can read my thoughts too?"

"Not quite," the doctor explained. "They give you a kind of input, different from anything you've experienced. You don't feel like someone else is in your head with you, if you're worried about that. It's more like one of your senses -- like a second kind of hearing -- and when we turn on the visual functions, like a second kind of seeing."

Jeremy considered that for a moment. "But how do you know? You've had the implants since you were a child, haven't you?"

"Yes," she said, "but I've done most of my work with people who come in from the outside, or get the implants late in life for some reason, so I know what you can expect to experience."

"Is that why the Advocate recommended that I see you?" Jeremy asked.

"Possibly," she said. "I'm also a damned good doctor." She smiled, and Jeremy began to relax. Dr. Berry's confidence put him at ease.

"The chief reason he sent you to me is that there can be complications when you receive the implant as an adult. I've dealt with those cases before, so I can keep you out of trouble. But that's for me to worry about. Let me run you through the usual process and I think you'll understand," she continued. "You get the communications implant at age one. That's pretty much so your parents can call you for dinner. It's almost like a second ear and a second mouth. It allows you to send and receive audio messages over the hole."

"The 'hole' is Society's communications system?" he asked.

"Yes. Although 'hole' is somewhat of a slang term. It's also called the net, or the CR, for 'communications relay.' *Everything* is interconnected by land lines, electro-magnetic transmissions ... you name it."

Jeremy couldn't name anything. The concept was completely out of his depth. In the Community, only the doctor, the schools and a few engineers had computers, and they had no communications system with the outside world. He knew a little about them from his basic science education, but he was sure Society had things beyond his wildest guesses.

"You said, 'everything.' So, if somebody wanted to," Jeremy asked, "he could find out that I just cleaned my clothes in that launderer?"

"Conceptually, yes. When I said everything, I really meant it. At least all electronic devices. But there's not much need for a launderer to have complete access to the hole," she explained. "And maybe I should explain that. Getting an implant doesn't mean that everybody has access to you at all times. You can turn off the communications relay -- input, output or both -- and you can filter who can reach you. It's not only rude to send unsolicited messages, it's difficult to do, since most people set their implants to ignore them. And you don't have to answer calls, anyway. People can't find you or contact you unless you let them."

"The implant is installed in early childhood," she continued, "but it isn't activated right away. It takes time for a child to learn to use it, so it's turned on in stages. It's not completely turned on until puberty, or thereabouts.

"Until the visual implant is activated, kids learn how to use the hole through terminals, and when the visual functions are turned on they have very restricted use. Their hole communications are supervised by their parents so they can monitor what the kids are doing, and decide when to give them unrestricted access.

"You can see the implant desktop because of a connection with the optic nerve. It looks like a semi-transparent tablet floating in the air," she said, and Jeremy noticed that her eyes suddenly took on that faraway look he'd noticed in the others in the waiting room. She looked back in his direction with her right eye while her left eye wandered slightly. "By sending the right commands -- that's something you'll learn to do -- I can call up anything I want.

"Watch this," she said, and she smiled as her eye wiggled slightly. A moment later Dr. Jenkins' voice came over a speaker somewhere in the room.

"Yes, Dr. Berry?" he said.

"Dr. Jenkins," Dr. Berry said aloud, "would you please bring me a portable workstation?"

"Right away, doctor," came the reply.

Jeremy smiled and shook his head. "So you were able to call him without even saying a word? And did he hear your call, or see it on his visual display?"

"That's a perceptive question," Dr. Berry said. "I sent a pro forma 'call' to Dr. Jenkins. It said, 'call Dr. Berry on the intercom immediately.' That message traveled through the hole to Dr. Jenkins' address. How he retrieved the message would depend on how he had his relay set. It could have been on audio, on visual, or he could have been offline, in which case it would have gone into his mailbox, and it wouldn't have been a very impressive demonstration for you."

Jeremy was beginning to grasp the concepts, but he was certain there was much more to know. *What if there's another Dr. Jenkins?* he wondered. *How does the hole know which person to send the message to?* As Jeremy was thinking, Dr. Jenkins entered the room with a dark gray object, about the size of one of the world atlases he used to study when he was a boy in school, but as thin as a piece of cardboard.

"Hi, Jeremy," he said. "How's it going?"

"Just fine, doc," he replied.

"Good," Dr. Jenkins replied. "Stop by and see me before you leave, okay?"

"Sure," Jeremy said, but he wondered what Dr. Jenkins wanted. The Advocate, who served as the intermediary and legal representative between the Community and Society -- both to make sure the Community was in compliance with all applicable laws, and to represent the Community's interests if they were threatened -- had warned Jeremy to be very cautious. Some of the people in Society might try to take advantage of him, he had said, and others might be unnaturally curious about people from the Community. "Remember the stories about country bumpkins buying the Brooklyn Bridge," he had advised. "You're the country bumpkin."

Dr. Berry took the gray, book-shaped object from Dr. Jenkins and set it on the table, gesturing for Jeremy to stand next to her and observe. She was wearing a perfume with a very distinctive smell. It reminded him of something back home. Something his mother used to grow in the flower garden.

Dr. Berry swept her hand over the flat surface of the workstation and it immediately lit up with a colorful and very complicated display. In the exact center of the screen was a bright dot with the words "Berry Clinic" displayed in dark lettering. Flowing out from the dot in all directions, almost like a child's maze, were lines to other "sites" -- that's what Dr. Berry called them. Each site seemed to have a unique graphic element, and some of them had explanatory text, holographic images, or animations.

"You select a site by touching it," Dr. Berry explained, touching a graphic of a small green cube, which immediately moved to the center of the screen. The network of interconnecting lines and graphics adjusted instantaneously. "This line," she said, pointing to a white line that extended from the green cube to the Berry Clinic site, "traces your path, so you know where you've been."

He studied the screen carefully, and then asked, "So this is what you can see when you have your visual display on? A screen like this just floats in the air in front of you."

"Somewhat like this, although I have my implant set up differently. It is a visual display, like what you see here, with color and graphics, and, of course, with sound."

She reached for the side of the screen and touched a figure that looked like a human ear. A piano concerto began to play very softly. Dr. Berry touched a new graphic element and the display rearranged itself to place the new site at the center of the screen. A voice said, *You have entered the learning station.*

Jeremy noted that the graphic at the center of the screen had the words "learning station" in bright orange letters.

"Now watch the upper left portion of the screen," Dr. Berry said. Jeremy looked at the dark corner, trying hard not to be distracted by all the other things on the screen. Suddenly a voice said, *you have one message,* and a bright red 1 flashed on and off.

"Touch the flashing number, Jeremy," she said.

When he did, the computer voice said, *voice or text mode?* and the display was overlaid with a white box, which contained two smaller boxes. In one was the word "voice," and in the other the word "text."

"You can answer by speaking, or by touching the right button," she said.

Jeremy touched the "voice" button and the computer said, *Message for workstation three. Doctor Berry wishes to see you immediately.*

Jeremy looked away from the display and smiled at her. "Pretty neat."

She smiled and swept her hand over the display again, causing it to go dark.

"I'll make you a deal, Jeremy," she said. "You let me insert the communications implant, and I'll let you borrow this workstation for a while."

"One last question first, please," he said.

Dr. Berry's smile faded a touch, and she looked disappointed. "Okay," she said, and her tone of voice said, "but only one."

"Show me how to turn it off before you put it in."

Her pleasant smile returned and she said, "of course," very softly. She grabbed the hand-held instrument, which reminded Jeremy of an air-powered nail gun, and opened a side compartment, showing Jeremy the pea-sized implant. It was to be implanted just behind his ear, under the skin. To turn it off or on, he needed only to push it with his finger.

"Can I ..." he began, but she interrupted.

"You have to be quiet. Your jaw moves when you talk," she said.

He closed his eyes and tried to think of something else while she put the medical instrument against his head. Jeremy felt a sudden, sharp pain, and then a warm, tingling sensation. He thought he might faint. Everything went black and his head began to swim, but then he recovered. Dr. Berry's hands were holding his head, and she was saying, slowly and gently, "it will pass, just be still. You'll be fine in a moment."

Jeremy closed his eyes and tried to sense any new sounds, or any change at all from a minute ago. Was this thing already connected to his brain? Should he hear something?

"It's not on yet," Dr. Berry said, as if she read his thought. She pushed very gently on the implant with her forefinger and he was suddenly distracted by a new sound.

You have one message from Doctor Berry, a voice said. Or was it a voice? It was like nothing he had ever experienced before. He didn't hear it, but he didn't imagine it either. It wasn't the sound of a thought -- it wasn't that intimate, that much a part of him. It was from outside, in some sense, but inside his own head.

"Has it connected itself to my brain that fast?" he asked.

"No. Some of the connections form almost instantaneously, but others will take a while to develop. The connections with the ear form very quickly, but you probably don't want to know the physiology of it."

Jeremy barely suppressed a shiver as he thought about it. He wasn't squeamish about blood, or operations, but he really didn't want to know about things inside his brain.

"So how do I get the message?" he asked.

"You have to train your implant to receive your own, unique signals," she said. "You're going to have to experiment with different mental images. One of them will trigger the implant. I can't tell you

21

which one, because every brain is different. This training process is a big part of what forms the connections between your brain and the implant.

"Go ahead and try something," she said.

Jeremy tried to picture the old computer he used to see in Dr. Elizah's office back in the Community. He imagined reaching his hand into the computer and pulling out a piece of paper. He was surprised by a voice. The first voice was the computer's voice, which was followed by Dr. Berry's voice, but he wasn't "hearing" it. It was coming through his implant.

From Doctor Berry. Jeremy, will you have dinner with me tonight? I'd like to check on your progress, and maybe you can tell me what it's like to live in a Community.

"Very good," Dr. Berry's real voice said. "You did it on your first try," she said with surprise.

"How did you know I got the message?" Jeremy asked with a suspicious look on his face.

"You're in diagnostic mode for a few days. I can monitor anything you do with your implant."

It seemed a rather rude intrusion, and something that she should have asked his permission for first. *But perhaps that's standard policy,* he thought.

Dr. Berry turned the display unit back on and, after a few practiced taps, the unit showed a document titled, *Learning to Use the MA7 Standard Communications Implant.*

"Take this home and study it," she said with the confident and authoritative tone of a doctor. As she handed him the book-sized display unit, she raised her eyebrows as if to say, "So?"

He suddenly remembered the message.

"Oh, that. I don't have any plans, so yes, I'd like that. Where do you want ..." he began, but she interrupted him.

"Study this until you know how to send a message. Then send me a reply, telling me where you're staying. I'll meet you there at seven o'clock."

Chapter 2 – Newbie

In his excitement about the implant, Jeremy forgot all about Dr. Jenkins and hurried out of the clinic to get back to his hotel room and try his implant. But his hurry was frustrated by his uncertainty on how to get a ride back. Unlike every book he'd ever read about city life, the robotic shuttles didn't respond to a call or a whistle.

"Can I help you?" a man asked, which surprised Jeremy a bit, since most people in Society didn't talk to one another on the street. The man was tall and powerfully built, dressed in a dark blue jumper suit. A web belt around his waist held a night stick, a pistol and several narrow strips of plastic, which Jeremy assumed were a type of handcuff. He was polite and friendly, but Jeremy sensed that this man knew his business.

"Yes, sir," Jeremy replied. "I need to call a taxi."

The policeman looked confused, until Jeremy clarified. "I just came from the doctor," he pointed back up the stairs toward the clinic, "and my implant isn't functional right now."

The policeman nodded. He looked away for a moment, and then back at Jeremy.

"I've called for an automated shuttle. It will be here shortly," the policeman said. "Do you know how to tell it where to go, and how to pay?" Jeremy nodded and the police officer went about his patrol.

No wonder the crime rate is so low, Jeremy thought.

The shuttle arrived within a couple minutes. It was, to his relief, the same model he had ridden from the Advocate's office to the train station. He pressed his right thumb against the identification plate, pressed the "voice-command" button and told the onboard computer to take him to his hotel.

The shuttle was remarkably quiet, which provided some time to read the file from the workstation Dr. Berry loaned him, although he had a hard time settling in to reading. He was still somewhat overwhelmed by the new experiences; riding in a vehicle that was driven by a computer, paying for his fare without cash, working on a computer that was no bigger than a large book, and certainly no heavier, and, the oddest thing, reading about a device that had just been installed in his head, which, at this very moment, was sending out microscopic filaments into the language and visual centers of his brain.

He tried not to think too much about that.

Jeremy read and re-read the sections of the tutorial that explained how his thoughts were transmitted to the implant, and while the concept seemed fairly simple, the technology it required fascinated him. The set-up program first asked him to "type" individual letters simply by thinking them. The implant's calibration routine simultaneously rewrote its internal programming and directed the neural connections to the most responsive areas of the brain. Since no two people responded to the implant exactly alike, the neural connections had to make a custom fit. All this took place in his head while the implant talked him through the whole calibration process.

Once Jeremy got over his initial disorientation, the procedure was simple, and even somewhat relaxing. The implant spoke a random letter and Jeremy pictured the letter in his mind. This process continued for several minutes until the implant recognized the neural responses that corresponded to Jeremy's mental images of each letter.

Once the success rate was acceptable, the implant changed modes. It spoke a word that Jeremy would have to spell by picturing the letters in the proper sequence. All of the words at this stage of the programming were commands: send, open, close, get, discard, save.

Before he was half-way through the second mode, the shuttle-car stopped at the curb in front of his hotel, the Armory and Alehouse. The weather being fine, he decided to take a walk around the block as he worked through the rest of the set-up program. He met with a few rude stares as he tried, sometimes unsuccessfully, to walk and train the implant at the same time, but he realized this was a skill he would have to develop, so he kept at it -- forming images of the basic words as he continued around the block a few times.

Jeremy's biggest adjustment so far was learning to walk the crowded Society streets without speaking to anyone. You simply didn't pass someone in the Community -- even a stranger -- without some form of greeting. But the Advocate had warned him that the opposite was the case in Society.

"Large populations develop different rules for social interaction, Jeremy," he had warned. "If you greeted everyone in Society, you'd never get anywhere."

That was true enough, Jeremy discovered, but it was a difficult mental habit to break, and just one among many. As he thought of that, he realized how intricately learned social custom and personal discomfort bound themselves together. Learning the mores of Society was going to be uncomfortable.

Manners and customs in the Community and Society had evolved on separate tracks over the course of decades. In order to function in this new culture, he would have to study its rules and adopt them, overcoming his discomfort. And that was going to require emotional distance -- an almost stoic indifference to the notions of propriety he learned in the Community.

By four o'clock Jeremy was comfortable enough with the implant to send Dr. Berry a message, but finding out how to send it was harder than he had thought. He discovered how to read the contents of his address box only to find it empty. To send a message to Dr. Berry, he had to provide her unique address to the mail routine. He turned to the workstation for help. There were lots of directories of people and businesses on the net, but they were huge, and he didn't know how to use them.

After 15 minutes of reading the help menu for basic mail service, he found his answer. Dr. Berry had sent him a message while he was at her office, and, fortunately, he hadn't deleted it. He transferred the address from that message into his mail routine's address directory.

To Doctor Berry from Jeremy Mitchell. I am staying at the Armory and Alehouse Inn. I will meet you in the lobby at seven o'clock.

The first rule of etiquette for net-messages, the terminal told him, was to keep it short. *I hope that wasn't too short,* he thought, but was suddenly interrupted by a voice.

From Doctor Berry. You're doing very well, Jeremy. See you at seven.

He almost looked around for her before he realized it was his implant speaking. *Wow, that was fast,* he thought, and began to daydream about the possibilities his implant would open up.

*   *   *

By 5:00, Jeremy had finished the set-up routine for basic audio communications and returned to his hotel room. By 6:45 he forced himself to stop playing with his new toy and take a shower. He was in the lobby, dressed and waiting for Dr. Berry at 6:55. He had almost brought the workstation with him, but since adults in Society had a "workstation" in their left eye, he didn't want to be seen with one -- it would be the rough equivalent of carrying a teddy bear, he reckoned, so he left it behind.

To pass the time he decided to check the restaurant's menu using his implant. To access the menu he had to address a message with the right syntax to the hotel's restaurant. It would send him an automated voice recording of the day's choices, along with a "printed" list, which required the implant's visual functions to read.

To Armory and Alehouse pub, **get** *menu,* he sent, putting the 'command' accent on 'get.'

As the recording was just finishing the list of appetizers, Jeremy noticed Dr. Berry entering the lobby.

"Hi, Jeremy," she said. "Did you get a table?"

"Oh, no," he apologized. "I didn't think of it."

"Then let's get one," she said and walked over to a small table near a large, plate-glass window that looked out onto the street. It had just begun to rain, and the pedestrians were adjusting their collars. Jeremy watched, wondering what technological marvel Society had invented to keep your head dry, and wasn't disappointed. He couldn't see any physical barrier, but it was obvious that the rain no longer fell on the people. It simply fell in a different direction, somehow diverted by the device in the collar.

So what's the big deal about getting wet, he thought, noting another cultural difference between Society and the Community. Society seemed so sterile -- so insulated from the real world.

As Jeremy watched the unnaturally dry pedestrians walking through the rain, Dr. Berry began to chat about the food at the hotel.

"Since you seem to know the territory, why don't you order for both of us," he suggested, but she shook her head.

"No, let me show you how. Have you learned the 'accept' command?"

"I've calibrated it, but I haven't used it yet," Jeremy said, but he wasn't sure he liked the suggestion. The 'accept' command allowed another person, usually a parent, to use a secure link to issue commands through someone else's implant. It was usually done as a training exercise. When Jeremy had read about it, it scared him. It was bad enough to have all those microfilaments boring holes in his brain, but allowing someone else to send commands through them seemed like too much of an invasion of privacy.

I don't want her to think she has to mother me, he thought.

Besides, he liked his privacy. If he gave Dr. Berry access to his implant, would she be able to read his thoughts?

He decided to try it once. He could always sever the link.

"I'm ready. Do I issue the command now?" he asked.

Dr. Berry raised an eyebrow in surprise. "You're very trusting," she said. "But no, you don't issue a blanket 'accept' command. There are predators out there, you know." Jeremy wondered what that meant, but she continued. "I will send an 'order message' to you, and you will reply with an 'accept' command. It's called an 'order message' because this function is usually used by parents, the police and the military. You can 'accept' it, 'discard' it, 'file' it, and maybe one or two other things I've forgotten."

Jeremy nodded. "Go ahead," he said, and once again, Dr. Berry raised her eyebrows in surprise at his trust.

A moment later he heard her familiar voice, mediated by his implant.

From Doctor Berry. **Order***, content unspecified.*

Without a second's delay, Jeremy replied.

Accept.

Again, her voice echoed in his mind. It was eerie to hear her speaking while her mouth was still.

I'm touched that you trust me so completely, but you should never accept an unspecified order. I mentioned predators, right? There are unscrupulous people who monitor the net, just waiting for someone to do something like that. They could transfer your money to their account, or send messages in your name. But let's continue.

Jeremy watched her face as her voice spoke inside his head, and he wondered how far inside she really was. Could she hear his thoughts?

From Table Twelve, ...

the message came through as Dr. Berry pointed to the small wooden block in the center of the table with the number 12 printed on it,

... to the Armory and Alehouse Pub, Attention Head Waiter, Two adult dinners.

It was a strange sensation. He could hear Dr. Berry's voice in his mind, but he had the feeling that he was sending the message.

Both as follows. Zinfandel. Whole wheat bread. Salad with vinegar and oil. Baked red snapper and mixed vegetables. Carrot cake and Coffee. End.

Jeremy looked at the doctor and she nodded. He sent the command 'break,' and she nodded again. The connection was severed.

"And no, Jeremy, I couldn't read your thoughts while the command mode was on," Dr. Berry said.

But then how did you know I was ...

She began to laugh. "Everyone wonders that, and it's an old joke," she said.

Jeremy shook his head. "One thing I was wondering. Why do I hear messages from you in your voice? Shouldn't it be in the computer's voice?"

"You can set up your mail routine to send messages with your own voice characteristics. All you have to do is talk into an audio-equipped workstation. Of course you can set your implant to read messages anyway you like. But I like to send personal messages in my own voice and business messages in a simulated 'computer' voice."

"Will the workstation you loaned me do that?"

She nodded.

"Can I buy one of those workstations to use until I get the visual functions turned on? I'd like to start thinking about a job."

She shook her head. "Don't worry about returning the workstation. You can hold on to that until we get you set up with your implant. But about a job, I have another option for you."

She explained that a local university had a grant program that would pay him a modest salary on a short-term basis if he agreed to discuss his experiences in the Community with the students and faculty in its sociology and psychology departments. The grant was enough to provide for his needs, with a little to spare, and it would give him the time he needed to get accustomed to the implant.

"Am I under any obligations to them?" he asked.

"What do you mean?"

"Do I have to tell them whatever they want to know?"

"Heavens no," she said. "If you're uncooperative, they might cancel the agreement, but it's not that big a deal. And if you find that you don't like it, you can back out any time you like."

Jeremy agreed to give it a try, and Dr. Berry said she would set it up for him.

The food arrived a minute later and conversation turned to lighter matters. The red snapper was the best fish Jeremy had ever eaten. The land-locked Community in which he had spent his entire life had to content itself with stream and pond fish. Jeremy had always thought a fresh trout was the best thing in the world until he tasted the snapper. The waiter noticed how much he enjoyed the fish and brought him a second helping.

Dr. Berry seemed to walk a tightrope in her comments about Society and the Community. On the one hand, she clearly had a message she wanted to get across, but she also seemed hesitant, as if she feared how Jeremy would react to the information. What she had to say certainly took Jeremy by surprise, since it was contrary to everything he'd learned about Society in the Community. But after all, Jeremy reasoned, the two cultures had diverged about 50 years ago, with little or no exchange of information, so there were bound to be differences.

The speculation in the Community was that Society had continued to follow the same trend it had been on when the Community separated itself -- a trend toward government control and a lack of personal privacy.

"This is incredible," Jeremy said after a few minutes of Dr. Berry's discourse. "Do you mean that Society hasn't been trying to get the Communities back into the fold all this time?"

"No, of course not. The Communities have the right to do as they please," Dr. Berry said with conviction in her voice.

Jeremy shook his head, either in disbelief or amazement. He had learned a very different history. When the Communities separated themselves from Society shortly after the turn of the last century, they were sure it was only a matter of time before a conflict developed. The communities had always assumed that after the government assumed complete control of Society, they would turn their eyes toward the communities. Some law would be passed — probably in the name of public security -- that would make the communities illegal, and they would be forcibly disbanded. It was the inevitable consequence of their different ideologies, and the Community would have no ability to fight back. It had a limited police force and no military.

"That may have been true of the old government, back before the riots," Dr. Berry explained, "but Society is completely non-interventionist now. If people want to live in their own world, with their own rules, they're welcome to it. Why should anybody else care?" She shrugged for emphasis, but Jeremy was still trying to take it all in.

"Then why did the Advocate tell us those things?" he said. "That virtually every session of the legislature had a new, threatening bill, and that the few representatives who were sympathetic to the Communities continued to block passage. Did he lie to us?"

Dr. Berry looked troubled. "I don t know why he would say that, but I do know that some sociologists have argued that the Communities require a belief in an external threat to retain their cohesion. I'm just guessing here, but perhaps he thought it was a lie told for your own good."

Jeremy expected surprises in Society. He knew the adjustment wasn't going to be easy. But this turned his whole world upside down. Was everything he'd learned as a boy a lie?

Or ... no. After all, Dr. Berry grew up in Society. She was, in fact, part of its machinery. Didn't Society depend on the implants, and wasn't she the leading specialist in that field? The government had to have its line – it's story. After all, they weren't going to tell their people that they were oppressive dictators.

So maybe this was all just a part of the Big Lie. Dr. Berry was feeding him Society propaganda -- and maybe she even believed it.

How could he know? He'd been raised to believe that the Advocate was a good and honest man who worked tirelessly for the interests of the Community. He'd always been told that the Society government was itching to make a complete takeover, once they had everything under control.

But for now, he'd play along and take Dr. Berry's story at face value. He could think it all through later.

He shook his head in disgust and said, "The Advocate is an official of both our governments. Are people allowed to lie like that in Society?"

"What's to prevent them?" she replied with a grin.

If he was lying, then I guess he fooled our government as well, he thought.

"I had always thought the government in Society watched everything you did. We have old records of how the government would take away people's land, or fine them heavily just because they cut down a tree, or dumped sand in a ditch. Is that all wrong too?"

"No, those things really happened, and that's part of the reason there were riots. But things have changed since then. Maybe you need to read up on your history."

Society history, he thought with disgust. *Why should I believe it?*

He sat still for a moment, lost in thought, and somewhat troubled. The next thing he knew he heard a sound beside him and noticed that the waiter had arrived with a second bottle of wine, which reminded him of a lesson from school. They were studying ancient wisdom literature, and the professor was discussing Solomon's quest to understand how and why the world worked the way it did, and how the effort ended in futility. We can't understand the ways of God, but we can't allow that to ruin life. Instead, men should rejoice in the good they have, enjoy what they can out of life, and leave the rest to God.

Let your garments be white, and let your goblet be filled with wine, he remembered.

He wasn't going to solve this right here, over dinner, so he might as well enjoy himself. He forced a smile and shrugged.

"I've got a lot to learn, I guess."

Dr. Berry sensed his change in mood and seemed more than willing to change the topic, so she asked him about the small things of life in the Community. Jeremy spent the next hour amusing her with stories about the constant presence of livestock, and the trouble the animals caused, the fascination with games of skill, and the tournaments that lasted much of the summer, the agricultural cycle, and the feasts and merry-making in Spring and Fall.

As the waiter cleared away the desert dishes, Dr. Berry brought them back to the issue of the implant. "Where did you leave the terminal I loaned you?"

"Oh, it's in my room. Was I supposed to bring it?"

"It's okay. We can go get it. I need to show you a thing or two."

On the elevator ride to Jeremy's room Dr. Berry questioned him about his implant operations -- how the implant voice sounded, whether there was any ringing, or pain, or other difficulties, and how he had done with the training exercises.

"No trouble," he said as he opened his hotel-room door by pressing his thumb against the security lock. "It was very easy."

Isn't it designed for children, after all?

The workstation lay where he'd left it on the desk in the sitting room that adjoined his bedroom. There was only one chair, so he stood while Dr. Berry called up several libraries he could use to study recent world history. She placed electronic markers in each location and explained the search functions, and then entered a series of questions about the political fall-out of the riots. She fed all the relevant information into a self-generating documentary program.

"This will make a useful little history lesson for you, so you can see what's been happening in Society since your Community broke away. You can watch this, or even read the files yourself if you like."

"Great," he said with a smile, but he still wondered how much of it was just Society propaganda.

Chapter 3 – No Way Back

Jeremy intended to take a brief look at the documentary and then head to sleep. He was always an early riser. But four hours past his usual bed-time he was still reading, watching video coverage of key events, and submitting new questions to the history library. The sheer magnitude of information overwhelmed him. Either Dr. Berry had told him the truth, or someone had invested a lot of time and effort in an incredible piece of propaganda.

In addition to the much-needed history lesson, Jeremy came away from his evening's study with an intense desire to get his visual implant activated. The terminal was amazing, and the idea that he could have all the same functions just a glance away was overpoweringly desirable.

As he thought about the appeal of the implant, Jeremy thought back on his simple life in the Community, where the most technology he'd see on an average day was a tractor. Back then he couldn't have long for what he didn't know about, but he wondered how he would have reacted if the Jeremy back then -- in the technologically unsophisticated Community -- had learned about the implants. He suspected the knowledge would have gnawed at him, making simple farm life very difficult.

Suddenly he remembered an incident from his youth. He was laying in bed, not quite asleep, when he heard his parents bustle around the house. His father was packing a few essentials and hurrying off to the north of the Community's territory. Jeremy listened to their hushed conversations -- he knew something important was happening -- but he couldn't make any of it out. Something inside of him longed to be in on the secret. He assumed that his father and mother were planning something important, or getting ready for something exciting, and he didn't want to be left out.

Later he discovered that an aircraft had crashed into the mountains. It was winter, and there was snow and high winds. His father and several other men found the survivors and kept them alive until a rescue team from Society arrived. When he heard what had happened, he ached for the missed opportunity.

Things like that were bound to happen, Jeremy knew, and sooner or later he might have found out about the implants, and maybe even the truth about Society. In fact, he began to wonder how much his father knew, or others in the Community. Might they have known, or suspected the truth?

Solomon's wisdom came back to mind. That was all water under the bridge now. His life in the Community was behind him, for good or ill, and he needed to get started on his new life. That meant moving forward with the implant and getting the visual functions turned on. Everything in Society assumed you had an implant, and the sooner he got his up and running, the sooner he would be able to get on with things.

And besides, he thought, *doctors always exaggerate risks.*

Dr. Berry had warned him that a small percentage of newbies develop a very dangerous illness called implant psychosis. Their brains aren't able to adjust to the implant and they become delusional and paranoid. The safest course was to introduce the implant slowly, under constant supervision.

Jeremy was unconcerned. He was still at that age where calamity always seemed to happen to other people. After all, he hadn't killed himself when he jumped his bike over Miller's canyon; he never got gored playing rough with the goats; studying at night under his cheap, desk-top lamp hadn't ruined his eyes; and getting the implants wasn't going to make him crazy. It was just another in a series of exaggerated risks.

He laughed to himself as he recalled the string of warnings, and his resolution was set. He would have the visual functions activated as soon as possible. He sent a message to Dr. Berry's office to set up an appointment and then turned his attention back to the terminal.

*   *   *

Later that night, Jeremy groaned and rolled over on the hotel bed. The 8th-floor window was open and the curtains were drawn, revealing Jeremy's pocket knife, resting on the sill next to the screws that had held the window shut. The cool spring breezes blew away the processed air of the hotel.

He was dreaming of a spring day a year ago. He had awakened in Amy's arms. The sun was shining through the white curtains of their bedroom, just recently furnished by Jeremy's and Amy's families. It was the most peaceful morning Jeremy had ever known. There was no work to do, no breakfast to cook, in fact, nothing to think about but the joy of being with his new bride. He caressed her shoulder and she awoke with a sigh.

Community custom exempted newlyweds from all work for a full month. Neighbors, family and friends provided food and drink while the newlywed's devoted themselves to learning all about each other.

As far as Jeremy was concerned, it was the best bargain he was ever likely to make.

*   *   *

"Jeremy, I think you're rushing things," Dr. Berry said. "I really think you should wait a week or two before getting the visual functions turned on," she said.

"What difference is a week or two going to make?" he asked, but his tone of voice said that he was sure of the answer.

Dr. Berry frowned slightly and shrugged. "Honestly, I can't say it will make any difference at all, but there are some neurologists who believe that the longer you let the brain get used to the implant's neural connections, the better chance you'll have of not rejecting the visual functions. But," she said as she saw the question forming on his lips, "it's just a theory. There's no solid evidence to support it, and there's really no reason why I can't turn on the visual functions today. In fact, if you really want it, I'm not allowed to refuse you.

"But I want to remind you of the danger of implant psychosis," she continued. "It's not something you want to fool around with, Jeremy. It is rare. Very rare, thank God, but it's a nasty business.

"If you start to get the symptoms, I want you to tell me immediately. *Immediately*, okay?" she stressed. "If we catch it in time, we can reverse it, but that's only before the patient becomes delusional. Then it's too late. So as soon as you notice anything odd in your vision you tell me. If you do get implant psychosis," she said in a stern voice, suddenly changing from caring doctor to public health official, "I'll have to have you restrained and probably drugged for the rest of your life. You'll be functional, in a minimal sort of way, but you'll be slow and dopey."

Jeremy's confidence wavered for a moment, but he set his jaw and looked Dr. Berry in the eye.

"I'm ready. Let's do it. What do I need to do?"

Dr. Berry sighed. "Just wait here, I'll be back," she said.

*   *   *

A minute later Dr. Berry returned pushing a small cart with a strange device on top. It reminded Jeremy of the eye-examining station Dr. Elizah had back in the Community, except this one was horizontal. The patient laid his head down, face first. A mask, like a ventilator, was in the center, and a complicated eye piece was at the top left, just below the padded, curved bar on which, Jeremy assumed, his forehead was to rest. On the left side, protruding up a few inches to about temple level, was an instrument similar to the hand-held device Dr. Berry had used to insert the audio implant.

"I thought the thing was already in my head and you just flipped a switch to start it," he said, trying not to sound afraid of the evil-looking device. "What's all this for?" he asked.

"We can just 'flip a switch' after the implant has been installed for several months, like it is with most people. If you want the visual functions now, we're going to have to help things along, which means manually installing some of the microfilaments." The look on her face told Jeremy this was supposed to scare him; that she wanted him to back out. "You can still wait, you know."

It can't be that bad, he thought. "So what do I do?" he asked, expecting that he was just supposed to lay his face down on the device and get zapped, like the day before. Dr. Berry raised her eyebrows and shook her head slightly.

"This procedure is a little more involved," she said. "We knock you out for a few minutes and strap you into this thing -- tight, so you won't move. It injects a series of microfilaments through the implant and into your optic nerve and the vision centers of your brain. The microfilaments are coated with thorohydrizine, which speeds up the connection time. By the time you wake up, they're pretty well connected.

"Are you ready?" she asked. Jeremy nodded.

"Place your forehead on the top bar and your chin on the bottom. Make sure the ventilator fits snugly around your face and breathe deeply."

Jeremy glanced at Dr. Berry and then did as he was told. There was no odor to the knock-out gas he knew he was inhaling, and he didn't even notice getting sleepy before he passed out.

*   *   *

When he came to he had a dull pain in his temple and his head was swimming. He tried to pull himself up but a hand restrained him.

"Don't try to move yet," a female voice explained. "In a minute you can lie on your back. After your head clears, Dr. Berry will give you your first implant lesson."

Jeremy felt nauseated and didn't want to speak. He relaxed against the pads on the implanting device and opened his eyes, expecting to see a wicked piece of medical equipment inches from his face, but he saw nothing at all.

"I can't see," he said, hoping he wouldn't throw up, and suddenly afraid that he had gone blind.

"The room is dark," the woman said. "Don't worry, you're fine. The microfilaments are all in place, but your eye will be sensitive to light for about an hour. Here," she said, placing one hand behind his head and another on his shoulder, "let's try to sit you up very gently, okay?"

He complied, again feeling a rush of dizziness and nausea, but it cleared soon enough. The nurse gently lowered him onto his back.

"Rest here a few minutes. I'll be back to check on you soon."

He heard a soft click and noticed a pale green light around the floor boards -- just enough for the nurse to see her way out. He closed his eyes and thought about nothing, wandering somewhere between consciousness and unconsciousness.

*   *   *

"How do you feel?" Dr. Berry's voice broke the silence. Jeremy wasn't certain if he had been sleeping or not.

"When I lay still I feel okay, except for a dull ache on the left side. I'm not sure if I should try to sit up."

His youthful confidence was subdued now. He didn't feel like the brash young man who wanted to charge ahead. He felt like the sick school boy who wants to be pampered.

"Don't sit up yet. Let's see how you do with light first. Are your eyes open?"

"Yes."

"Tell me if they begin to hurt," she said as she slowly raised the intensity of the ceiling lights. Jeremy looked steadily at the instrument table against the side wall. He remembered that a few of the handles were different colors, and he wanted to watch them change from shades of gray in the darkness to their natural colors as the light increased, but he never got that far.

"Ah, that's beginning to hurt," he said when it was just light enough for the white walls of the room to appear a dull gray.

"That's good. Try to sit up now, slowly, and see how you feel."

He took a deep breath and cautiously sat up, keeping his hands ready to catch himself if he fainted.

"I'm okay. Better than I thought," he said. "Does everybody go through this when they get these things?"

"Not everybody does it this way, remember? If you're patient, and let the implant secrete the microfilaments at its normal rate, there's no discomfort at all.

"Are you ready to start with some basic lessons?" she asked.

Jeremy nodded and then shook his head, confused.

"What is it?" she asked.

"Your lips are red."

Dr. Berry looked confused by the comment.

"You can't see colors in the dark. You stopped turning up the lights when everything was still black and white, but I can see colors now." He wondered if the implants had altered his vision.

Laughter and surprise touched the corners of Dr. Berry's eyes.

"That's because I didn't stop turning up the lights. I just set them on a more gradual increase."

Jeremy nodded and laughed at himself. "Okay, I'll stop playing junior detective."

Dr. Berry reached for his temple with her index finger. He noticed a subtle, fresh, floral scent as her arm passed by.

"Okay, this is the start-up switch and the emergency off button," she said as she rubbed her finger around the circumference of a lentil-sized disk. "Put your hand here so you can feel it." He did, and could just feel it under his skin.

Dr. Berry pushed his finger down, compressing the switch. There was a sudden buzz in his head, followed by a moment of dizziness and confusion while Dr. Berry's hands gently held his head still.

"It's alright," she said, much as she had the other day. "Just relax. Everything's fine. It'll pass."

The sensations that filled his head when the implant turned on were like nothing he had experienced before. It felt as if he were extremely drunk, and yet more wide-awake and alert than he had ever been. His head swam, but he felt as if all his senses were more keen, more acutely aware of everything they felt. Nothing in his line of sight changed, but he was sure he could discern more colors and detail in everything he saw. Even the skin of Dr. Berry's arm seemed to hide a myriad of hues and shades that he had never experienced before, and every pore and hair on her skin was sharply in focus.

But almost as suddenly as it began, the altered vision faded and colors returned to normal. The sensation was not unlike a rush of adrenaline, which sharpened the senses for a time, but quickly faded. He wondered if he had really seen those things, or if it was a trick of the implant. He was tempted to think that for a moment he saw things as they really were, and was now disappointed that his normal vision had returned.

As the odd sensations faded, he noticed something that looked exactly like the screen of Dr. Berry's workstation floating in the air about two feet in front of him. He reached out to touch it, and then stopped, realizing it was an image from the implant.

"So you can see it," Dr. Berry said. "Good. I'm going to ask you a series of questions about what you see. Are you ready?"

Jeremy nodded.

"Is it moving or still?" she asked.

"Still up and down, jiggling slightly left to right."

"You'll learn to control that. Is it translucent or opaque?"

"I'm not, ... I think it's translucent, but it changes. When I try to look at it, it seems opaque, but I can lock straight through it if I try."

"Very good. Can you read the date and time in the upper right-hand corner?"

"Barely. Eleven ten a.m. June 5th, 2065, I think."

"Very good. Now I'm going to lead you through some of the set-up programs, but that means I need to be able to see what you're seeing, or rather, what you're supposed to be seeing."

She picked up a portable terminal from the cart that held the implanting device and powered it up. Jeremy watched the screen as Dr. Berry keyed in a series of commands. The screen on the terminal changed to match what he was seeing in his own, internal monitor. It was odd to see both screens at the same time.

"First, Jeremy, you need to send the 'cursor' command."

He hadn't used that one, but the procedure was simple enough. He had to think the word with the proper command accent. He had chosen for his command accent his father's tone of voice when he was calling Jeremy, or one of the animals, in from the fields. His voice had a characteristic ring to it, and Jeremy could imagine it easily, but, as with so many other command words, it was a little hard to imagine his father yelling 'cursor,' so he pretended it was the name of one of the goats.

Immediately a bright orange dot with a subtle, dim cross-hair appeared in the center of both screens -- the one in his left eye and the one on the terminal. He tried to move it with his eyes and it shot to the left of the screen. He tried to compensate and it continued to jump around, out of control.

"That's the idea. Practice that for a while. I'm going to get us both a glass of water. You're supposed to drink a lot of fluids for the next 24 hours while the implant tries to talk to your brain."

*   *   *

The nausea and discomfort from the implant faded quickly as

Jeremy continued the hour-long training session. He finished the introductory lesson and learned how to find the remaining five lessons in the self-tutor program, which he could finish on his own time. Dr. Berry was about to usher him out the door, but he had one more question.

"How do I sever the link with that terminal over there?" It still displayed an exact replica of what he saw on his implant, and he found it disconcerting to be monitored like that. People in the Community were instinctively resistant to the idea of submitting to someone else's supervision and care.

"What are you planning on watching tonight, Mr. Mitchell, that you don't want your doctor to see?"

"That's really not the point, is it?" he asked, becoming slightly suspicious. "Am I supposed to leave that connection on?"

"Why don't you leave it on for a little while. It's my job to monitor how well you adapt to the implant, especially for these first few days. I'll check in on you from time to time today, but you can cut it off before you go to sleep. You can shut off everything with 'clear all,' but the right way to do it is to place the connection in your active window and send 'discard.' You'll still be in diagnostic mode with me, but I won't be able to see everything you're doing."

He didn't like being in diagnostic mode either, but he didn't want to push things too far. He nodded his assent, smiled at Dr. Berry and went to say good-bye to talk to Dr. Jenkins. He'd neglected to see him last time, as he'd asked, and wanted to make it up. Besides, in the Community you never left until you said goodbye to everyone you knew.

*   *   *

"Occasional dizziness is an understatement," Jeremy said aloud to no one in particular as he walked down the five brick stairs from the landing of Dr. Berry's office to the concrete sidewalk. His mental focus on the implant training lessons had taken his attention away from his discomfort, but now that he was back on the street, it was returning.

He gripped the black, wrought-iron handrail and steadied himself, taking a few breaths to clear his head. He tried looking around, up and down the street, afraid that even casual head movements might bring the nausea back.

Satisfied that he was okay for the moment, he started walking carefully south, towards the Armory and Alehouse, which was ten blocks away. The dull throb in his left temple made him wonder if he should get a taxi, as Dr. Jenkins had almost insisted.

I'll just go slow.

But his short interview with Dr. Jenkins had left him a few things to think about. He seemed unnaturally curious about Jeremy's case, and asked him to report anything unusual.

Either implant psychosis is more common than Dr. Berry has led on, or there's something else strange about me.

He suddenly remembered Dr. Berry's comment that he had a slightly enlarged occipital region. Might that be a cause for concern?

A sudden jab of pain took his attention back to his implant. Dr. Jenkins told him that the best medicine for the pain was going through the training exercises. He had a theory, he told Jeremy, that using the very portions of the brain that were affected by the implant ameliorated the side effects.

Jeremy was relieved to discover that all the commands he had learned for the audio implants were subsumed into the functions of the visual implant, but they were magnified. When he put the command accent on 'send,' a blank screen, like a sheet of note paper, appeared directly ahead at about chest level. As he thought a message, the words typed across the page. But the entire image was translucent, as if the page were a lightly frosted glass and the letters were light streaks of charcoal. If he concentrated on the paper, it would become more substantial, almost blocking his vision of the things beyond, but never quite, since the images from the implant were only in one eye. The paper seemed opaque when he closed his right eye and concentrated on it, but he couldn't be certain, for as soon as he tried to see the things behind the paper the image would fade. The implant knew what he was looking at and automatically adjusted its imaging system to compensate.

"Hey mister, would you mind standing someplace else," a voice said.

Jeremy looked up and realized he was standing in loading zone. He had no idea how long he had been there, looking at one thing or another with one or both eyes. He gave the driver a sheepish grin and moved along.

*   *   *

He walked for hours, finding it easier and easier as the day went on. As he became more proficient with the cursor, he began to follow links all over the hole. He could hardly believe how much information was out there.

In the late afternoon he found a library of old movies. Some of them were things he had watched with his parents, and since the copyright had expired, they were available free of charge. He sat on a park bench and watched "To Catch a Thief."

Chapter 4 – Hanna

"Where's my appetite?" Jeremy said to the ceiling as he lay in bed at 7:30 -- an uncharacteristically late hour for him to rise. In the Community he would have been up by 5:30 to see to his father's goats before heading off to work. But he wasn't expected at the university until 10:00 -- so late in the day, he thought -- and he didn't have much to do until then.

Well, I guess I better eat, he decided as he rolled out of bed and made his way toward the shower. In five minutes he was washed, dressed and out the door. He left the Armory and Alehouse and headed south on North Capital Street to a restaurant he had seen on one of his walks. It looked clean, popular and cheap, and that was what he wanted. After a few minutes he spied the telltale emblem -- two yellow curved structures that formed an 'm.' It almost smelled like breakfast at his dad's house, just a little more sanitized.

The rush-hour traffic had stacked the street three deep with hovercars in both the north-bound and south-bound lanes. Jeremy stared for a few minutes at the odd site. One row of vehicles remained at ground level, the next lined up at 15 and the next 30 feet off the ground. Each row formed a perfect line, as if the cars were riding on an invisible road. Most of the windows were dark, but every once in a while Jeremy could see a rider through the window, as if he was in his own little world, drinking a cup of coffee or just staring -- probably reading the news on his implant, Jeremy thought -- or napping. The vehicles passed each other like cogs in a huge machine, and not at all like people.

Horses are better than hovercars, Jeremy thought. At least you could smell the air and see the world and talk to your neighbor when you were on the back of a horse. The stark contrast between riding Billy, his Palomino, and sitting in one of these automated contraptions seemed like an icon of the reason the Community broke off from

Society. It wasn't as if the Community couldn't have built a hovercar --
it had the scientific knowledge and the mechanical capability -- it just
wasn't the way people in the Community chose to live. They had
machines for some jobs, but for most things, horses or other animals
were simply better; more personal, more natural, more humanizing.
You couldn't be kind to a hovercar, or care how it felt on a cold
winter's day. Jeremy was sure the lack of horses had a darkening effect
on the collective mind of Society.

Technology simply wasn't the answer to everything. The
Community knew that; Society didn't. In Society, technology was the
unquestioned means to achieve any goal. More than that, technology
often separated goals from their natural means. If someone in Society
was concerned about his weight, he ate specially engineered diet food.
In the Community, he just ate less, or he lived with being fat. No-
alcohol beer, caffeine-free coffee, fake sugar and fat, contraception --
they were all Society's efforts to strip the undesired elements from the
natural world. The Community hadn't rejected that principle *per se* --
they used suntan lotion to protect their skin -- it just wasn't the way
they saw life. Life was a matter of participating with the natural order --
cultivating it and training it -- not cheating it, or breaking it into its
parts and rearranging it.

As he thought about these things, walking itself became a kind of
sacrament to Jeremy. It was his affirmation of Community values -- of
living life the way it ought to be lived -- in the midst of hovercars.

He also realized that his walks were getting a little easier. He was
less distracted by the implant, but there were still a few things to get
used to. Ghost images, for example. Sometimes, especially on his first
day, noise in the communications signal came through the implant as
strange, black blobs. As his brain learned to communicate with the
implant, and since the implant was connected to his optic nerve, the
"noise" was visible. The first time he saw one he thought it was a huge
bird. Dr. Berry assured him that they were common and would go
away after a while.

As Jeremy passed the huge yellow m,' he wondered what he was supposed to do to get some food. He entered slowly and looked around, trying to take in as much as possible. To his relief, there was a printed menu on the wall near the kitchen. He supposed he could have ordered ahead of time with his implant, but he wasn't sure how all that worked yet. Besides, he was in no hurry, and he craved some kind of human interaction, even if it was just placing an order.

He decided on coffee, juice and a muffin, and he chose to pay with cash: he didn't need it anymore, and he wanted to use up what he had left. When Jeremy offered his coins, the attendant smiled at the novelty, and Jeremy noticed that several other people in the restaurant watched as he handed over the three blue disks. The attendant looked at them carefully, as if he hadn't seen any for a long time, and then handed back two yellows and one red. Jeremy took his change and his food and sat down, ignoring the eyes that followed him to his seat. He looked up, on pretense of watching the passers-by through the window, but intending to cow some of the more curious spectators into minding their own business.

The packaging on his breakfast had him fooled, but he wasn't willing to fumble with the coffee while half the restaurant was watching him out of the corner of their eye, so he started with the juice, which was more straight-forward. When he was confident that interest in his visit had worn thin, he began to experiment with the white plastic lid on the coffee cup. He wasn't getting anywhere.

"Hi. Can I help?" a friendly female voice interrupted.

Jeremy looked up to see a slightly bedraggled but cheerful-looking girl -- or was she a woman? -- smiling at him. He motioned to the chair opposite the small table. "Please, join me," he said, craving some company. Besides, she was pretty, if a little young. Jeremy still hadn't met many people in Society.

"Thanks," she said, and took the coffee cup out of his hand, tilting it so the cap faced him. "You do it like this," she said as she held the bottom steady and twisted the top in a counter-clockwise direction. Steam poured out of a half-inch hole on one side as she handed him the opened cup.

"I need a cup this morning," Jeremy said. "Thank you. And by the way," he continued after a moment's pause, "my name is Jeremy."

"Hi Jeremy. I'm Hanna," she said, and her voice told him that she was not a girl, but a young woman. It was not the pitch of her voice, which sounded as young as she looked, but something else; her inflection, perhaps, or something behind her eyes. Or maybe it was the way she drank from her gigantic cup of coffee. It was the relentless assault of someone long-accustomed to the need for a morning jump-start.

"Nothing else to eat, Hanna?" Jeremy asked. "Would you like some of my muffin?" As soon as he said it he wondered if that was a little too odd an offer to make to a stranger, but she seemed to take it in stride.

She smiled at him and shrugged. "Maybe just a small piece, for fellowship," she said, and reached across the table, taking a pinch off the side and popping it into her mouth.

"I don't usually eat breakfast," she said. "I just study, or sleep."

Jeremy noticed a book in her coat pocket, and suddenly realized he hadn't seen one since he'd come to Society. "You're a student?" he asked between bites. "Where do you go to school?"

"Right here at the Capitol University," she said, pointing vaguely to her left. "I'm studying anthropology." After a pause she added, "Pretty useless thing to study, huh?"

"I wouldn't know," Jeremy said quickly, but he didn't want to get into that, so he continued. "You wouldn't happen to have a 10:00 lab in sociology in the Powell Building, would you?"

Hanna's eyes lit up with surprise. "As a matter of fact, I don't. But I have a friend in that class. Are you a guest lecturer or something?"

Jeremy laughed. "Nothing so grand. But I'm supposed to be there today." He looked up and studied Hanna's eyes for a moment. He noticed that she was looking straight at him with both eyes. Neither of them wandered. Perhaps her implant wasn't on, he thought, or perhaps she just had good control of her eye muscles.

His gaze was suddenly distracted by something moving along the sidewalk outside the restaurant. He glanced away from Hanna in time to see a man's form glide past the main plate-glass window. Something about the figure troubled him, and he wanted a second look. It was as if he couldn't focus on the man, or as if he was walking in a mist in the otherwise bright and sunny weather.

A mirror on the left wall of the restaurant reflected a view of the sidewalk where the man should appear, if he continued in the same direction along the sidewalk, but he wasn't there. Jeremy continued to look for some time.

"Is something the matter?" Hanna asked.

"I just saw someone float by, outside. It was really weird."

Hanna smiled. "It's probably one of those hover-board things. They're all the rave at the university. You get yourself going and you just float along, about a foot off the ground."

"Maybe," Jeremy said aloud, but he continued to watch the sidewalk. Why did the man look so funny, and why didn't he see him in the mirror?

"So, uh," Hanna said, struggling not to giggle with embarrassment, "why did you use cash to buy your breakfast? Are you from Australia?"

Jeremy looked up. *Australia? What does that have to do with it?*

"No, I just had these coins and I wanted to get rid of them," he said.

She shook her head disapprovingly. "You could have traded them in with a collector for four times their face value. They're hard to get these days."

"I didn't know that," Jeremy said, feeling stupid.

"What time is your first class?" he asked to divert conversation.

"Nine. And if that means you want me to go, that's okay."

"No, no, I didn't mean that. Please stay," he said earnestly. "I just ..."

"You just wanted to change the subject," she finished his thought. "That's okay. But whether you meant it or not, you're right. I need to get going to class." Jeremy watched as she showed the first visible sign of checking her implant. Both her eyes moved up and to the left -- the default position for the clock.

"I'm sorry," Jeremy said. "I didn't mean to be rude."

Hanna smiled warmly at him. "You seem like a nice guy, Jeremy. I come here every morning at about eight. Maybe I'll see you sometime." She picked up her coffee cup and left.

Jeremy sat for a minute, staring into space. He might have gone on like that for some time, but his implant called him back to life.

From Doctor Berry. Reminder. Ten o'clock, Powell Building, Room Twenty-three A. There's a map in the university page.

Jeremy activated his clock. He still had about an hour before he'd have to leave. Not another walk!

To Doctor Berry. Acknowledged.

He accessed the university page on the hole and located the Powell Building. There was a large park about a quarter of a mile from the building. He packed up the remains of his breakfast and headed outside to take a leisurely walk in the general direction of the park. Perhaps he could study for a while. He still had a few more lessons to do, and he wanted to read as much as he could about the implant and hole communications.

Back on the sidewalk, Jeremy turned from North Capital Street onto H Street, generally watching the pavement immediately in front of him as he continued to work on walking and working his implant. As he turned the corner Jeremy froze in mid-stride to avoid a collision. He'd almost walked right into someone's back. He was about to excuse himself when a sudden, irrational fear gripped him. It was that same pale, floating creature he had seen through the restaurant window. It wasn't a foot in front of him, facing away, drifting down the sidewalk.

There was no hover board or anything else to explain its odd, mid-air movement. Its feet moved slightly, but it wasn't walking -- the legs just stretched from time to time. The head moved about, left to right, up, down, taking in the surroundings, apparently unconcerned about where it was going.

But it wasn't just the unearthly movement that was so shocking. The body itself looked like a shade, or a mirage of a person. Jeremy could make out the form distinctly, but he could also see through it, which is why he nearly called out when the form looked as if it was going to collide with a man walking the other direction, towards Jeremy.

He could see the man through the body of the phantasm, and then there was the awful moment when they touched, then occupied the same space, then separated, both seemingly oblivious to the union they had for no more than a second. Somehow it seemed disgusting. Jeremy had one last thing he had to do before it got away. He closed his left eye.

The image vanished. There was nothing on the walk but normal pedestrian traffic. He tried alternating eyes, and there was no question about it; he could only see it through the eye that the implant was connected to. But why didn't anyone else see it? Or did they?

He had to know.

"Pardon me," he said to the man who had just shared space with a ghost, "did you see that?"

"Did I see what?" the man asked, clearly not pleased about being disturbed and eager to be on his way.

"I'm sorry, but did you see the form of a man floating along down the sidewalk?" He felt foolish asking the question, but he felt he had to be direct.

The man scowled at him. "Is this some sort of joke?"

"No, but I'm sorry to have troubled you," Jeremy said and immediately turned away, walking slowly down the sidewalk. The creature was nowhere to be seen, but Jeremy continued to scan the street, hoping for another look.

What could that have been? he thought. He checked to make sure he didn't have any odd programs running on his implant. He had been playing a spy game the night before, and it was possible there was some odd visual effect from that. But his implant was on standby: only the clock was running, and of course the mail system was on.

Could that be it? Can you send a ghost image by mail?

Jeremy ran a series of searches in the help sections of the mail database as he continued to walk toward the university. Tracing down his hypothesis had a calming effect. The adrenaline was wearing off, and he began to breathe more regularly. Seeing that thing had been a jolting experience, but he wasn't sure understand exactly why. It had frightened him at an almost animal level.

From what he could tell in the help database, it wasn't possible to send visual images by mail. You could send a message with a tag to a visual image stored on the hole, but the recipient would have to activate the tag before the image would appear. He had just received a message from Dr. Berry, but there had been no tag.

He arrived at the park and paused from his frantic thoughts to take in the beautiful lawn and stately oak trees, of all different varieties. In the center of the park was a reflecting pool, complete with a dozen or more ducks and geese. Jeremy sat on one of the wooden benches next to the pool and tried to calm himself and gather his thoughts.

First things first. I don't want to be late.

He sent himself a delayed message to remind him to leave for the Powell Building on time. With that out of the way, he began to concentrate on figuring out what in the world he had just seen, and why.

He first suspected, and hoped, that seeing strange images was another common problem for newbies, like the floaters he had seen before. But Dr. Berry's warnings about implant psychosis were still ringing in his ears: one of the symptoms was seeing strange images. Jeremy refused to believe there was anything wrong with him, so he had to try to figure it out for himself first. If he couldn't solve it on his own, maybe he'd talk to Dr. Berry, but the risk was that she'd say he was sick and start "treatment."

After a few minutes searching the hole, he found a database of research articles on the experiences of newbies with the implants. He scanned the headers and noticed that one name occurred again and again in the studies: Dr. Anne Berry. She was clearly the expert in this field, just as the Advocate had said. She also had Jeremy under supervision.

A disquieting thought occurred to him. What privileges did "diagnostic mode" give Dr. Berry? Could she know that he had seen those images? Would she know that he was looking into implant psychosis? Would that make her suspicious of him?

Jeremy disliked going to doctors in the first instance, and he really didn't want her to put him through all kinds of fool tests. He decided to keep things to himself until he was fairly certain that he really had a problem, so he ratcheted up the security on his link to Dr. Berry, cutting her off from everything except mail and chat. The trouble was that if she tried to access his account while the security was up, she might wonder what he was up to.

Let her wonder, it's my business, he decided after changing the link status. She couldn't get any information on his account without his approval.

He tried to calm down, but he couldn't shake a sense of urgency. He couldn't risk locking her out for too long, but he had to make some progress. As he struggled to find the right information on the hole, he noticed that his hands were shaking.

After a half-hour's reading, aided by sophisticated search engines, Jeremy found that several other young newbies had reported "seeing things," and had been subsequently diagnosed as suffering from implant psychosis: each time by the same physician, Dr. Anne Berry. The reports never recorded what they had seen, only that they became obsessed with certain illusions, presumably generated by neurological rejection of the implant.

They also became paranoid, unable to trust anyone, especially their doctor. Dr. Berry's thesis that such paranoia was the major indicator of the advent of implant psychosis had been universally accepted in the scientific community: mistrust of the supervising physician was the first sign of trouble and called for more careful supervision and testing.

For the second time that morning Jeremy felt his adrenaline rush. This woman had too much control over his life. The supervisory link with Dr. Berry was still secured, but now he had to decide which course had the most risk. What would make her more likely to suspect that he was becoming psychotic, that he was reviewing the literature on imaginary images, or that he had shut down his link to her? His mind raced for a solution, and then his pre-programmed message came.

It's time to go.

He quickly shut down his search and accessed the university's map site, then he re-established his link with Dr. Berry.

He gazed across the pond and watched the ducks for a minute, breathing deeply. As he felt the jitters fade, he got up and followed the map to the Powell building. He walked through the campus, his mind engaged in that non-verbal thought that sometimes seems like no thought at all.

*　　*　　*

Anticipation formed a knot in his stomach as he walked down the final corridor of the Powell Building to Room 23A. He paused briefly at the door, forced a casual smile, and walked in.

He expected to see scores of college students staring at him, watching his every move, wondering how they grew 'em in the Community. Instead, seven students sat, engaged in light conversation, in a rough semi-circle of chairs that Jeremy would have expected to find in a living room. Refreshments filled a small table against the wall to his left. He rechecked the room number against Dr. Berry's message.

A moment later Dr. Berry herself emerged from a back office with another woman, who, after seeing Jeremy in the door, immediately rushed to greet him.

"I'm so glad you could make it, Jeremy," she said, pumping his hand. "My name is Phyllis, and this is my class," she waved to the students, who meekly smiled. "Did you have any trouble finding the place? Well no, of course not, because you're here on time. That's great. You already know Dr. Berry, I think. Can I get you something to eat?"

Jeremy smiled at the torrent of babble and allowed Phyllis to lead him to the refreshment table. He picked some sort of fruit-filled cookie as Phyllis told him who made what, what Jeremy might like, and gee, isn't he old enough to make those decisions for himself.

Phyllis continued to pour out a stream of words as Jeremy smiled indulgently, and nodded and grunted when she seemed to need encouragement. Esther, back home, had a similar manner. She was pleasant enough, in small doses.

The flow of words was suddenly stanched as Phyllis ushered him into his seat and handed the class over to the students. Phyllis retired to the back and continued to unload her daily supply of words in whispers to Dr. Berry. Jeremy prepared for the worst, expecting to be asked embarrassing questions about mating rituals, or some other sociological nonsense, but there was none of that. The students wanted to know what school was like in the Community, and how the founders of the Community were able to resolve tensions between the secular and religious elements of their culture, and whether it had really worked. They wanted to know how criminals were handled, which made him a little nervous, and about taxation, and decisions on spending public money. Jeremy often turned the questions back on the students, asking them how the same issues were handled in Society.

The 50-minute class was over too soon, and Jeremy wished they could continue, especially since that constituted the extent of his work-load for the day. The students promised they would have some tough follow-up questions next time.

"You did a great job, Jeremy," Dr. Berry said after she managed to pull herself away from Phyllis.

"Thanks. You know, I didn't expect to see you hear today." He tried not to sound suspicious.

"I'll let you in on a little secret. I organized this school program for newbies, and I like to come along from time to time to make sure it's working okay. It's not technically part of my practice, but it helps me a lot."

Jeremy nodded his head, looking down at the floor. After an awkward pause he said, "One thing that didn't come up in the discussion today was personal privacy. People in the Community can be fairly zealous about that."

"And you don't like being in diagnostic mode," she quickly interjected. "I understand. Let me make you two promises. First, I won't pry into what you're doing. I'm too busy for that kind of thing anyway. But I do need to maintain the connection so I can run some standard analyses on how your implant is functioning. It's just medical data. I don't know or care what it is you're doing with your implant."

"But you can see, if you want to," Jeremy clarified.

"I can, but I don't, and I won't. I have hundreds of patients, and I can't spend my time monitoring what all of them do."

"And the second promise?"

Dr. Berry smiled. "I'll turn you loose as soon as I can. I'm obligated by law to keep you under supervision for at least a week."

Jeremy sighed. "Okay. I'm not thrilled with the idea, but if that's the way it's gotta be ...."

Dr. Berry grimaced and nodded. "I m afraid so. If you want to get an implant as an adult, those are the rules."

Promises, promises.

Well, maybe that's the end of it. If I don't see those things again, it really doesn't matter if she can monitor me for the next week.

Curiosity would have to wait. The prospect of Dr. Berry suspecting that he had implant psychosis was worth putting it all behind him. Submitting himself to the care of a psychiatrist was about the scariest thing Jeremy could imagine, since they had the ability to take away his independence -- even independent thinking -- with their "therapy."

*　*　*

Jeremy had the rest of the day free, and nothing much to do. He didn't know anyone to meet for lunch, or, for that matter, any idea where to go. And besides all that, his late breakfast made lunch seem unnecessary.

He absentmindedly checked the university site on his implant, just to look for inspiration, and noticed a reference to the Washington subway system. The visual effect as he moved from one hole site to another took some getting used to. The implant desktop remained motionless, floating a few feet in front of him, at head level, just to the left, but the graphic display of most sites had 3-D elements. If he watched the display too closely as he was linking to another site, it seemed as if he was moving through his implant desktop. Images flowed off the screen as if he was flying toward, and then past them.

Viewing the hole location for the subway was an experience somewhere between watching a model train and riding in one. When Jeremy queried the site on how to get from the university to the Armory and Alehouse, a video showed a map of the city, highlighting each location. It zoomed in on the stop closest to the university, showing what the street entrance looked like, how frequently the trains ran, with a host of related video clips, including a view of the tunnels as the train sped down the track.

Hovercars accounted for most area traffic, but the subway still moved a substantial portion of the local population. The cars were clean, and the fare was less than half the going rate on a hovershuttle.

Since it was the middle of the day, traffic was light. Jeremy called up a few hole pictures of Metro operations during rush hour and was glad he had missed it. Things were never that crowded in the Community, except maybe at the Spring dance.

Jeremy descended the entrance tunnel and waited on the platform. A silver and black train arrived in a few minutes. As he got aboard and glanced around at the passengers, something caught his eye. A fiber of insulation from the overhead panel dangled down from the ceiling, a machine screw caught on its end. It was the first sign of disrepair Jeremy had seen in any public facility, and he knew that it wouldn't last long. A cleaning robot would eliminate the string and report the misplaced screw to maintenance.

He watched the screw as the subway car sped through the tunnels. It swayed to one side, then the other, as the car took a wavy path to the next stop.

At the next stop, Jeremy watched the passengers get on and off. The man in the flight jacket brushed past the woman in the blue coat, seemingly unconcerned that she had a conscience, and a soul, or that a bright word might make the difference between hope and despair. Few made eye contact, and no one spoke. But Jeremy saw the loneliness in the woman's eyes and thought he'd break taboo and speak to her. He rose from his seat and headed in her direction, and then noticed something funny a few meters ahead of him on the train. It made his heart stop.

It was the form of a man, floating horizontally in the air -- another of his ghosts. It lay just above and behind a woman who was seated, facing away from Jeremy. The ghost appeared to be studying something intensely, but Jeremy couldn t decide what it was. The woman was completely oblivious.

Jeremy closed his left eye and studied the empty space with his right. He could see no sign of the creature. He considered asking if anyone else on the train could see it, but he didn't want to look like a fool.

The thing was facing away from him, and Jeremy had a sudden urge to touch it. He got up and wandered toward it as casually as he could manage. He stood right next to it, and then he noticed something odd about its movement. The subway car took a sharp right turn and Jeremy almost lost his balance. He remembered the screw. But unlike Jeremy, or the dangling screw, this image wasn't affected by inertia. It remained completely still relative to the wall of the subway car, despite the irregularities of the ride.

The car stopped at his station and the doors opened. Jeremy reached out and put his hand through the image, then he turned and got off the train without looking back.

As he came out of the subway station near his hotel, he configured his favorite search engine to look up everything available on angels.

Greg Krehbiel

Chapter 5 – The Study of Ghosts

When Jeremy walked into the restaurant at five after eight the next morning, he was thankful to see Hanna in her usual seat. He had ordered his breakfast through his implant and knew it would be waiting for him in the autodispenser, but he didn't know how to get it out. Of course he could download the instructions, but instructions were never any good because they were always written by people who understood the process too well. Instead of saying "open the big orange door," it would say "open the dispenser lid," and there would be five things that might qualify as a dispenser lid.

"Hi," he said as he took a seat opposite Hanna at a small table.

"Good morning, Jeremy. No breakfast today?"

"No. I'll eat just as soon as you tell me how to get my food out of that contraption over there."

Hanna rolled her eyes, but explained anyway, very carefully. "You just open that big door, the orange one, put your right thumb on the big button-shaped thing that says 'identification plate,' and the inside door will open up. Your order will be inside."

"Sounds easy enough, but please don't watch me, okay? I'm tired of being a spectacle in this place." Hanna laughed and hid behind a book.

The dispenser worked just as Hanna described, and he was back in a minute, handing her a muffin and a bowl of fresh fruit from his tray. She gave him a grin and picked at the fruit.

"Thanks, Jeremy," she said.

As Jeremy opened his coffee and unwrapped his muffin she continued. "So, my friend MacKenzie told me about you. She's in that sociology class you've been visiting. She said you did a good job."

"MacKenzie" is a girl?

"I'm flattered that you asked about me," he said, looking squarely into her eyes, noticing how the blue gave way to bright green around the edges. Her eyes seemed to sparkle under the attention. "And I'm glad she gave a good report. I didn't expect to like the class, but I did."

Hanna's cheerful face took on a serious aspect. "Yeah, I suppose you would be a little nervous about it, huh? It must be weird to be in a totally different culture, and then to be placed under a microscope. But," she continued with a happier expression, "I think this is a great way for you to learn the ropes. You can ask them about Society stuff while they ask you about the Community."

"Yes. It was helpful," he said.

"Feel free to ask me anything you want to know. I won't bite."

"I wouldn't mind," he said, and then, seeing her confused expression, shook his head. "Never mind. But let me take you up on your offer. My first question is, why do you have a book? Are some titles not unavailable on the hole?"

"Just about everything is available, although some things are expensive, so if you can get your hands on a book you can save some money. But this one you can get for free," she said, patting the left hip pocket of her oversized vest. "I just like real books. They're easier on the eyes."

"So do I. Can I see it, if you don't mind?"

"Sure," she said. She reached into her pocket and handed Jeremy an exquisitely bound, leather volume. It was the perfect size for a coat pocket, felt substantial in the hand, had gilded pages, a satin marker and an embossed title. Jeremy thought it was a Bible, but it was titled "Call to the Unconverted," by Richard Baxter. He'd never heard of it, but the title scared him. *Is she some kind of religious nut?* he wondered.

"I'm taking a class in English Puritan theology and this is one of the books we're supposed to read," she said. "I saw the title in my pastor's library, so I thought I'd read the real thing, instead of burning my eyes out on my implant."

Jeremy smiled at her as he glanced at a few pages.

"I'd noticed that your eyes don't wander, like a lot of people's do."

Hanna grimaced. "It used to be a sign of poor discipline -- 'implant eye,' they called it, and you were considered somewhat of a slob if you couldn't control it -- but people seem to have given in. Not me."

Jeremy looked up and smiled again as he paged through the book. He was a very fast reader, but this book made for heavy work. Baxter's style seemed tedious, and the subject didn't interest him at all, but the book itself was a beautiful thing. The text was in a flowing script that forced the reader to take it slow. It might even have been hand-written.

He handed it back.

"I wouldn't have suspected that an anthropology student would have to take English Puritan Theology. It sounds more like something in a divinity program."

"You're right, it's not in my curriculum. It's actually a class offered at my church."

That brought to mind his late-night study from the day before. "Do you know anything about angels, Hanna?" he asked in a subdued voice, looking down into his food.

"Some," she said. "What do you want to know?"

"Well," he looked up at her eagerly, but kept his voice low, "how would you know if you had seen one?"

He steeled himself for the inevitable laughter, but it didn't come. Instead, Hanna wore a thoughtful expression and looked away for a minute. "I've never really thought about that," she said. "From everything I've read, angels look like regular people. Sometimes they look like huge regular people, like when David saw the angel that was attacking Jerusalem, but most of the time they are just taken to be men."

If you believe that stuff, Jeremy thought, and found it somewhat odd that she hadn't questioned his interest.

"I was studying this question last night, and I came to the same conclusion. They just look like regular people most of the time." She didn't reply, and there was a minute of silence as he pondered what to say next. "What do you know about ghosts?"

Hanna suppressed a laugh. "Far less than I know about angels, I promise you. I would say that I don't believe in ghosts, but frankly I'm not dogmatic on that one. I don't think there are ghosts, but I wouldn't rule out the possibility."

Jeremy nodded, and his respect for Hanna shot up a few notches. It was one thing to believe that angels were real if you thought there was sufficient evidence. It was a completely different matter to believe that ghosts were not, and it seemed that she knew the difference.

"Aren't you dying to know why I'm asking these questions?" he finally said.

The edges of her mouth curled in a conspiratorial smile. "I figured you'd get around to it if you wanted to. And besides, I have other ways of finding out about you."

MacKenzie.

He shuffled in his seat a bit, scratched the back of his head and looked around.

"I have a lot of things I'd like to talk to you about. Can we go for a walk?"

Hanna raised her eyebrows in surprise, put her half-eaten breakfast on Jeremy's tray, and they left together.

*   *   *

At the 10:00 sociology lab, Jeremy asked for another round of introductions and was careful to associate names and faces, especially MacKenzie's. She was modestly dressed, unlike some of the people in the class who wore elaborate hairstyles and fantastic clothing. Her brown hair was neat, but not overdone. She was pleasant-looking, but not beautiful, and she looked thin, although her clothes made it hard to tell. He smiled and nodded at her when her turn came, and she winked back.

The class went on much as it had the day before. Most of the questions focused on the socialization of children in the Community. This was the seminar topic for the semester, and the students asked about some things Jeremy had never even considered before. Was there an average age for weaning and potty training? Were boys encouraged to be more athletic than girls? Did fathers prefer their boys, or mothers their girls?

It was a much harder interview than he expected. Jeremy had to stop and think before almost every answer, and he was surprised how much he didn't know.

When class was over, Jeremy had one piece of business to attend to.

"Hey MacKenzie," he said before she could get away. "What are you doing for lunch?"

*   *   *

"Double duty today," Dr. Berry said to Jeremy as he grabbed a cup of coffee at the psychology lab later that afternoon. The room was much larger than the intimate settings of the sociology class -- which Dr. Berry had missed that morning -- and there was a correspondingly larger audience.

"Yes, but it's been very helpful," he said. "I've learned a lot about Society. I've even learned some things about the Community. I'm a little more worried about these guys, though." He pointed to the assembled crew of nine psychology teachers and 15 students.

"You'll do fine," Dr. Berry said. "But if things get difficult, or you feel uncomfortable, remember that you don't have to answer the questions. And one other thing. Doctor business this time. I need to see you for a follow-up visit. You can come to the office, or I can just meet you somewhere."

"How's this evening in the lobby of my hotel?" he said,

uncomfortable with the idea of going back to her office, unless he had to.

"Sure. How's seven?"

*   *   *

A moment later there was an exchange of pleasantries and introductions, but the teacher of this psychology lab came from a different mold than Phyllis.

"First of all, Jeremy," he said as he began the interview, "we should tell you that we've read the transcript of your conversations with the sociology class." Jeremy didn't know there was a transcript. "You've given us some very useful information about the Community, but I believe our approach will be slightly different, and perhaps our analysis will be a little deeper."

He smiled self-assuredly and glanced around the room. A few of the other professors returned his arrogant smirk while others rolled their eyes.

As the professor's voice droned on in the background, Jeremy received a message over his implant.

From Doctor Berry. Chat mode requested.

"Thank you, professor," he said aloud. **Accepted,** he sent.

Be careful with this guy. He likes to impress his class by being tough on people, Dr. Berry's voice said through his implant. It was the first time she had sent him a message during one of these sessions, and the first time Jeremy had used chat mode.

Thanks for the warning.

"I'd like to start the questions myself, if you don't mind," the professor began. He liked to be called "professor," while most of the other teachers went by their first names.

Jeremy nodded.

"There is one striking omission from your anecdotal accounts of life in the Community," the professor began. "You explain that you grew up believing Society to be oppressive and invasive of personal liberties, and that you've found that not to be the case." He said this with the condescending tone of a teacher who has exposed and corrected a foolish error. "But you never mentioned why, if you felt that way, you left the Community."

Jeremy swallowed hard and tried not to show the sudden panic he fought to suppress. Did the professor know the real reason?

You don't have to answer, Dr. Berry's voice told him after his delay was becoming obvious. He nodded, almost imperceptibly, to Dr. Berry and turned to look at the professor.

"It was a difficult decision, of course, and not one I wish to review right now for complete strangers."

The professor didn't react, but it was clear that he was not used to being spoken to in that tone of voice. He made another attempt.

"Surely there is something you can tell us about your reasons for leaving the Community. Or do you wish to leave a room full of psychologists to speculate?"

There were subdued chuckles.

"You can speculate all you like. It doesn't make a bit of difference to me what you think."

The professor shook his head and made an impatient gesture to one of the other faculty members to take over the questioning. He then immediately scribbled something on a pad of paper in his lap. Pads of paper had been rendered obsolete by the implants, and Jeremy expected the pad was some sort of affectation. Paper was usually reserved only for special correspondences.

Jeremy looked away from the professor and toward the rest of the assembled teachers and students, as if to say that he was dismissing the professor from further consideration. He noted that one of the other psychology professors discreetly gave him a thumbs up. He was the next one to speak.

"Jeremy, I don't know if you're aware of this, but the Communities came to differing decisions about how completely they should sever their ties with Society. Some continued to watch our television broadcasts, for example, or listen to the radio, back when we had such things. But yours was different. The Community you are from severed all contact from the very beginning. Why was that? What was so wrong with the radio? Were you afraid that Society ideas would undermine your Community?"

Jeremy laughed good naturedly. "Hardly. No, it wasn't the fear of the conspiracy theorist. The founders of our Community didn't listen to the radio because they were completely uninterested in anything anyone was saying, and because they had more pressing matters to attend to, like building a new culture, a new government and all that. Society ideas seemed both useless and sophomoric." He stopped himself at that, and then said, "no offense meant to the sophomores."

A young man in the back of the room said "none taken," and there were a few scattered chuckles.

"In fact, years later, part of our education was to listen to tapes of the broadcasts from that era," Jeremy continued. "Perhaps you never have?"

The questioner, Bob, as Jeremy remembered from introductions, said that he hadn't.

"You ought to. It's complete drivel; pure propaganda. Some of the shows complained about oppressive government tactics and some defended them. But it was just a lot of wind, and nobody seemed to get to the heart of the issue. People competed as if they were ideological enemies, but they didn't realize how much they had in common. In fact, it was some of their common assumptions that were the real root of Society's problems."

He paused and took a drink of water, discreetly surveying a few faces in the crowd before he continued.

"There were a few voices of reason from those days, but many of those were the very people who ended up founding the Communities, so we were left with the impression that the brain trust had left." He laughed at that. "And we were content to leave you folk to quarrel among yourselves. We had no idea that things had straightened out."

"Very interesting," Bob said, "but you also made no effort to check back with us. Why was that?"

"At the time we split, the government had its fingers into everything. We thought it was inevitable that they'd take over every institution and organ of power. We were just waiting for the government to come and close us down. We didn't expect you to reform, but in that hope we established the Advocate as a kind of ambassador, or legal counsel, for the Community. He was supposed to be let us know what was going on, but it turns out, in our case, at least, that our Advocate has been lying to us for decades, feeding us stories that the government was still knocking on the door, threatening to disband the Communities."

Heads around the room shook in disgust and anger, and there were a few murmured conversations.

"But now I have a question," Jeremy said. "Didn't the other Communities have Advocates? That was the original model. Did they all lie, or were we the fortunate ones?"

"Sad to say, we know of at least three who did, but most of them told the truth," Bob explained. "Some of the Communities disbanded when they heard how things had changed in Society. Some stayed together, preferring their simpler lifestyle. In fact, some of the Communities grew as the people from Society emigrated. The new government restored the liberty of citizens in Society, but some people still longed for a simpler life. Yours is one of the few communities that remained completely isolated."

Jeremy shook his head. "Amazing. And why didn't anyone try to let us know what was going on?"

Dr. Berry spoke for the first time. "Because you had stormed off into your room and closed the door, put up a 'do not disturb, go away' sign, and never came out again. Why should we have bothered you?"

The room grew quiet and several heads turned sharply to glare at Dr. Berry, but Jeremy just smiled.

"I guess if I can accuse Society of being sophomoric, you can call the Communities temperamental adolescents. But these things happened two generations ago, and, for better or worse, I'm no longer a citizen of the Community. Maybe we should stop saying 'us' and 'you.'"

"Agreed," Bob said.

The allotted time passed quickly, but several people remained afterward and continued to question Jeremy about their pet theories regarding the communities. As he had discovered from the budding sociologists, he hadn't considered many of the questions very deeply.

After a while he said, "it may be that you know more about the psychology of the Community than I do. You've studied it and thought about it. I never really questioned it." To which they replied, "but you have thought Community thoughts. No matter how much we try, we're still aliens looking in."

*　　*　　*

Jeremy rested his head in his hand and rubbed his temple as the hovercar took him back to the hotel later than afternoon. Almost as soon as he left the university campus, all thoughts of his twin interrogations left him -- but the tension remained, as well as a kind of mental weariness. Would he see another of these ghosts, or angels, or whatever they were? Or was it all madness? Was this the kind of thing Dr. Berry had warned him of?

An hour later he was no closer to a sensible course of action. "The trouble with being deceived is that you don't know it," he said aloud as he lay on his bed, staring at the ceiling. It was a saying that was used in the Community to explain why people in Society had allowed themselves to be trapped and enslaved by their brutal, bureaucratic, meddling captors. Jeremy now knew that it was the Community that had it all wrong; that Society was nothing like they imagined. In fact, it was all quite ironic. It was the Community that was deceived, and didn't know it, after all.

Was "implant psychosis" the same thing? Was it like being deceived?

Objectively speaking, he had the symptoms: he was seeing things that nobody else saw -- which, arguably, could be taken to mean that they weren't really there -- and he was beginning to mistrust his doctor. But the self-fulfilling nature of the symptoms bothered him.

If I see something, I have to hide it from my doctor unless I want to live the rest of my life under medication and psychological supervision. And there is no objective test to prove that I haven't seen anything.

He began to replay in his mind the two experiences with the phantom images. Was there any element that could not be explained by madness?

He laughed out loud.

What can't be explained by madness?

After all, he reasoned, you can't prove that all of your experiences aren't a grand illusion. You simply have to assume that your experience of the world is generally valid.

But that doesn't rule out illusions. Some people develop defects in their perception of the world, either from accidents, or liquor, or drugs, ... or, mental illness. The brain has diseases just like the rest of the body, and some people are just sick. They're psychotic.

Am I psychotic? he wondered.

Implant psychosis resulted from the brain being overloaded by stimuli, and since the implant is connected to the optic nerve, the brain malfunctions appear as strange visions. That seemed reasonable enough, but something bugged Jeremy about it. The things he had seen couldn't really be described as errors in vision: that would make them cloudy, or dark, or distorted. But he saw distinct forms, acting in a rational fashion. Images created by "noise" in the connection between his implant and his brain wouldn't be like that, he guessed.

Furthermore, he only saw them with his left eye. Why would a mental illness manifest itself only in the vision of his left eye? And how had he so quickly developed the ability to generate such elaborate hallucinations. Where did he get the idea that the ghost on the subway would act independently of the inertia of the train?

If that was all part of an illusion, then his visions must have been generated from his higher reasoning centers, and not just the visual part of his brain. But the implant didn't connect with those areas.

Fortunately, he'd seen maps of brain activity in the victims of implant psychosis in the literature. Some of the studies, he remembered, included detailed maps made while the patient claimed to be "seeing something." If they showed evidence of activity in the higher reasoning functions, that might indicate that the images were, in fact, elaborate hallucinations, like his. But if the brain activity was primarily in the visual centers, Jeremy would have to conclude that his visions couldn't be the same kind of thing.

But what if my visions are different? The other cases never talk about the content of the illusions.

This seemed like a nasty problem. What he really needed was a map of his own brain while he was having a "hallucination." But how could he get one without tipping his hand to some doctor?

He pondered that for a moment, and then decided that doubt could only go so far. "Philosophy is a conclusion from the preponderance of evidence," he remembered one of his teachers saying. "Trying to dot every 'i' and cross every 't' is a mistake that has destroyed many hopeful theories."

Still, he wondered. If his visions were of a different kind from the other patients', he might have no reason to fear disclosing his experiences to Dr. Berry. But as his supervising physician, she had the power to have him forcibly restrained and drugged, if she thought that was necessary, and he didn't want to change it. All she needed to do was have one other doctor agree with her diagnosis, and as the world's expert on the subject, who would resist her?

"Ah," he said, pounding his aching head, and remembering that he was still in diagnostic mode with Dr. Berry. The real problem, he realized, was doing his search of the medical database without allowing Dr. Berry to find out about it.

His mind raced. There had to be a place where he could access the hole without being monitored. He glanced at the terminal she'd loaned him, which he had forgotten to return. Was it safe? And then he remembered a public terminal in the lobby of the hotel. She couldn't monitor that.

The weariness and strain of the last couple hours faded as his mind focused on a clear, discreet task. Jeremy left his room and started for the elevator, more and more confident that he was neither paranoid nor psychotic.

If I was paranoid, I'd be afraid that she had the lobby terminal monitored.

*   *   *

After the stress of the last couple hours, Jeremy happily fell into one of the deep, leather seats in the Armory and Alehouse pub. A slight scent of ale and stale tobacco called back memories of the publick houses in the Community. Smoking was quite rare in Society, but the Armory and Alehouse used a synthesized imitation of tobacco smoke to help set the mood. The whole place looked like a colonial armory, with heavy, carved wooden furniture, antique lamps, several fireplaces, and rack upon rack of muskets. The minutemen had their own muskets, Jeremy recalled, but it added to the atmosphere. The bar even served hard cider in wooden mugs, and Jeremy ordered one from a period-costumed waiter.

The public terminal was connected to the base of a brass lamp on an end table next to the corner fireplace, as he recalled. He looked in that direction and his blood ran cold. A phantasm was sitting at the terminal, looking straight at Jeremy.

Chapter 6 – Implant Psychosis

Jeremy hoped the poor light in the pub concealed the sudden fear on face.

How did it know I would be here? Why is it watching me?

As soon as the thoughts crossed his mind, he knew he had to avoid meeting that gaze. No one else could see these things. He couldn't let on that he did. He also had an instinctive feeling that this was no creation of a psychotic mind. This image -- this ghost, or angel, or phantasm -- was real.

He decided to go ahead with his plan as if the thing weren't there. Perhaps it didn't know that he could see it. He had to play to that possibility. Perhaps the thing would lose interest and leave him alone.

Jeremy walked over to the terminal as casually as he could manage, focusing on the plaid fabric of the couch and the brown wood stain of the paneling -- anything to avoid making eye contact with the ghost -- and then he sat down, right on top of the ghost. He didn't look at his legs, but his peripheral vision told him that the creature was taller than he: its knees stuck out a couple inches beyond his own.

He turned to the maple-wood end table on which the public terminal sat and suddenly didn't know what to do. He didn't want to do a search on the visual oddities of implant psychosis while this creature sat in his lap. Instead, he did something impulsive and looked through the entertainment directory for a listing of live shows within walking distance of the hotel.

As he spoke his requests to the terminal, the phantasm moved itself behind the end table. Jeremy struggled to keep his eye on the terminal as the thing moved around. First, it was to his left, horribly close, then in front, with its eyes just above the terminal screen, peering at him intently, but Jeremy didn't dare to look at it and give himself away. It reached its hand through the terminal and into Jeremy's face. The hand passed through him harmlessly, as he suspected it would, but it was revolting, and it took all his self-control to keep from reacting.

As Jeremy tried to concentrate on his search, the waiter arrived with his cider. He turned to thank him, trying his best to seem natural and undistracted by the ghost who was passing his hand through Jeremy's head, trying to provoke a reaction. It was obvious the waiter didn't see it.

"Thank you," he said to the waiter, looking deliberately in his eyes and resisting the temptation to look back at the phantasm. "For your trouble," he said, giving him his last piece of cash, a red coin.

The waiter nodded his thanks and turned away, while Jeremy turned back to the terminal. The phantasm wasn't there, anymore. He resisted the desire to look around the room and see where it had gone and forced himself to read three pages of a boring review of a local musical before he let his eyes leave the terminal screen.

He couldn't chance allowing his eye to be distracted if the ghost reappeared. When he looked up from the terminal, he stared directly at his cider mug, picking another safe object with his peripheral vision. He sat for five solid minutes, sipping his cider, staring blankly at a musket on the opposite wall.

The phantasm seemed to have gone. Jeremy made a casual sweep of the pub and saw no signs of it, but he still feared to continue his search in this place, so he got up and headed back toward his room. As he went, he experienced a profound pang of loneliness. He desperately wanted to confide in someone -- to tell his story and talk it out. He needed someone he could trust, but he didn't have many options. Dr. Jenkins, perhaps, but he was too close to Dr. Berry, and she was the last person he wanted to know about this.

The clock on his implant told him it would be another hour before his appointment with Dr. Berry, and he needed something to distract him. He hurried back to his room and changed into swimming trunks, put on the hotel's robe and followed the signs to the hotel's indoor pool. Swimming always set his mind at ease, and the monotony of a few miles of 25 meter laps would give him time to think it all over.

Another public terminal caught his eye, mounted on the wall beside the showers. Two men were using it to consult a movie schedule. He wondered why people with an implant would ever need a public terminal, but ... clearly there were aspects of all this he still didn't understand.

He kept an eye on the two men as he stowed his things in a locker. When they were gone, he casually glanced around the room to make sure no one was watching, and then quickly keyed in the search he was unable to do in the lobby.

Jeremy located the library of research papers on implant psychosis and called up his favorite search engine, which allowed him to describe his search in plain sentences and asked for clarification if it had difficulty with the parameters.

He typed his request on the pull-out, touch-pad keyboard: "Search the entire database for studies that include maps of the brain patterns of the victims of implant psychosis made while they were having hallucinations. Do any of these show unusual activity in the higher reasoning centers?"

An instant later the screen printed a reply.

"Of the 45 cases that meet the stated parameters, only one showed unusual brain activity in the higher reasoning centers," the terminal replied. He accessed and quickly reviewed that case. The patient had a history of mental illness before receiving his implant.

That's good enough for me, he thought, and headed for the pool, confident that whatever else might be going on, "implant psychosis" was not causing him to see these images.

*   *   *

"Four hundred meter I.M.," he said to himself as he stood on the coping of the pool at lane three. "Four laps each of butterfly, backstroke, breaststroke, and any other stroke not previously swum," he recited, remembering how the announcers did it when they had

Saturday-morning competitions at Beaver Lake. "Bang," he said, and dove in to the almost sickeningly warm water.

Beaver Lake, he reminisced. It had so much more class than this sanitized, indoor thing of concrete and chemically purified water. At the lake, the entire swim team had to show up early to scrub the algae off the starting blocks and make sure the lanes were clear of sticks and leaves. After summer storms the officials had to measure the distance between the two piers to make sure all the lanes were still precisely 25 meters, and more than once a meet was postponed due to a passing water snake. Once there was even an alligator.

The hotel pool, by contrast, had no spirit. It was a 'facility,' and so very tame. Both the air and water would always be warm. Children wouldn't cry in fear the first time they saw a snake, or set their feet down on the muddy bottom. They wouldn't have to get used to eddies of warm and cold water, or changing visibility, or watching a keeper trout swim under them. This concrete thing was sterile and bland, and although he could see the lane markers underwater from 25 meters away, Jeremy would rather be at Beaver Lake.

He was so caught up in his reverie that he almost forgot his troubles. He was relaxed now, on his third lap of backstroke, and decided it was time to figure out what was going on. What was he seeing, and what should he do about it?

Of the three times he'd gotten a good look at the phantasms, at least two of them were spying on someone. One was scrutinizing a woman on the subway train, one, of course, had been watching him, and the other seemed to be scanning the streets, perhaps looking for someone. He had no way of knowing if there was a connection between himself and the woman, so the only apparent common element was the act of spying itself.

Invisible spies, he thought. *What government wouldn't kill for them?*

The riots that had forced the government out of its intrusive, paternalistic ways, Jeremy recalled from his history lesson, were over computer security. No one had felt that their privacy, or property, was secure because so much information flowed over the world-wide computer network, and there were too many cases of information piracy. At the same time, everyone knew the military had encryption routines that secured vital information, and when the New Congress convened for the first time, they made that technology available to everyone. Ever since then, security on the hole was the unquestioned operating assumption of Society. Hackers tried to break into the system from time to time, but they always failed. The encryption seemed fool-proof.

That was the assumption, anyway. *But what about these ghosts?* He could only see them in his left eye, which had to mean that they were somehow connected to his connection to the hole, and that might mean that the network was not as secure as everyone believed. But why did he see them at all? What were they?

He was shooting in the dark. He simply had to know more about the technology of the implants, and Hanna's friend MacKenzie seemed like the natural choice. Hanna said she was a genius with computers, especially communications systems. But could he trust her? Should he let someone else in on his secret? What if she turned him in?

As he finished his last lap, he decided he had no choice. *I have to trust somebody.*

*   *   *

Exercise was exactly the right thing for him. Meeting Dr. Berry, the doctor who had the power to commit him to an institution, in the Armory and Alehouse pub, where a short time before he'd been harassed by a phantasm, might have been a test of his mettle. But after a couple hundred meters in the water, he felt clean and refreshed, and he had that comfortable, slightly tired feeling in his muscles that followed exercise. It put a confidence in his stride that ghosts and doctors couldn't easily shake.

A waiter brought the complimentary tray of bread and cheese to their table, and Dr. Berry had ordered a bottle of wine and two glasses.

"Busy day?" Jeremy asked.

"Always," she said. "If it's not patients its research, or speaking engagements, or little annoying things, like renewing the lease on the office."

"I'm sorry to put you out, then, making you come all the way over here."

She shook her head. "Washington's still a small town, and I have to get out some time. Besides, I have to keep up with my patients, and this is the most dangerous time for implant psychosis. You're doing very well learning how to use the implant, but some of the data I've been getting concerns me."

"Like what?"

"You've been under a lot of stress, and you've been overly excited the past few days. Especially earlier today -- a couple hours ago. Sometimes those readings can be a bad sign." She paused for a moment to read his face. "So what's been bothering you?"

Jeremy laughed. He tried to make it sound natural, but it felt contrived.

"I thought I'd already had my psychoanalysis for the day."

"And I noticed that you resisted it."

"People from the Community like their privacy."

"Even with their doctors? You're not doing yourself a favor if you don't let me know what I need to know to help you."

Jeremy shook his head. "Who says I need help? You're acting as if it's a foregone conclusion that I'm going to get this 'implant psychosis.' I thought it was rare."

"It is. Perhaps you don't remember, but you do have an enlargement in the occipital region of your brain."

"I do. I also remember being told it wasn't a problem." He didn't say that he'd also checked it out in the literature, and found absolutely nothing to indicate a connection with implant psychosis.

"It probably isn't," she admitted without meeting his gaze. Her face showed suppressed concern, but she shrugged and took another piece of cheese. "If you don't trust me, there's not much I can do for you."

"It sounds to me like the shoe's on the other foot. You don't believe me when I say that I'm doing fine."

"It's not out of the blue, you know. I can access your implant while you're in diagnostic mode, and the data I'm getting concerns me. And it's even more of a concern that you're developing an attitude."

Ah. The last refuge of the manipulative woman.

Jeremy knew there was no response to that charge. Any conceivable response would be cast as confirmation of his 'attitude.'

He took another sip of wine and waited for her to take the next step.

"You're playing a dangerous game here, Jeremy," she said after a minute, with clear signs of irritation. "You're beginning to show classic signs of implant psychosis, and the longer you wait, the worse it will get. If you trust me -- if you let me take you back to the office and run the tests I need to run -- then we can catch it in time, and you'll do just fine. But if you continue with this passive-aggressive attitude, things will just go from bad to worse, and then I won't be able to help you."

Jeremy smiled and took another sip of wine.

"More?" he asked, offering to refill her glass. She scowled, but then turned her gaze away and seemed to be listening to a message. She sat up straight as her eyes flickered about.

"They need me. I have to get back to the office. But don't forget what I've said. I think you ought to reconsider your course."

*   *   *

Once she left, he sat back in his seat and took a deep breath. A faint smile struggled for mastery with an expression of weariness. Through drooping eyelids he watched the light of the lamp sparkle through the deep red wine as he swirled it in the glass. He also noticed that his hand was shaking slightly.

His implant startled him out of morose self-reflection.

From Hanna. Hi Jeremy. Remember me? MacKenzie and I are bored. Can you meet us?

He shook his head and sat up straighter in his chair.

To Hanna. Chat mode requested, he sent.

Accepted.

Your timing couldn't be better, he sent. *My schedule just freed up and I'm wondering what to do. What did you have in mind?*

MacKenzie wants to go skating. I want to watch a movie. How about you?

Neither of those options had the slightest appeal to him. His mind was consumed with questions about the phantasms, and this might be his best chance, although it would require letting Hanna and MacKenzie in on his story. If he could sit down and talk with them for a while, maybe he could make sense of everything that had happened to him in the last few days.

Actually, this may sound boring, but I've got something on my mind. He remembered Hanna's offer to help him adjust to Society. *It has to do with the implant. Would you and MacKenzie mind talking me through it? I'll buy you a drink, or we can get an ice cream or something.*

Just a minute, she replied, and then continued a moment later. *There's a great chocolate bar at 11th and Massachusetts. Can you meet us there?*

A chocolate bar is a place? I thought it was a kind of candy.

It's both. It's a bar, you know, like ... a bar, but they serve chocolate in just about every way you can imagine. As long as you don't make me eat a sausage for breakfast, I can budget the calories.

Jeremy grinned. Hanna wasn't close to having a weight problem.

I'll meet you there in ten minutes, but I've got one or two things to do, so do you mind if I turn off the chat mode?

No. See you soon. **Chat mode discarded by remote host.**

*　　*　　*

Looking at the evening sky brought Jeremy a sense of calm. The fading light promised to hide him in a blanket of darkness. Childhood ghosts grew more fearsome at night, but he had a feeling that the ghosts that had been following him needed the light to see. He might not have believed that if he had thought it through, but he wasn't thinking now, he was just walking and allowing his mind to wander in nothingness as his body enjoyed the cool breezes of a Spring evening.

He pulled his thoughts back to the present when he turned the corner onto Massachusetts Avenue and saw a row of retail establishments. They were all one- and two-story enterprises that comprised the bottom floors of the traditional 13-floor, D.C. office building. A series of old-fashioned wooden signs hung from the eaves. The one he wanted stood out by its plainness. Amidst oranges and purples and bright greens, the sign for the chocolate bar was chocolate brown, and bore in white letters the name of the place. It was, literally, The Chocolate Bar.

The restaurant was divided into a self-service facility for carry-out and an eat-in area with waiters. Everything sparkled clean and bright, reminding him of pictures he had seen of old-fashioned soda fountains. The tiled floor, the metal hand railings, the white tables and red chairs all gleamed to a polished perfection. A quick scan uncovered no robots, but it had to be their work. Jeremy couldn't imagine that human hands could make a place look so immaculate.

"Hi Jeremy," Hanna called from a table near the center of the eating area. She and MacKenzie rose to greet him, although MacKenzie timidly hung back a little, somewhat unlike her manner in class, or at lunch.

Does she think she's on Hanna's turf?

Jeremy greeted them both warmly and took a seat on a three-legged stool.

"So what's good?" he asked, speaking to the ceiling as he called up the bar's hole address and accessed the menu.

When all the orders were placed they fell into an easy chit-chat. Jeremy felt suddenly light-hearted. The cheery surroundings, the company -- they recalled his school days. His dad always told him it was important to be a fun date, and he began to realize how much he craved simple, friendly time with people about his own age.

The orders arrived remarkably quickly and they started right in. Hanna ordered a chocolate fudge cake, MacKenzie a thick bar of slightly warmed dark chocolate, which she ate with a fork, and Jeremy tried out the thick malted milkshake, complete with a motor-driven straw. After the novelty of the straw wore off, he began to notice the flavor of the shake. It was the best thing he'd tasted in his life.

Hanna and MacKenzie both offered him a bite of their desserts, but although sharing a dish with one woman might be romantic, just swapping food around the table didn't appeal to him.

"So what's on your mind, Jeremy?" Hanna asked as a bus boy took their empty dishes and a waiter poured steaming coffee into gleaming white, porcelain cups.

Jeremy looked down at the table to gather his thoughts. His suddenly serious expression took Hanna and MacKenzie by surprise. "Actually," he said, "I have some important things to ask you both about, but first I need to ask some computer-related questions. Do you mind?" He looked back and forth at both of them, but they all knew MacKenzie was the computer expert. Hanna pointed to MacKenzie with her open hand, as if to say, "ask her."

Jeremy rubbed his eyes as if the afternoon's headache was returning just by thinking about it again.

"Okay, as I understand it," he began, "everybody's implant is connected to a network of millions of computers, and all the implants and computers are tied together by a zillon communications links."

"I won't vouch for the numbers, but go on," MacKenzie said.

Jeremy shrugged and grinned. "Okay. So when I send something over the net, my message goes to some computer somewhere, the computer gives a reply, and that information is sent back to my specific address, to my implant, which formats the information in whatever mode I've selected, ... visual, or whatever."

"Keep going," MacKenzie said approvingly.

"Question number one. Everything I see in my implant is on my desktop. Is it possible to see things from off the hole that appear in your normal field of view -- not on the desktop at all?"

"What have you been reading?" she asked with some surprise. "Just today I read about some really advanced work on that very subject. You see, the early implants had a tendency to get mixed up with people's regular vision. In the left eye anyway. But it was all cloudy and hazy and confusing, and gave people horrible headaches, so they had to move everything into a very limited frame -- what we know now as a desktop. But somebody's been re-evaluating that question, and there have been some breakthroughs."

"Frankly, I think it would be an irritation," Hanna chimed in. "I like keeping things on the desktop."

"You wouldn't say that if you'd seen some of the simulations. It's really amazing what they might be able to do with this. Just ...."

Hanna reached over and took her hand to cut her off.

"I think Jeremy has a couple more questions for you. You can tell us the geek stuff later, okay?"

MacKenzie tried to scowl, but a smiled peeked through at the corners. She looked back at Jeremy.

"Question number two," he said. "Could one of those computers send me some visual information that I didn't request?"

"No."

Her abrupt answer surprised him. "Just flat-out 'no'? No maybe's, or possibilities, or anything?"

MacKenzie shook her head. "Sorry, just, ... 'flat-out no.'" She looked at Hanna and they both giggled. Apparently it wasn't a Society expression.

"Privacy is sacrosanct on the hole," she continued. "Nobody can send you anything, except mail, unless you want it. And you can even filter mail."

"But isn't there some information that goes to everybody? Like the clock, or, ... I don't know, emergency stuff. Civil defense. Warnings about invading dragons. That kind of thing." Hanna laughed.

"Yeah, there's lots of stuff that comes off the hole to everybody's implant, but it's not visual information. It's kind of background noise." Jeremy took note of that. "You don't see the embedded messages unless you want to. What I mean is, your implant gets notice that there's an emergency message. You get that notice however you have your implant set, and then you have to access the file. Nothing comes to you automatically."

Jeremy asked about the black floaters he saw the first couple days he had the implant.

"Well, okay," MacKenzie conceded, "some of the noise is 'visual,' in one sense. But that's an accident, first of all, and it's just noise, not information. Most people don't see it, and if they did, it wouldn't be anything recognizable. Maybe our brains learn to ignore it."

He remembered Dr. Berry's comments about his enlarged occipital region -- a region that does visual processing. Could there be some connection?

"Is that noise at a special frequency, or something like that?" he asked.

MacKenzie shook her head. "'Frequency' is the wrong word, but it has a characteristic signature to it. We just automatically filter it out, ..." She paused for a minute and looked hard at Jeremy. "But you might not, since you're a newbie. It's possible, I guess, that some visual information could be coming through, like the noise that makes the floaters."

She looked down at the table, hard in thought. Jeremy looked over at Hanna to make sure she was doing okay while he and MacKenzie monopolized the conversation. She reached over and grabbed his hand, which was resting on the table-top, and gave it a friendly squeeze. She nodded her head at MacKenzie, as if to say, "She's the one to figure this stuff out."

"Jeremy, I have an idea," MacKenzie said after a minute. "I just wrote a little program that can test what we were talking about."

Jeremy looked at her in surprise. "You just wrote it?"

"She's amazing," Hanna said.

MacKenzie rolled her eyes. "It's no big deal, guys, but listen -- I'm going to send a message to you and Hanna, and I'm going to put some noise in it. I want to know if you can see anything when you get it."

They both nodded, and a second later Jeremy heard MacKenzie's voice through his implant. At the same time he saw a small dark patch, like a storm cloud, hover over his chocolate malt. He looked quickly at Hanna, whose expression told him all he needed to know. He looked up at MacKenzie and smiled. She mouthed 'wow' and stared off into space, deep in thought again.

Greg Krehbiel

Chapter 7 – MacKenzie

"This is amazing," MacKenzie said after another minute of stunned silence. "Jeremy, this is ...." She shook her head at a loss for words. "I just have to show this to my professors. Nobody has ever been able to make this kind of communication work. I don't think you realize the implications of this. I could do my doctoral thesis on the message I just sent you. I need to ...."

Jeremy cut her off, shaking his head and holding his finger to his mouth, asking her to be quiet. "I'm sure I don't understand the technical aspects of it, MacKenzie, but there's something else we need to talk about, before you tell the world. And this isn't the place. Can we get out of here?"

Hanna and MacKenzie looked at each other as if they didn't quite understand why he was being so mysterious, but they were willing to play along. They shrugged and got up to leave. Jeremy didn't speak until they were a block away from the Chocolate Bar and on a somewhat lonely stretch of pavement.

"I've got a story to tell you both, but I need your word that you won't repeat any of it to anybody." Jeremy looked seriously at Hanna and MacKenzie, who almost laughed at him. MacKenzie was still thinking of all she could do with what she had just learned, and how it would impact her academic schedule.

"What? You want me to keep this secret?" MacKenzie protested. "This is the biggest discovery in hole communications in a decade."

Jeremy hung his head and thought for a minute. He spoke without looking up. "I couldn't ask you to keep what we've just talked about secret. That wouldn't be fair." He looked up and stared MacKenzie in the eye. "But I want you to swear to me that you won't tell anybody what I'm about to tell you Both of you," he added, looking at Hanna. "And I think that after you've heard my story, you'll want to keep quiet about the other stuff as well. At least until we can figure it all out."

Hanna and MacKenzie shared a meaningful look. They whispered something to one another, and then Hanna looked back at Jeremy.

"Well, it turns out that your luck is better than you know," she said. "We're both Covenanters."

She might as well have said they were newspapers for all the good it did Jeremy. He looked at her with a blank expression.

As they turned aside to sit on a park bench, Hanna briefly explained what she meant. Covenanters were a religious group whose devotional practices centered around a series of covenants, or oaths, made with God, and in some cases, with others. Putting it in terms Jeremy would understand, they were a modern form of Puritanism.

Hanna didn't explain the details, but both Hanna and MacKenzie were sworn to keep confidences sacred at all costs. It had something to do with the initiation rites they started back during the riots. The survival of the fledgling Covenanter movement depended on secrecy.

Jeremy didn't understand it all, but he got the idea that they would rather die than reveal something they had promised to keep secret, and they both promised to keep his story to themselves.

Religion didn't have much of a hold on Jeremy, and he was not a little disappointed that Hanna had caught it -- he was sure it would put a damper on future dates -- but a sacred promise of silence sounded just perfect for his present situation. He told them everything.

*　　*　　*

They were still on the park bench well after dark. It was a warm, late-Spring night, and it would have been much more enjoyable if they didn't have such serious things to discuss. Jeremy finished his story about his experiences with the images, and Hanna and MacKenzie were still trying to take it all in. Hanna was the first to speak.

"It seems to be more than a coincidence that Dr. Berry had you under surveillance, and then there was one of those things at the public terminal, watching you."

MacKenzie nodded. "Yeah, that seemed just a little too coincidental to me, too. And you said that she went off suddenly after your meeting tonight?"

"She said she received an emergency call. She is a doctor, after all."

Hanna and MacKenzie were silent for another minute, thinking things over, but then Jeremy got a message through his implant.

From Dr. Berry. I need to see you right away.

Another coincidence? he wondered. This was getting uncanny.

To Dr. Berry. I'm a little busy right now. I'll make an appointment with your office. He didn't know what else to say.

From Dr. Berry. This is urgent. I've just received a new batch of analysis of the data from your implant. I need to see you right away.

Hanna and MacKenzie realized something was going on and they looked at him, curious. "Are you seeing something?" Hanna asked. Jeremy ignored her and began searching around for something on the ground. They looked at him like he had gone mad. He grabbed a stick and started writing in the dirt.

"It's Dr. Berry," he wrote, and then realized how silly he was being. "Why am I doing this? She can't hear what I'm saying."

MacKenzie shook her head and suppressed a laugh.

"She says she needs to see me," he explained.

MacKenzie immediately lost her mirth and shared a concerned look with Hanna. They both shook their heads.

"No way, Jeremy," Hanna said. "I don't trust her. Don't see her."

From Dr. Berry. Please respond. I need to see you right away.

Jeremy didn't know what to do, and he was beginning to fear that Dr. Berry could get a lot more information from him through her supervisory link than she had told him. He made a rash decision and cut the link. Hanna and MacKenzie were still looking at him, waiting for some explanation, but Jeremy had no time. He wasn't accustomed to managing his implant and talking at the same time.

There was an almost immediate response over his implant.

From Dr. Berry. This is not a game, Jeremy. Restore the link and come immediately to my office.

He reset his mail server parameters to block all incoming messages from Dr. Berry. He fumbled about, looking for the right settings. He was beginning to get frantic, and Hanna and MacKenzie could see it.

The three of them caught the eye of a passing policeman. He slowed his hovercar to watch what was going on.

"What's the matter, Jeremy? What can we do?" Hanna and MacKenzie asked. Jeremy's eyes were darting back and forth, trying to decide how to reconfigure his implant so Dr. Berry couldn't get to him. He was so absorbed in what he was doing he couldn't even hear their questions.

MacKenzie looked away for a minute while Hanna grabbed his shoulders and looked into his eyes. "How can I help you? What's the matter?"

Jeremy looked at her with far away eyes. "She's getting really serious," was all he said before he was interrupted by another message.

From Workstation 10 at the Berry Clinic. **Order.** *Surrender yourself to police custody immediately.*

Did she know there was an officer nearby? How could she?

The officer turned on his lights and got out of his car.

MacKenzie finished whatever she was doing and grabbed Jeremy's arm. "Trust me," was all she said.

From MacKenzie. **Order.** *Content unspecified.*

Accept, Jeremy immediately replied. He knew he was in way over his head with the implant, and MacKenzie would know what to do. He watched as his implant performed a dizzying sequence of unfamiliar functions. All his mail and privacy settings were reconfigured. There was nothing for him to do but sit back and watch. Hanna realized that MacKenzie could handle the technical side of things, so she walked toward the policeman. He was an older man with a kindly face.

"Hi, officer," she said in her sweetest voice, with just a hint of apology. "Thanks for helping out, but it's no big deal. We were at the Chocolate Bar tonight." Some of the desserts offered at the Chocolate Bar were intoxicating, and it was not uncommon for college students to get ill after a visit. The officer gave Hanna an understanding look.

"You young ladies take care of him for me," he said, seemingly satisfied. He shook his head at Jeremy and walked back to his car.

"No, not again," Jeremy groaned. He had rolled his head over the back of the park bench and was looking into the sky. The officer apparently thought he was having a wave of nausea from over-indulgence and chuckled to himself. But what pulled the color from Jeremy's face was what he saw.

Another phantom was slowly cruising down the street about 100 feet in the air, scanning the ground, looking for something. Jeremy quickly got up from the park bench and sat under a tree, but as he did he saw another image coming up the street from another direction, several blocks down. They hadn't seen him yet, and the tree wasn't going to provide adequate cover.

"I need to hide," he said aloud, eyes darting back and forth. Fortunately the police officer was in his car now and didn't overhear him. "There're two of them right now, floating along up there," he said, pointing discreetly up with his head. MacKenzie foolishly looked up, and the phantom noticed her. It stared down at the three of them for a moment and then dove toward them at incredible speed. The other, still a few blocks away, followed.

Jeremy panicked. He got up and ran into the park, looking for somewhere to hide, darting from bush to bush. Hanna and MacKenzie followed as fast as they could. When MacKenzie caught up to him she just about screamed, "just close your eye. They're not really here. They can't hurt you."

Jeremy stopped and stood up straight, closing his left eye. He gave a weak smile, but kept opening and closing his left eye. "It's no use," he said in a defeated tone. "I can choose not to look at them if I want, but they still see me. They're right here," he said, pointing just to his left and right. The ruse that he couldn't see them wasn't going to work anymore. The images were staring at him intently, studying his face. Jeremy plopped down on the grass in surrender.

"What can I do?" he asked MacKenzie.

"I don't know, Jeremy, but they can't do anything to you, can they?"

"No, they have no substance," he said, swinging his arm right through one. It smiled at him and did the same, but it was not a pleasant smile.

"Jeremy," Hanna said, looking around a bit nervously. "Doctors have the authority to have you committed to a hospital. If Dr. Berry knows where you are, she can have you arrested and sedated."

"But how could she know," MacKenzie began, "unless ..."

She didn't have time to finish. The three of them felt a sickening feeling in their stomachs as a police siren started to wail just half a block away. In a minute, the police officer stopped his hovercar in the middle of the street, just 20 yards away, and opened the back door. A huge German Shepherd stepped onto the street and stood at the officer's heel. They both walked toward Jeremy at a deliberate pace.

"Run, Jeremy," Hanna said. "There's nothing else to do."

Jeremy agreed, but he hesitated for a moment. He took Hanna's hand and looked into her face.

She smiled at him. "Go, while you still have a chance."

He squeezed her hand and then sped off like a deer.

Jeremy was at the other end of the park almost before the police officer could respond. He pointed, whistled, and let the dog go. It shot off at a tremendous speed.

Hanna and MacKenzie watched the foot race, terrified. Jeremy apparently knew he couldn't outrun a dog and decided his only chance was to lose him in the traffic on I Street. He ran in and out of cars, often coming dangerously close to a collision. But the dog wasn't fooled. Jeremy was recklessness, but the dog had absolutely no concern for itself. It was intent on its prey, and nothing else mattered.

Hanna bit her lip and clenched her fists. It looked now as if it was just a matter of time. But suddenly the traffic patterns changed. A hovercar stopped, trying to avoid the dog. Another car swerved to miss the first car, bounced off a bus and slid sideways into Jeremy. He was thrown 10 feet onto the pavement and crashed into a light pole.

Greg Krehbiel

Chapter 8 – Captured

"Listen to me. I know he checked in here. I was here when they brought him in," Hanna persisted. She was starting to lose her temper. Normally she would put a check on her emotions and back off, maybe even apologize and try to start over, but it was 3:00 in the morning and she had been through a lot in the last six hours.

"Ma'am, I'm sorry," the woman at the information desk replied, trying to keep cool herself. "I've checked the records three times. There is no Jeremy Mitchell in this hospital. There has never been a Jeremy Mitchell in this hospital. I'm not disputing what you saw," she said, raising her hands as if to ward off a blow as Hanna again opened her mouth to talk. "If you say they brought him in here last night, I believe you, okay? They brought him in here last night. All I'm telling you is that I have no record of it."

Hanna stood silent with her mouth open. After fifteen minutes of arguing with this woman, something finally made sense.

As soon as she and MacKenzie had seen that Jeremy was okay after his collision, they discreetly disappeared in the crowd before the policeman tried to track them down for questioning. They hired a hovershuttle, darkened the windows and moved out of the way -- just far enough that they could keep an eye on things, then they followed the paramedics to the hospital.

On the way, MacKenzie theorized about the technology that must be at work behind those ... images -- or whatever they were. Whoever could pull off all of that could easily change the admittance records at a hospital, Hanna reasoned. But they couldn't cover up everything. Nurses had to have seen him. Doctors had to have worked on him. She had to be able to find someone who could tell her what had happened and where they had taken him.

"I'm sorry," she said to the tired woman at the information desk. "You've been very kind and I've been very rude." She turned and walked away before the relieved desk clerk had a chance to respond. Hanna picked one of the lobby chairs and collapsed into it.

MacKenzie had left her hours ago. She was at her lab at the university, working on her theories about how to detect, or block, the images Jeremy had been seeing.

Hanna felt profoundly alone.

She sent Jeremy several messages, but he hadn't replied.

How am I going to find him? she wondered, and absent-mindedly called up the hospital's hole location on her implant, seeking inspiration. She saw the hospital's staff roster and thought about sending messages to everyone on the list, asking if they'd seen or heard of Jeremy. It would be a rude thing to do, but she couldn't think of any other option, so she composed a generic letter. It took some doing to find the unique address for all the staff people -- names, of course, were not precise enough -- but she got through half the list before she fell asleep.

*   *   *

"Pardon me, Ma'am, you're going to have to come with us," the voice kept repeating in her dream until she realized it was not a dream and that she was being roused by two men in military uniforms. Hanna sat up quickly, and looked around. She was still in the hospital, asleep in the lobby chair.

She had no intention of going anywhere with them. She stood up and headed toward the elevator, but they wouldn't have it.

"Not that way, Ma'am," the younger one said. He was polite, but firm, and without laying a finger on Hanna the two men managed to turn her around and get her out the front door of the hospital. As soon as she was out the door she picked up her pace and deliberately headed away from the military vehicle that was parked at the curb. She didn't recognize the insignia, but she didn't expect to.

The two officers got on each side of her, and two more came out of the over-sized hovercar. "I'm sorry, Ma'am, but you're going to have

102

to come with us," the younger one said again.

She turned around sharply and planted her foot on the sidewalk to emphasize her words. "I don't have to go anywhere with you, and I'm not. Good bye." She turned again and walked away. By this time the two men from the car were ahead of her. They made no threatening move, but it was clear that she was not going to get past them if they wanted to detain her. It was early morning and she didn't see any pedestrian traffic. Even if she screamed it was unlikely that anyone would hear her or try to help her.

Hanna walked straight towards the two men who were waiting for her on the sidewalk, and then suddenly stepped to the side and ran on the street. She didn't fool anybody, and they had her surrounded again in a few seconds. The four men now formed a close wall around her and ushered her toward the car.

She gave in and walked with them, wondering if it made any sense to make a break at the last second. There really wasn't anywhere to go, and she was sure she couldn't outrun them.

"Before I get in this car," she said after one of the men opened the door, "who are you and what authority do you have to treat me like this?"

"Special services, Ma'am," said the same officer, the only one who had spoken so far. Hanna remembered the designation: they were an investigative branch of the military that also performed special security functions, such as guarding heads of state. "We just want to talk to you."

"And what if I don't want to talk to you? I don't have to talk to agents of the special services. What you're doing is illegal."

"I'm also an officer with the Capitol Police," he said, unimpressed by her efforts to distract him but nevertheless showing her his badge. "You're not under arrest, and technically you can refuse to go with us, if you want, but if you decide to do that, I'd file charges against you for hindering a federal investigation. I can have that charge filed and approved in about a minute, and on that basis I can take you into custody. It's your choice."

Hanna had heard enough about the special forces to know that they often cooked up stories like that to badger people into obeying them, but she also knew that when they had authorization from high up in the organization, they usually had all the legal details arranged ahead of time.

She sneered at the man and got in the car.

*　　*　　*

"This is outrageous," Hanna screamed at her interviewer after the third consecutive hour of questioning. "I have told you everything I'm going to tell you, so let me out of this place." She had tried to send messages to Jeremy and MacKenzie, but ever since she had been taken from the hospital they had her in a communications black-out. The implants relied on radio signals to communicate with the hole, and Hanna had been cut off since she got into the car at the hospital, which was hours ago.

More and more she doubted that her captors were actually special services agents. Once off the street, the official demeanor quickly disappeared. The room she was in now -- what she could see of it in the dark -- was not impressive. The floor was dirty, and her seat was rocking from legs not quite matching.

"You haven't told us what we want to know about Jeremy Mitchell," the voice said again. It was such an irritating voice, a study in monotonous, atonal drone. She couldn't even see who was speaking to her, if it was a real person. The questioner might be in a dark part of the room, or it might be a computer-simulated voice. She was so sleepy and disoriented that she couldn't tell.

After another half hour Hanna had had enough. She had tried to be reasonable with this thing -- it had to be a computer, she thought -- but it refused to respond reasonably. She made up her mind to ignore it and take a nap. Her last sleep had been long hours ago in a chair in the hospital lobby, and that hardly counted. She had been in this place far too long. As she tried to get comfortable in the small wooden chair, the droning voice kept talking, probing, prodding, searching for a way to draw her back into a conversation.

*   *   *

When Jeremy opened his eyes he was looking through a window at two palm trees bending under a stiff wind. The clouds behind them were very dark, almost black, and a few raindrops bespeckled the window pane. He remembered the mad race across the park, the dog, and the frantic game of dodge with traffic. He also remembered the shock of his collision with the car, and he had a vague recollection of emergency personnel tending him.

He assumed he was in a hospital, but the window dressings seemed too domestic for that, and the furniture, as his eyes strayed from the window, seemed too homey. It was well-polished maple, and looked more like a private guest room than a room in a public facility. He wondered if this might be the style of recovery rooms in Society hospitals, but then he realized, seeing the ground extending beyond the palm trees, that his window was on the first floor and he could see two hovercars parked in a driveway out front. Everything spoke of a private residence.

He propped himself up in bed to take a better look around, and then he suddenly realized something else: there were no palm trees in Washington, D.C. Clearly he had been moved, and moved a long way. But why? He lay back down and wondered if Dr. Berry had won. Was he in a mental institution? If Dr. Berry had reported him to the police, they certainly would have turned him over to her care.

This spawned a new concern. He felt slightly drowsy, and it was unsettling to think that he might be on the "slow and dopey" drugs Dr. Berry had warned him about. Was he being treated for "implant psychosis"?

The locator function on his implant should tell him where he was, anyway. But his implant didn't respond. A blank, almost transparent desktop floated in front of him. It didn't respond to any network commands, so he turned it off.

Jeremy's expression grew grim, and he began to look for an escape. He tried to sit up and get a better look, and then noticed the cast on his leg. *Well, no more running for a while,* he thought, *and so much for an easy escape.*

Just then the door opened. Jeremy prepared himself for a struggle, but as soon as he saw his visitor, he relaxed.

"So we're up, I see," an older woman said. She was about 60, Jeremy figured, somewhat heavy, and grandmotherly, with that kind of face that could be radiant with joy or stern with disapproval on a moment's notice. She wore a plain, pale blue dress, not unlike something Jeremy would expect to see on his own grandmother.

"Where am I?" he asked.

"You're in my home," she said. That sounded good, Jeremy reckoned. It was unlikely that patients in the lunatic asylum were farmed out to people's houses. "And I don't think I should tell you any more than that."

"Why not?" he asked, somewhat indignantly. Who did they think they were, whoever "they" were who had taken him here, to cart him off somewhere and not tell him where he was?

"I'm told it's for your own safety," she said, and then held up her hands in the universal "stop" sign. "I don't want to argue the point with you, young man, but they didn't even tell me your name, so we're both in the dark about your situation. I've been hired to take care of you until you're ready to be moved, and that's what I'm doing."

Jeremy thought about that for a minute and then smiled at her. "My name is Jeremy Mitchell. I'm sorry. I shouldn't take it out on you."

"That's okay," she said. "I'm sure you're out of sort. They tell me that someone will be by to speak with you this afternoon, so maybe you'll get your answers then. But in the meanwhile, you haven't had any solid food for a while, so eat this." She pulled a cart in from the hallway and set a serving platter on a table in the corner. A breakfast-in-bed tray appeared from somewhere next to it. In a minute she had him set up with beef stew, steamed vegetables, black bread, coffee and some sort of pudding. It reminded him of dinner back home.

"How long have I been here?" he asked, taking a napkin from the tray and tucking it into his shirt.

"Just since yesterday," she answered, helping him prop himself up on the pillows, "but they tell me your accident was two days ago."

"Why doesn't my implant respond?" he asked, hoping this wouldn't be a secret.

"That was part of the deal," she said. "Mine doesn't work either. They set up some sort of black-out around my house, at least for a day or two. Eat up, young man. You need to get your strength back."

Jeremy smiled again. She seemed kind and a little bit crusty, just like an old lady should be. He thanked her for the meal and started with the stew. After the first bite, he realized he was starving.

Greg Krehbiel

Chapter 9 – Inside

"No," Jeremy yelled as he sat bolt upright in his bed, sweat dripping down the sides of his face. The room was dark and the gentle breezes of the midnight air toyed with the curtains. A bright moon cast dim shadows of palm trees on the carpeted floor and the peach-colored walls. The silence of the room was broken only by Jeremy's heavy breathing as he made the difficult transition from his nightmare to being alone in a dark, strange place.

He had seen it again -- the wandering eye -- but, as usual, he couldn't figure out what it was, or why it was there, haunting him. All he could remember was the eye, twitching unnaturally, just like Weatherstone's had when the knife penetrated his lung, and then the dream switched to the horrible vision of his wife's dead body lying in the grass, her bare arm etched with her own blood as, with her last strength, she had written the first letters of a name before her life slipped away. Jeremy had seen it, he was sure of that. The memory of that horrible night had never faded. But when the body was taken to Dr. Elizah for examination, the bloody writing was gone, except in Jeremy's nightmares.

It was the only solid evidence identifying Amy's murderer, but he was the only one who had seen it, and under Community rules it was inadmissible as evidence. Had it wiped off against his shirt as he carried her dead body back to the house? Or had someone in Dr. Elizah's office washed it off to cover for Weatherstone?

Jeremy lay back on the pillow, reliving the grim decision that twist of fate had forced him into. He, alone of all people in the Community, had known who the killer was, but the evidence was gone. He could never get a conviction under the Community justice system, which required at least two reliable witnesses. Besides, the fact that it had been his wife would cast a shadow on his veracity. His testimony would be dismissed. "You're just looking for someone to blame," they would say. Bloody writing that mysteriously disappeared was just too coincidental, and nobody wanted to speak against Weatherstone.

The dark despair of that late summer's night settled over him again. He had been through it a hundred times, but it never lost its poignancy. His mind drifted in dark thoughts as he lay back, staring at the ceiling, indifferent to life, or death, or love, or hate, wishing only for an opportunity to seek further vengeance for the loss of his beloved.

*   *   *

Jeremy awoke again facing the window. The sky was clear now, and the palm trees moved under a slight wind. There was nothing to do but lie in bed, so he simply stared out the window, wondering what state he was in, if he was in the United States at all, and what was going to happen to him.

He had tried the door during the night, but it was locked, and he couldn't open the window. Overpowering the old woman was an option, but it didn't seem like the right thing to do as long as he was in no danger, and he didn't know who or what was on the other side. He made up his mind that he was going to try to escape sooner or later, but for now he was content to let his leg heal and eat the free food.

Still, he wondered who had done this to him. Not Dr. Berry, he figured. She would have put him in a regular hospital or, rather, in a mental institution. And besides her, he couldn't put names on any suspects. There were, of course, the phantoms, but what did he really know about them?

That he had been taken here, "for his protection," the old woman said, implied that someone was after him, or watching him -- someone with sufficient resources to make it necessary to travel far away to hide him. It also implied that someone else was protecting him.

So which side were the phantasms on? Were they looking for him, or hiding him? He pondered that for a while, enjoying the view from his window and wondering what he had gotten himself into, but a voice from the other side of the room interrupted his reveries.

"It's a nice view," it said. "Much nicer than anything in Washington. Don't you think?"

It was a man's voice, and Jeremy rolled onto his back to look at him, but as he turned to look he saw the last thing he expected -- a head. The disembodied head of one of the phantasms that had haunted his life for the last few days was floating two feet above him, staring down at him.

"Not again," Jeremy said, and closed his eyes, dropping his head on his pillow in resignation.

"So it's true," the voice said. "Don't worry, the image is gone, Jeremy."

Jeremy opened his eyes. The ghostly head was gone.

He wondered how MacKenzie would explain this. He'd turned his implant on last night, in case his network connection returned, but he still had no service. But MacKenzie said the images must have been coming through his hole connection. Was someone generating the images -- the phantasms -- locally? Perhaps it was created by something very close by? He knew that his implant was connected to the network by a very high-frequency, low-watt radio transceiver embedded in his skull, so it was a simple matter for someone to block his access to the hole by jamming the radio signals, but he needed to know more if he was going to figure out what was happening to him. He wished he had done more research on the communications technology that made his implant work.

Jeremy sat up and glanced around the room to make sure the image was really gone, and then looked at his uninvited guest. He was a middle-aged, unremarkable man, except for a slight irregularity in his features that made his head look slightly crooked, as if his left ear hung down lower than his right. His manner betrayed the confident, efficient, hopelessly bored attitude that a genius might have when he was forced to address the general public.

He produced a pair of cups from a tray at the bed-side and poured black coffee for the two of them.

"I'm sure you're wondering who we are."

He had Jeremy's full attention as he sat back down in the room's only chair, took a noisy sip from his cup and proceeded to explain things in a dull, lecturing tone. He worked for the government. "No, no branch you're familiar with," he explained, which implied national security or defense, Jeremy thought. His specialty was network security. Recently, the test routines his organization periodically ran on hole communications had turned up some possible breaches of security. As he tracked them down he discovered a complicated web of false signals, phony addresses, decoys and other tricks to hide some kind of high-level shenanigans. He feared that someone was getting ready for a major operation, and it was his job to stop it.

He reminded Jeremy that if anyone could crack the multi-layered encryption codes that protected all hole traffic, they could make a mint in stock and commodity speculations, getting an edge on competitors, leaking trade secrets, extortion or just plain old theft. The possibilities were endless. Even worse, if a breach of security became common knowledge, commerce would grind to a halt, and there wasn't a convenient back-up. Even though a breach was unlikely, the signals he had been getting from his search routines indicated that somebody might be on the verge of breaking a few of those codes.

More research confirmed that something big was going on, but he couldn't nail it down. It was clear that more than one person was involved. This group was very careful, very shrewd, and very well financed, according to his theory. So far, there was no hard evidence of wrongdoing by the organization -- he only had an operating profile from some detailed analysis of hole traffic. He couldn't make any arrests, and even if he could he couldn't make them stick. He had a few suspects, but there was way too much of the puzzle missing to make any moves at this time.

Some of his agents -- he must be some kind of supervisor, Jeremy thought -- had been keeping an eye on one of the main suspects in this organization, and that's how Jeremy got tangled up in things. When he was taken to the hospital after his accident, Dr. Berry gave orders for him to be sedated and taken to a mental institution, but the people who came to take him away weren't staff of the mental institution, they were employees of one of his main suspects. Assuming that Jeremy was somehow involved with the organization, he had Jeremy taken away from the phony mental institution staff and brought to his house for questioning.

In the meanwhile, they started doing background work on all of Jeremy's friends and acquaintances. They monitored MacKenzie's lab work and found out she was working on a process very similar to some of the techniques used by the organization they had been tracking. Putting it all together, they developed a few working hypotheses, one of which was that Jeremy was working for the organization and was able to monitor hole traffic in some special way. Taking a cue from MacKenzie's work, they tried to send an image masked as noise and, as they had just proved, Jeremy could see it.

"But it seems, despite everything, that you're not a spy at all," he said. "In fact, you just recently left one of the Communities and got your implant, and Dr. Berry wanted you committed because you've been seeing things, and seeing things is a symptom of 'implant psychosis.'" He seemed to regard the concept with contempt. "But you don't have implant psychosis, Jeremy. What you have done, without trying, is become a very important player in a very big game."

His analysis was too precise to dispute, even if Jeremy had the desire. It seemed that he had become a pawn in a much larger game.

Jeremy fell back on his pillow and let it all sink in for a minute. Why did this have to happen to him, of all people? Hadn't he had his share of intrigue for a while? He had left the Community to get away from trouble, not to get a double dose of it. But then he wondered if it was truly only him. Were the other "victims" of implant psychosis really seeing the same things, only they weren't lucky enough to escape Dr. Berry's pharmacy? Such speculations would have wait for another time. Now he just wanted to get on with his life.

"Since you've decided that I'm not a spy, I guess you're done with me now," he said. "Can I go?"

"Go? Go where? I'm sure you realize you don't have a job any more -- Dr. Berry will have seen to that already -- and of course you've still got a cast on that leg. But if, as I hope, you are speaking somewhat figuratively, as in, 'can I be done with your investigation,' then the answer is a little more complex." He looked down and thought for a moment, but Jeremy didn't let him think for long.

"So I just have a cast on my leg, is that it? It's not broken? You put a cast on my leg to keep me still until you got around to me?"

He looked up nonchalantly, as if he had just asked about the time. "You're in perfect health. I'll have it removed this afternoon, if it bothers you," he said, and began to pace the room, as if the liberties they'd taken with him were of no consequence.

Jeremy rolled his eyes and shook his head. "And what is to keep me from walking out the door when you do, Mister, ... what is your name by the way?"

"Peter," he said, still pacing. "And what kind of answer do you want?" he continued. "We could still hand you over to Dr. Berry for 'treatment.'"

Jeremy shook his head. "No, actually you couldn't, because I imagine she's on your list of suspects and you wouldn't want me telling her about this little conversation we've had."

Peter stopped pacing and looked at Jeremy with a sudden, keen interest. "You have the right instincts, Jeremy. You just don't know the game." He shook his head and continued. "The truth of the matter is that we have drug treatments that can scramble your short-term memory so badly they're effectively erased, so we could still hand you over to the care of your precious doctor without much risk to my investigation."

Jeremy was appalled at this man's crass use of people. It didn't matter to him that Dr. Berry would medicate a healthy man into a fogged, useless existence, so long as it didn't impede his work.

Jeremy had always been taught in the Community that Society had become so large and so dependent on its industrial technology that it had to view the individual the way a machinist would view a screw -- just a piece that can be replaced when it's broken. Peter seemed to embody that attitude, and it disgusted him. His face had an almost inhuman detachment from emotion, as if only a machine could look that way. Jeremy wondered what series of circumstances and decisions led him to where he was today.

"Actually, Jeremy, I'd like you to consider working for me. You've got nothing else to do, nowhere else to go, and I've only told you one reason why you need me. No, my young friend," he said, the words sounding more than hollow from his unfeeling face, "you're stuck. If I'm right about this organization and what they're trying to do, you have an ability that threatens them. They'll want you sedated, or dead. Preferably dead. At the very least you need our help in keeping away from them."

And you can use me too, he thought.

"If that's the very least," Jeremy said, "why don't you tell me what the very most is."

*   *   *

MacKenzie lounged in her favorite chair in the lobby of her dorm, finishing up the homework for her noon lab and wondering, for the thousandth time, where Hanna had been for the last week. She did her best to cover for Hanna's absence from classes, but she was getting to the end of her options. She sighed, finished the last line of computer code and was interrupted by a message from her implant.

Forty three incoming messages from Hanna.

MacKenzie usually had her mail system send all messages into her inbox. She didn't want to be bothered with a mail notice while she was in the middle of a deep, theoretical computer question -- which was most of the time -- but ever since Hanna had disappeared she reset her mail parameters to put a priority on any message from Hanna, or any that mentioned her name.

Forty three? MacKenzie wondered, and before she had a chance to read any of them she saw Hanna herself stumbling in the front door to the dorm.

"Hanna," MacKenzie said as she saw her friend come in the L Street entrance. "Where have you been? I've been looking for you for a week. Everybody's been worried sick."

Hanna shook her head and looked at MacKenzie unsteadily. "A week?" Her eye wandered as she checked her calendar. Her face, already showing signs of severe stress and fatigue, grew pale, and MacKenzie quickly put out her arms to hold her in case she swooned.

"Here, sit down," MacKenzie said, lowering her into a couch in the dorm lobby. A crowd was starting to gather and MacKenzie resented the intrusion. She picked someone she vaguely knew and sent her for a glass of water, and then tried to get the rest of the onlookers to find something else to do. Hanna just closed her eyes and rested her head on MacKenzie's shoulder. "I don't know where I've been," she said, "but I feel horrible."

MacKenzie knew Hanna was going to need her for a while, so she attached her homework to a message to her professor and explained that she would have to miss class today. She let Hanna rest for a minute, made her drink the glass of water and then took her up to her room to sleep.

*   *   *

"Have you seen Jeremy?" Hanna asked as soon as they were in the privacy of her room. She sat on the bed and tried to give MacKenzie her full attention, but her head nodded and her eyelids drooped. MacKenzie gently pushed her down onto her pillow.

"No," she said. "I haven't heard a word, and I've checked all the mental institutions I can find, just in case that doctor woman got her way. He's just gone. Maybe he's had enough of Society and went back to the Community."

That was a thought Hanna hadn't considered. It would have been a natural way for him to escape, returning to his own people. The doctor couldn't get him there even if she tried. Still, Hanna hoped he was around, somewhere.

"But what about you?" MacKenzie asked. "Where have you been?"

"I don't know." Hanna shook her head. "I have a few, faint images, but it's like snatches of a dream you can't remember." She shook her head wearily, but MacKenzie told her not to worry about it.

"You rest," she said. "We'll worry about that tomorrow. Right now, you need to sleep. But I might be able to get some clues if you give me access to your mail headers. At least I might be able to figure out what zone you were in, and that sort of thing."

Hanna mustered up enough energy to adjust her security protocols so that MacKenzie could do her wizardry, and then she fell asleep.

*   *   *

Late that afternoon, MacKenzie was still working on Hanna's mail, trying to get a clue where she had been. Because implants had a limited communications range, the network had relay stations all over the country, spaced about a half a mile apart, to manage traffic. Each station had a unique code, and as signals passed from one relay into the main, high-capacity lines, the code from each station was embedded in hidden headers. If you knew about such things, as MacKenzie did, you could read those headers and trace the path of incoming messages.

It was the headers that allowed the mail routines to screen incoming mail, but clever programmers could get around that. Once MacKenzie went to a summer retreat in Colorado Springs and met a guy who just wouldn't leave her alone. He kept sending her mail, asking her personal questions, even telling her about his life and his dreams. She set her mail filters to screen for his name and automatically delete anything he sent, but he got around that quickly enough by using other user names, or sending from public terminals. But when MacKenzie found out about the hidden codes in the headers, she simply blocked out the state of Colorado and never heard from him again.

As Hanna slept the afternoon away, MacKenzie ran every analysis she could think of on Hanna's messages from the last three days. She had sent several from the hospital that made it into hole traffic, but for a week after that everything she sent was queued up in her out box. Wherever she had been, she had no contact with the hole at all. There were only a few places where blackouts occurred naturally, and none of them were close by. But it was an easy enough thing to contrive by jamming the radio signals.

Hanna's mail routines had automatically tried to re-send the queued messages every ten minutes. They continued to be rejected until just before she came into the dorm. That was why MacKenzie received a flood of messages from Hanna just before she saw her. Apparently, she had been kept in a communications blackout until just before she came into the dorm.

Having done everything she could with Hanna's mail log, she started reading the 42 messages she had just received. Fortunately, Hanna had kept her wits about her during her confinement. She mailed updates on her situation periodically. Those messages could have been erased from her implant outbox if her captors had had the right equipment, but apparently they hadn't, and MacKenzie was able to read the journal of her ordeal from the messages. It would have been fascinating reading except that it had happened to her best friend.

Chapter 10 – The Network

More relentless questioning. I wish I could send you something more substantive, MacKenzie, but I've been sitting in this chair in this same room forever. I eat here, I sleep here. Fortunately they let me go to the bathroom and stretch my legs a little, but it's just me, the room, and the interrogator's voice. They keep asking about Jeremy, and of course I tell them nothing, but I'm afraid they'll use drugs on me before too long.

That's it for now.

That was the 42nd and last message, but it had been sent three days before MacKenzie received it. The 41 previous messages detailed Hanna's experiences from the moment she got into the car with the security officers, whom she later suspected of being phonies. They had taken her only a little way before one of the guards covered her face with a smelly handkerchief that knocked her out. When she awoke she was tied to a chair in a dark room, completely alone. In the 40 remaining messages, Hanna detailed the same, monotonous, endless questioning about Jeremy: who was he, what did he know, what had he said about Dr. Berry, what had he said about the images he claimed to see, why did he see them, did anyone else see them -- and on and on it went for hour after hour and day after day.

At first, Hanna was full of questions and complaints about her treatment, but after she decided that her questioner was a machine, she tried not to reply any more. She found that as the questioning wore on, she occasionally found herself responding. She didn't answer the questions, but she was talking back, arguing, complaining and protesting her innocence. As soon as she was aware that she had started speaking again she would be silent, compose another message to MacKenzie and resolve to keep her mouth shut, but it was only a matter of time before she found herself arguing with the questioner again.

After what seemed like an eternity of questions she fell asleep in her chair. When she awoke she found herself untied and in a different room: one with bathroom facilities and a very meager serving of vegetables and rice. She was ravenously hungry and ate the bland food quickly, then used the facilities. As soon as she was done she heard a hissing noise, became disoriented and passed out. She awoke in the same chair, listening to the same questions, going through the same mental torture.

And so it went until the final message. They probably did resort to drugs, MacKenzie assumed, and that explained why Hanna hadn't sent any more messages, and why she looked so terrible when they finally let her go. MacKenzie had to assume that Hanna's captors knew everything about those things Jeremy had been seeing -- or at least they knew everything Hanna could tell them.

MacKenzie turned her attention from her implant screen and looked around the darkened bedroom. Hanna was sleeping peacefully in her bed, and MacKenzie's own head started to nod.

She was the perfect computer student. As long as she had a project to keep her busy, she could stay awake and remain productive for days. But as soon as the job was done, she crashed, recuperating for the next marathon session. It was midnight now. She knew she wasn't going to last much longer now that there was nothing else to do, so she slid her chair next to Hanna's bed and tried to cover herself with the corner of Hanna's blanket, then fell asleep.

*   *   *

Hanna's alarm went off at 7:30.

"Shut up!" she yelled. It was a programmable alarm clock, and she could have programmed anything she wanted as an off switch, but her previous attempts at gentler commands never seemed to work. It was too easy to say "off," or, "good morning" and roll right back over on the pillow. Yelling "shut up" at the decibel level she had programmed into the off switch helped to wake her.

MacKenzie slept through the alarm and the yell. Hanna headed for the shower, suddenly realized that she had been wearing the same clothes for a week, tossed them into the launderer, then retrieved a new outfit from her dresser. Three minutes later, clean and dressed, she tried to shake MacKenzie awake. After a Herculean effort of shaking, tickling and prodding, MacKenzie woke up enough to mumble "coffee" and went back to sleep. Hanna remembered that MacKenzie's alarm clock didn't make a sound -- it was set to brew a strong cup of Jamaican coffee at 8:00. It was the smell that woke her up. Usually, it was a nice arrangement. The only problem was when she spent a few days in the computer lab; then she had a nasty mess to clean up when she came back to her room and found a few days worth of coffee spilled all over the machine. The cleaning robots would take care of the carpet and the furniture, but the appliance itself would have to be scrubbed by a microbot. They were expensive, and the university didn't provide them. Hanna thought she might buy one for a Christmas present.

Hanna looked down at her friend, slumped over in the chair, only half covered with the corner of the blanket. She realized how much MacKenzie had been through in the last several days. She bent over and kissed her on the cheek and then went down the hall to the food concession to get a cup of coffee. When the smell reached MacKenzie, she took a sip, rolled off the bed and stumbled toward the shower. Hanna set the cup of coffee on the narrow ledge where the launderer stuck out from the wall and sat in the room's only chair. She had a lot of back-logged mail to go through and she wanted to see if there was anything from Jeremy.

MacKenzie stepped out of the shower and went for her coffee before she even touched her clothes -- such was the power of her addiction. A few minutes later they both ran a brush through their hair and set off for McDonald's. Except for a few necessary grunts, neither of them spoke until they were out the front door and into a beautiful spring morning.

"So what did you find out?" Hanna asked as soon as they left the building, as if she had been eagerly waiting to be out of the dorm before she spoke.

MacKenzie wasn't sure how to answer. She had two concerns. On the one hand, she wanted to figure out what was going on so they could find Jeremy and help him if they could. On the other hand, she wanted to help Hanna restore her memory of the last few days, and she wasn't sure about the best way to do that.

"I didn't find out much that is useful, actually," she said, clearly disappointed in herself. She was used to working miracles. "Have you started to remember anything from your experience?"

Hanna slowed down, as if walking fast and deep memory work didn't fit together, and shook her head. "The last thing I can remember," she said deliberately, "is watching that dog tear off after Jeremy." She turned and looked up at MacKenzie. "Did he get away?"

"Are you starved?" MacKenzie asked. "Do you mind if we try something before we go to eat?"

It wasn't like MacKenzie to be evasive, or to postpone breakfast, so Hanna figured she was up to something. She shrugged and MacKenzie pulled her somewhat bewildered friend off in a different direction. She took Hanna to the park where they had their long talk with Jeremy a week earlier. MacKenzie walked to the place they were standing when the police dog started running after Jeremy, and she asked Hanna to visualize the whole scene in her mind. Hanna closed her eyes and thought for minute, then opened her eyes and looked around, imagining the sound of the officer whistling at the dog, and then seeing the dog take off after Jeremy. Suddenly she put her hands to her mouth.

"He was hit by a car and thrown into that sign," she said, and started running toward it, just as she had a week ago. It was starting to work. Her memory was starting to come back, but she couldn't remember what happened next.

"That's enough for now," MacKenzie said. "Actually, it's better than I expected. Let's go get something to eat and come back, okay?"

*　　*　　*

MacKenzie picked up some food at the bagel shop across the street as Hanna put her thumb on the identification plate of the autodispenser to get her large coffee and two egg muffins. A familiar voice from behind her said, "Eating a real breakfast for a change? That's good."

"Jeremy!" Hanna said in surprise. She threw her arms around his neck. "Where have you ..." She couldn't continue. Jeremy put his finger to her lips to keep her quiet, then pointed outside with a nod of his head. Hanna followed him out and they found MacKenzie waiting for them in the alley, all smiles, with a touch of cream cheese on the corner of her mouth.

"Sorry to hush you like that, Hanna," Jeremy said, "but I need to keep a low profile. Come with me."

He led them deeper into the alley between McDonald's and the office building next door, then behind a large cargo vehicle and a few trash receptacles, through a door and into the physical plant of the office building. The hallways were like a maze, but Jeremy picked his way through quickly and confidently to another door that said "Janitor" on a small, red nameplate. He pressed his thumb to the locking device, opened the door and led them in.

The room was clearly not for a janitor. An attractive, very busy woman sat behind a large desk, working meticulously on a very small electronics device with a pair of hand-held instruments, not unlike surgeon's tools. She greeted Jeremy with, "Hi, Mr. Mitchell." Jeremy nodded and hurried Hanna and MacKenzie past the reception area into a small conference room and shut the door.

"Jeremy, what's going on?" Hanna said, looking around in wonder at the room. It was posh in the extreme, unlike anything she had seen in Washington.

"I really hate to say this, especially since you've probably been worried about me for the last week, but I can't tell you." He looked sheepishly at both of them, expecting a torrent of righteous indignation, but MacKenzie just shrugged and said, "We should have expected as much."

"So what *can* you tell us, then?" Hanna asked. "And can I eat my egg McMuffin in this place? I'm starved."

Jeremy nodded and held out a chair for her at the conference-room table. "What I can tell you is that I wasn't hurt too badly by my run-in with the car, and that I still need to keep clear of Dr. Berry, and probably the police, for a little while." He looked them over for a minute and then continued. "But you both look like you've got your own story to tell."

MacKenzie had been riding on an emotional high since Jeremy spirited her out of the bagel shop. Her best friend was back safe, and now Jeremy seemed okay as well. She wanted to talk so badly it hurt, but she realized that she needed to work with Hanna on recovering her memory, and she believed, based on something she'd picked up in a psychology class, that associations were the key to memory, and lost memory had to be recovered very carefully. Anything she said here might make the process more difficult.

She composed a private message to Jeremy. Just at that moment, Hanna started speaking.

"Yeah, something weird has happened to me," she said. "I can't remember anything from the time you were hit by that car until yesterday afternoon." Jeremy looked at her with concern and remembered Peter's words that her organization had checked up on his friends. He had received a few delayed messages from Hanna yesterday at about noon, but they didn't say anything about being kidnapped, and he assumed they had been delayed because of his situation, not hers.

His implant chimed an incoming message.

From MacKenzie. Chat mode requested.

Accepted, Jeremy replied.

"You can't remember anything?" he said.

Don't push her, Jeremy. I've got a strategy for helping her get her memory back, okay?

"Nothing, really," Hanna replied, "except little pieces of images from here and there." She paused for a minute and looked at her McMuffin. "I remember that I didn't like the food."

"That's not saying much, knowing your habits," MacKenzie said disdainfully, and then sent another message to Jeremy.

She was kidnapped by somebody. She composed lots of messages to me that explain what they did to her.

"I'm so sorry, Hanna, it must have been terrifying," Jeremy said.

Can you send me copies? I got five messages from her as well. I'll forward them to you.

"I guess it was, but, ... I don't remember," Hanna said.

"That's okay, Hanna, don't worry about it now," MacKenzie said. "We'll work on it."

I guess that's okay, MacKenzie replied. Secretly she was pleased that Hanna had sent 42 messages to her, but only five to Jeremy. She forwarded the messages.

The room was suddenly quiet, and then Jeremy laughed. "This is maddening. We've all got these tremendous stories to tell, and we can't say a thing."

*   *   *

"Okay, this is where he left us, right?" Hanna said to MacKenzie as they went over the events of that fateful night for the fourth time. "Then he ran that way," she pointed, "then the cop sent the dog after him, and it looked for a minute like he was coming after us, but then right here," she walked forward about 30 feet, "the dog veered off toward Jeremy." MacKenzie nodded and the two of them started walking toward the street, following the path of the dog. Hanna munched on a candy bar, still trying to catch up from a week on a starvation diet.

"Then there was all that foolishness in the street, and the collision, and then Jeremy came flying through the air and hit his head against this post," she said, laying her hand on it. She had reviewed this scene enough to be fairly dispassionate about it now, but the first time she remembered that Jeremy had been hurt she begged MacKenzie to tell her what happened. MacKenzie refused, and Hanna finally decided to play along.

"That's right," MacKenzie said, leaning against the post herself, "and what did the dog do?"

"It came right back here and started growling at Jeremy, but then the cop called the dog off. I think he knelt down next to him like this," she did it, "and started looking Jeremy over." By now they were both immune to the curious stares of passersby, and continued to act out as much of the events of that night as they could. They had informed their professors that they would be out of class for at least a day. MacKenzie hoped they could get this over with soon. She was dying to talk to Hanna about what happened during her interrogation, but she had committed herself to trying to rebuild Hanna's memory one step at a time, and she was pleased to discover that the method was working.

"And then I saw the emergency vehicle hovering over that building there, and I waved to it," Hanna said, "but it was already on its way. I guess the cop had already called for it."

They continued like this, working on every scene in the park until Hanna could remember everything as well as MacKenzie, or better. Then they went to the hospital and repeated the procedure. The process picked up momentum: the more Hanna remembered, the easier it was to remember more. By dinner she was able to recall some of her experiences in that dark room. MacKenzie decided she had done her job, and that she would go over all the messages with Hanna later.

The day's work drained them more than either expected, so they decided to treat themselves to a fancy dinner and relax. When the wine arrived, Hanna made a toast. "To my best and truest friend, MacKenzie," she said, holding up her glass.

"Wherever you go, I go," MacKenzie replied.

*   *   *

"What kind of a perverted, criminal outfit do you run here," Jeremy yelled at Peter. He had finished reading about half of the messages MacKenzie had supplied him and he couldn't contain himself any longer. The rest of the staff, loitering around on the edges of the main suite were in shocked silence, afraid to show any interest, but too intrigued to miss hearing this confrontation. Peter was not a man you yelled at.

"You kidnapped me and put a cast on a healthy leg, and you kidnapped my friend and half tortured her. I don't care who you work for or what kind of high-and-mighty moral principles you have, you can't treat people this way."

Peter stared at him for a solid minute, completely unperturbed by his rampage. He could have been considering what to have for lunch, or whether or not to kill him on the spot, but you couldn't tell it from his face.

"How do you know we kidnapped her?" Peter asked in a calm voice, and then walked away.

Jeremy was so boiling with rage that Peter's words took a few minutes to sink in. He stood there, not sure whether to yell or throw a punch. Finally he stomped back to his office and shut his door. He wished he could slam it, but Society doors didn't work that way. They slid out from a cavity in the wall and were opened and closed by pulleys and engines.

Jeremy fell into his chair and closed his eyes, allowing the torrent of emotion to flow unrestricted through his mind. After a few minutes he began to calm down and systematize his thoughts. It embarrassed him to explode like that. He knew he had a violent temper and he preferred to keep it under control. So far in his life it had only caused him grief, but part of him still believed it was a hidden asset that served him well, somehow.

From Peter to Jeremy. Come into my office in five minutes.

That was the last thing he expected to hear from him. *So, he has to dress me down now,* he thought. He looked for an object to hurl across the room, but there was nothing available. Instead, he took a deep breath and began to analyze what he knew about Hanna's situation. He had five minutes to get his thoughts in order and decide whether to yell at him again and quit, or whether he had jumped to a wrong conclusion.

$$* \quad * \quad *$$

"Give me five reasons why it probably wasn't us who kidnapped your friend, and five why it probably wasn't the Network," Peter said as soon as Jeremy entered her office. He did his absolute best not to look sheepish, but Peter had such an austere look about him, he wasn't sure he had pulled it off. Ever since Jeremy had signed on with his organization, Peter had been a rigid taskmaster. The last four days had been the most intensive experience of his life as Peter ran him through a series of lessons and drills. He had learned more in the last 48 hours than he thought possible.

"One," he began. "When you told me you had checked up on my friends, you didn't mention Hanna. That could indicate that you were unaware of her, or that you hadn't tracked her down yet. Two. You used completely different techniques on me. The operation against Hanna seemed low-budget by comparison. Three. You admit that you checked up on MacKenzie, but you didn't kidnap her. Why would you kidnap Hanna but not MacKenzie?"

"Reasons why it probably wasn't the Network," he continued, "Why didn't they kill her?"

Peter nodded. "I'm glad you didn't make up a bunch of nonsense just to fill your quota," he said. "Based on what you know of the Network, that's a decent analysis. Now," he said, moving on, "I want a full report of what they did to Hanna, with your opinions on what it all means, and I want you to tell me everything you think they could have learned from her. I want it before tomorrow morning."

He didn't say "dismissed," but he might as well have. Jeremy left, trying very hard not to look like his tail was between his legs.

I guess that's initiation, he thought.

Greg Krehbiel

Chapter 11 – Duncan

"Eunice MacKenzie?" a man with a heavy Scottish accent asked as she was heading across campus the next morning. She and Hanna still had a lot of work to do to restore Hanna's memory of her ordeal, but they had decided to go back to class before Hanna got too far behind.

"Sort of," she said, stopping to talk to the powerfully built man. She didn't recognize him, and his demeanor didn't inspire confidence. He reminded Hanna of a Scot she had once seen in a movie -- stern, strong, someone you wouldn't want to cross, and who might be a saint or a devil. "I go by MacKenzie, if you don't mind." He nodded.

"I'm an admirer of your groundbreaking work on hole communications," he said with no hint of a smile.

How could he possibly know about that? she wondered. She hadn't told anyone what she had been doing, and none of her other projects could really be called "groundbreaking." Had someone been looking over her shoulder in the lab? MacKenzie wasn't sure if she should play dumb, ignore him and walk away, accuse him of violating her privacy, or what. They stared at each other for a few seconds, and then he asked if they could talk privately.

"Privately?" she laughed. "No, we can't. But I would be willing to meet you somewhere, in public, with a friend."

The man thought about that for a minute and then agreed. They made arrangements and he hurried away. He walked with the confident stride of a man who knew his business and would neither expect nor tolerate any interference.

*　*　*

That evening, Hanna and MacKenzie sat in a corner booth at the Chocolate Bar, waiting to meet the strange man who had approached MacKenzie earlier that day. The rainy afternoon gave way to a brilliant, clear evening sky, and the light from the setting sun on the wet pavement made the view of the Massachusetts Avenue pleasant and relaxing.

"Do you really think this is a good idea?" Hanna asked. "It seems like we're getting sucked into something that I don't want to be involved with. And from your description, I'm not sure this man is entirely safe."

MacKenzie shook her head. "I think we're involved whether we like it or not," she replied. "I don't think he's safe, but I haven't made up my mind whether he's good or bad. But don't worry, I've taken precautions." Hanna could only guess what she had done, but she trusted her friend completely. MacKenzie had the rare gift of knowing her limits. If she said she had taken adequate precautions, then there was nothing more to say.

"Here he comes," MacKenzie said as she saw the man come in the door. He was alone, as they had agreed. Not a few eyes were drawn in his direction. He was a man who commanded respect, or at least notice, but he was a willful man -- you could see it in everything he did -- and, despite his general good looks, the women who sometimes went to the Chocolate Bar looking for dates weren't interested. They were looking for a good time: he was far too serious.

MacKenzie caught his eye and he came to their table.

"I know about your experiments in the computer lab," he said to MacKenzie after the barest of introductions. He said his name was Duncan. "Your command of hole communications is quite impressive. I wish you were working for me."

MacKenzie's first thought was to question how he knew about her work, but she decided to hold off on that one for a little while. "What kind of work do you do?" she asked.

"It involves hole communications," he said in a very quiet voice.

"Doesn't everything?" MacKenzie asked.

The edge of his lip curled into a slight smile. "I *monitor* hole communications," he said, pausing slightly after the second word.

"Isn't that both illegal and impossible?" Hanna asked, slightly irritated with Duncan's manner. Before he had a chance to answer, a waitress delivered three chocolate sundaes. By common consent they were all silent while the waitress was within earshot.

"I hope you like chocolate sundaes," Hanna said after she left.

"The answers to your questions are yes, yes, and yes," Duncan said as he drove his spoon deep into the dessert, pulled it out, overflowing with chocolate, and shoved the oversized helping into his mouth. "At least that's what you're supposed to believe."

"How did you monitor my work?" MacKenzie asked in as level a tone as she could manage. If he was able to do what he seemed to be claiming, it was rude, illegal and unbelievable all at once.

"I can do lots of things," Duncan said, "but I'll give you a demonstration. Call up something on your implant. Anything you want."

Did he expect to tell her what she was seeing? The very idea that someone could monitor what she was seeing on her implant was absurd, and a week earlier -- before she met Jeremy -- MacKenzie wouldn't even have played this game, but now she was ready to give him a chance. She tried to pick a hole address he wouldn't guess, just to make it a fair test, so she looked up the concert roster of the Baltimore Philharmonic Orchestra. As soon as the page was visible on her desktop, which seemed to float in the air just above Duncan's chocolate sundae, MacKenzie suddenly turned in the booth, faced the wall behind her, and started waving her arms as if she were shooing a very large and active fly.

"Go away, go away," she said. "It's not your business." Hanna looked at MacKenzie as if she was crazy, but Duncan stared at her in shocked disbelief. He recovered quickly and began to look behind him and around the room, searching for someone.

"Is *he* here?" Duncan said, and without waiting for an answer he got up and left.

"What in the world was that all about?" Hanna asked after Duncan had left the Chocolate Bar.

"I played a hunch and it paid off, that's all," MacKenzie said, "but we can't talk about it here. Let's finish these sundaes and I'll tell you about it later." MacKenzie had that smug look on her face of someone who had just pulled off an incredibly good practical joke.

*   *   *

The alley entrance to Jeremy's office didn't look at all the same in the dark, and it took Hanna and MacKenzie a few minutes to find it, and several more to find the door labeled "Janitor" once they were inside. MacKenzie sent a message to Jeremy that they had arrived and he quickly opened the door and let them in. He was still peeling some kind of plastic mask off his face.

"So, now do I get to find out what this was all about?" Hanna asked in a frustrated tone.

Jeremy smiled a conspirator's smile at MacKenzie and then looked at Hanna. "Think about it, Hanna. That big fellow you met tonight claimed to know what MacKenzie had been doing at her workstation. MacKenzie suspected that those images I've been seeing had been spying on her in the computer lab, and that was how Duncan knew what she'd been working on, so she asked me to come along and see if any of them showed up tonight." While he was talking he took something out of his pocket and plugged it into a port in a workstation. MacKenzie looked on with keen interest. "When Duncan asked MacKenzie to look something up on her implant, one of the images appeared right behind her head. I sent a message to MacKenzie telling her it was there and she pretended to try to shoo it away." He laughed. "You should have seen the expression on its face when it thought she could see it."

Hanna noticed another patch of plastic material stuck to Jeremy's face, and she picked it off. "So you were in disguise?" she asked. "Where were you? How did you hear our conversation?"

Jeremy smiled and glanced at the workstation, keying in a few simple commands. MacKenzie watched everything he did very carefully. "Yes," he said, "I was in disguise. Some of those phantom things know what I look like, and I didn't want them to see me. But I could hear what was going on from this," he held up a small gadget about the size of a matchbook, "and MacKenzie and I were in chat mode." Hanna took an interest in the listening gadget but Jeremy put it in his pocket with an apologetic look. "Sorry," he said.

Hanna shook her head at him. "You're in this stuff pretty deep, aren't you, Jeremy? But then again, it looks like we are, too. Who is this Duncan character? And what's he going to do now? Was it you he meant when he asked if 'he' was here?"

"I'm sure of it," Jeremy said, looking at the workstation again, which now displayed an image of Duncan sitting at the booth in the Chocolate Bar. Jeremy had taken a micro camera to the Chocolate Bar as well as the listening device. While they looked, the workstation matched the image from the camera with an internal database. Next to the image of Duncan appeared a series of links to other information about him.

"Duncan is heavily involved with these net spies," Jeremy said.

"Is that what you call them now? Net spies?" MacKenzie asked.

Jeremy thought for a minute before answering. "Actually, I think that was the first time I used the term. It just came to me, but it seems appropriate, doesn't it? The one I saw tonight was right behind you, looking just over your head and, I presume, directly at whatever you were viewing on your desktop. That's how Duncan expected to be able to tell you what you were looking up."

"That means that Duncan was in contact with the net spy, just like you were in contact with MacKenzie," Hanna said.

MacKenzie shook her head and sat down with a faraway expression on her face. Jeremy was about to ask her something, but Hanna stopped him. She knew that look. MacKenzie was in genius mode, filtering everything she had just learned through her encyclopedic knowledge of the implants and hole communications. Jeremy and Hanna stood still, watching her for a minute, then Jeremy turned to the display on the workstation and began following a couple of the links.

Peter's either going to love me or kill me tomorrow, Jeremy thought. Duncan was one of Peter's main suspects with the network. Tonight's work had established that Duncan was connected with the net spies, but, unfortunately, he had also spooked him. He didn't know which would be more important.

*   *   *

"Jeremy's into this in a big way," MacKenzie said as they walked back to their dorm around 1:00. They were the only people on the street, so the patrolmen on each block followed them at a discreet distance, tag-team escorting them back to the dorm. Crime was almost unheard of in Washington, and the patrolmen wanted to keep it that way. Hanna loved them. They were respectful and always polite, but it would be foolish to mistake politeness for weakness or a lack of resolve. Patrolmen were required to be black belts and expert marksmen.

"That workstation he was using back in his office had some high-end stuff on it," MacKenzie began. "And that camera and listening device weren't cheap, not to mention the mask he was wearing. He's linked up with somebody who has a lot of resources."

Hanna pondered that for a minute. "So there're at least two groups out there," Hanna said. "Whoever Jeremy's working for, and whoever Duncan's working for."

"It seems that way," MacKenzie said. "And the 'net spies,' as Jeremy calls them, seem to be on Duncan's side." She stopped and looked at Hanna. "Do you think we should go to the police and tell them what we know?"

Hanna shook her head. "We can't. We promised Jeremy not to talk."

"But we know enough on our own now," MacKenzie continued. "We wouldn't have to tell them anything about Jeremy."

"Wouldn't we?" Hanna asked. "How could we tell our story without mixing in some of what we've heard from Jeremy? And if they thought something serious was going on, they'd summon us to testify, and we'd be required to talk or face obstruction of justice charges. Besides, I imagine one of these two groups is connected with the government. I doubt they need us."

MacKenzie always deferred to Hanna on theory, just as Hanna deferred to her on computers. They walked the rest of the way home in silence, each considering what they had learned and working on their own suspicions and theories.

*   *   *

The excursion to the Chocolate Bar ate up a lot of the time Jeremy had to work on the report Peter expected by morning. He had the office concession pumping out coffee, but he could already begin to feel the diminishing returns. Useful brain power was running out, and he was less than half done.

Two hours later he was finishing up his report with the last of his mental energy. He had to get some sleep before morning, so he began tossing his clothes into the launderer and looking for the right address to send the report. Now that he was an employee of Peter's organization, he had access to the roster, but as he looked for the address, a name caught his eye.

Carl Maria Lenzke, known in the Community by his title, the Advocate. *The lying rat works for Peter.*

Jeremy followed the link to Lenzke's name and found his office address. He was temporarily assigned to one of the smaller agency offices in Fairfax, Virginia. Jeremy had to meet with Peter at 10:00, but he had a hovercar at his disposal, if he needed it. It would be possible to be in Fairfax as late as 9:45 and still make his meeting with Peter. Jeremy quickly planned his itinerary for the morning, reserved one of the hovercars for the 8:00 to 10:00 slot, set the alarm in his implant and went to sleep.

*   *   *

"I thought you didn't usually eat breakfast," MacKenzie said as she set her coffee and bran muffin on the table across from Hanna.

Hanna had just stuffed her sausage muffin in her mouth and couldn't answer for a minute. "I've been so hungry," she said after a moment. "They didn't feed me very well, you know, and I think those drugs had some effect on my appetite."

"You don't look any worse for it," MacKenzie said, and Hanna smiled, "but it hasn't improved your taste in food." Hanna gave her a dirty look and took an over-large mouthful of hotcakes just for spite.

"Okay, okay," MacKenzie said. "Actually, I've got some theories I want to bounce off of you."

"Computers just aren't my thing," Hanna protested, taking another bite. "But go ahead," she mumbled through her food, forgetting her manners, and then giggled. MacKenzie glowered at her.

"Okay, first of all, why did that ghost thing, that 'net spy,' as Jeremy would call it, get behind me and look over my shoulder as if it were watching my implant desktop? I mean, it was acting as if my implant was really there, in front of me."

Hanna set down her fork, picked up her coffee and thought about that in silence for a minute. "The ghostie wasn't really 'there,' in any meaningful sense of that term," she said. "If you're on the right track with your research, then the 'net spy' is just some background noise that Jeremy can see, for whatever reason. So maybe we need to back up and ask why the ghostie appears in a particular place at all -- behind you, or anywhere else."

MacKenzie smiled. "You were always good at this kind of thing. Questioning assumptions, I mean. Let me see," she thought for a minute, but Hanna was ahead of her.

"Here's what I mean," Hanna continued. "If somebody has figured a way to crack the security codes on the hole, then it seems they should just be able to access that information at a terminal or something. They shouldn't need to be sending these images all over the place."

"But?" MacKenzie prompted.

"But what if they're not accessing the data stream itself? That's what you call all that glop that carries the information around, right?" MacKenzie tried not to be irritated when Hanna's silly side came through, but "glop" was annoying, and she gave Hanna a disapproving grin.

"Oh lighten up. I'm getting the theory right, and you know what I'm saying," Hanna said. "So here's what I'm thinking: the implants are in our eyes, ..."

"Connected to our optic nerves," MacKenzie corrected.

"Same thing," Hanna said, knowing it was wrong. She was in the mood to offend MacKenzie's technical sensibilities, and it was too easy when MacKenzie was in her hyper-analytical mode. "So maybe the feed works both ways," Hanna continued. "We 'see' the desktop that the implant feeds into our optic nerve, so how do we know that what we really see -- photons hitting our eyes, and all that -- doesn't feed back into the implant and onto the net?"

MacKenzie's trained response was to shake her head no. That was against all the canons of hole communications. But so were "net spies." She stopped shaking her head and looked back at Hanna. "It can't happen," she said, and Hanna couldn't tell whether she was stating that as a fact or trying to convince herself of it.

MacKenzie continued. "I have to admit that your theory would explain what we know so far," she said. "The best way to process visual information is in 3-D. You just can't get it all otherwise, so if you had a huge database of visual information, the best way to analyze it would be through virtual reality. You'd suit up and just walk around inside the images, looking at things." She nearly choked on the last words.

"Looking at things," she repeated, "just like those things were looking at my desktop." MacKenzie's face turned white. "This contradicts everything I've learned about the implants, but it has to be right." She swallowed hard. "Hanna, this is terrible. This means that somebody has the capability of looking at anything and everything that anybody does."

"Duncan?" Hanna asked.

*   *   *

"Jeremy, it's good to see you again," Carl Lenzke said, standing in the doorway of his modest office, which was part a series of row houses converted into offices. The tone of his voice was friendly -- even cheerful -- but his face was somewhat grave. "I figured you'd get around to visiting me one of these days."

Jeremy was marching up the walk to the office like a man on a mission. Lenzke stood still, waiting to see what Jeremy was going to do. He walked up to the door and stood on the mat, being careful to stand a little too close to Lenzke, showing just a touch of belligerence and disrespect. They both stood eye to eye for a minute. Neither blinked nor spoke.

"Why did you lie to us?" Jeremy finally asked, spitting out the word "lie."

"I don't have to explain my actions to you," Lenzke said. Jeremy tensed up to spring at him, but Lenzke stepped back into the brick foyer of the office, opening the heavy wooden door wide and gesturing for Jeremy to enter. "By all means stay outside if you'd rather fight, but if you wish to talk about something, please come in. I am at your disposal, either way."

Jeremy was a young man, physically fit, agile, and hopping mad, but Lenzke, although more than 30 years his senior, was no slouch. He was powerfully built and had that calm, serious air of a man who knows how to handle himself in a fight.

Jeremy stepped in, once again careful to invade Lenzke's space just enough to be rude. Lenzke pointed him to a small, lounge-like room to the right and the two of them went in. The office was an old brick row house, tastefully decorated on the inside and out. Its formal look was designed to inspire calm confidence, but it wasn't having any effect on Jeremy.

"So you're above explaining yourself to one of your Community guinea pigs, is that it?" he asked. "What kind of an experiment were you working on, Mr. Lenzke?"

Lenzke looked up at a painting of a fox hunt that hung on the wall above the fireplace. He showed no sign of concern about Jeremy's remarks. He looked like a wise tutor who is saddened that he can't get through to one of his favorite students.

"All I can say, Jeremy, is that there were things going on that you don't know about; things I wish you would never, ever know about." A slight look of distant fear filled his eyes. "Or me, for that matter," he said with a lighter expression. "I wish I didn't know what I know. But every man has to do what he can with the hand he is dealt in life. I'm not playing this hand with you, Jeremy, so you don't get to see my cards. All I can tell you is that I did what I thought was best, and I still believe it to have been the best decision, just as I believe that you made the right decision."

Jeremy looked at him with a confused expression. "In coming here?" he asked, continuing to look out the window and refusing to make eye contact, except to threaten.

"No, in leaving the Community. You would never have received a fair trial in there. The man you killed was too well connected, and Community justice has a very narrow view of justifiable homicide."

Jeremy looked at him sharply. The Advocate knew all about his case, of course, but Jeremy didn't like to be reminded of it. "The man I killed was a nut and a murderer. He should have been locked up years ago." He looked Lenzke in the eye now.

"Of course he should have," Lenzke replied. "If it makes you feel any better, I urged that myself, but the council wouldn't hear of it. His father wouldn't allow it, and his father exercised more power than you know." There was something in his voice, or his expression, that told Jeremy there was a deeper meaning to that remark. "It was only after his son killed your wife that the Community started to recognize how much control he had over them. But still, you would have been convicted of murder by any jury in the Community. You did the right thing to leave."

"And you want me to believe that you did the right thing in lying to us all those years? In telling us that Society was ready to storm in and take over?"

Lenzke didn't reply, he just looked at Jeremy, and his face said everything. He had no remorse, and he was confident he was in the right. For a second, Jeremy softened in his judgment. Lenzke seemed so sincere, and so empathetic. It was hard to believe that he was quite as bad as Jeremy had imagined. For a second, he almost believed that there were extenuating circumstances, but only for a second.

"I don't know why I came here," he said, and stormed off.

Chapter 12 – The Dragon Lady

"So what can I do for you today, young lady?" Dr. Berry asked after MacKenzie came into her office. The large, exquisitely decorated room was designed so that a guest's attention was drawn to the exact center, which is where Dr. Berry sat in her chair behind a large desk.

A doctor's ego, MacKenzie thought.

She had seen Dr. Berry in the sociology class, but she hadn't paid her much attention. Here, it was unavoidable. Even the furniture had been altered to make Dr. Berry stand out. MacKenzie realized that her seat was several inches lower than Dr. Berry's, which, added to the fact that Dr. Berry was a fairly tall woman, made her dominate the room.

"I'm a hole communications major," MacKenzie explained, "and I've been doing some research on how the implants interact with our brains. I have some ideas about ways to expand the range of things we can do with implants, but I need to know a few things about the connection between the implant and the optic nerve." MacKenzie was very nervous about this meeting and wasn't completely convinced it was the right thing to do. She needed some information about the implants to follow a few of her theories, and Dr. Berry was the most accessible local expert on the subject.

Dr. Berry nodded. "Haven't I seen you somewhere before?" she asked.

"You visited our sociology class when that guy from one of the Communities was there. Phyllis -- my teacher -- told me that you were an expert on implants." That was as close as she wanted the conversation to get to talking about Jeremy, but Dr. Berry wouldn't have it.

"Speaking of your class, have you seen Mr. Mitchell since then?" Dr. Berry persisted. "He seems to have disappeared." MacKenzie got a lump in her throat. This woman seemed to be the center of all the 'coincidences' involving Jeremy recently. It was hard to predict what she might know and MacKenzie didn't want to have to lie to her.

"Is that the guy from the class?" MacKenzie asked innocently. "I'm sorry, I'm not very good with names. I'm somewhat of a computer fanatic. I don't recognize people too well."

"You recognized me," Dr. Berry said, and MacKenzie felt she was being interrogated. She had to play to the good doctor's weakness.

"You're hard to forget," she said in a shy voice.

"So what can I do for you?" Dr. Berry asked again.

"About the optic nerve, I don't understand how the connection with the implant works. Obviously the implant feeds visual information to the optic nerve for the visual interface, and we know there is some feedback from the optic nerve to the implant, but I'm curious how much."

"How much?" Dr. Berry asked. "Everything. When they designed the implant, they had two options for the connection with the optic nerve, exclusively one-way, or two-way. There was no sensible way to filter it, and no need. Since the implant needs some feedback from the user to be able to adjust brightness, sharpness and color, and to create the illusion of 3-D, the one-way connection was out of the question. So the implant gets everything the optic nerve has to tell it. But of course it isn't sophisticated enough to interpret that information the way the brain does. The microcomputer in the implant just disregards that part of the data stream."

But what if it doesn't? MacKenzie wondered.

"That's great," she said aloud. "All of our computer simulations of the implants don't register that feedback at all. Somebody in class asked about it one day and the professor said that was a physiology question, not computer science, but it got me thinking. Maybe my project will work after all."

"What are you trying to do?" Dr. Berry asked with some interest.

"I want to design an implant utility that can take photos. I think it would be cool to be able to take a snap shot of what we see and send it as part of a message."

Dr. Berry shook her head. "Good luck. Nobody really knows how the brain processes all that information, so it's pretty ambitious to think that you could design an artificial system to do it. And besides, the implants aren't designed to do that. You'd need to design a new implant, and who would want to have a new one installed just to be able to take pictures?"

A new implant, MacKenzie thought. *Maybe that's the secret.*

"So why can we design an artificial system to give visual information to the brain, but we can't build one that uses the visual information the eye collects?" MacKenzie asked, wondering if she was playing this correctly. *Hanna's the one who should be doing this kind of thing,* she thought.

"That's just the point, really," Dr. Berry said. "The visual information we feed to the brain through the implant is quite different from what the brain normally receives from the eye, but somehow the brain figures it all out and we see the image. The implant can only do what we program it to do, but the brain has the ability to adapt to differing kinds of sensory input. It's really quite remarkable."

MacKenzie was lost in thought for a moment. Hanna would have said she was in genius mode. Dr. Berry just watched, patiently.

"You might talk to a friend of mine," she said in an odd tone of voice after more than a minute. "He does a lot of contract work for me when I need a special analysis of implant problems. He knows more about the technical side of implant communication than anyone. His name is Duncan Douglas." She paused and studied MacKenzie's face. "Do you know him?"

MacKenzie was certain she had lost some color in her face. It was just too coincidental. "Know him? I don't think so. I may have heard the name around the lab. But there's one more thing I'd like to ask of you. Can I borrow an implant? A new one."

"Sure, but why would you want to?" Dr. Berry asked. "There are computer simulations available that are 100 percent reliable. If you tried to set up an interface between a workstation and an actual implant, you'd probably get noise in the signal."

"I just want to be thorough -- just in case something was overlooked in the simulation programs."

"On one condition," Dr. Berry said. "When you're done with it, come back and tell me about your research. That is, if you find anything. And be sure to talk to Duncan."

"Deal," MacKenzie said

Dr. Berry's expression was inscrutable as she led MacKenzie to the storage closet, gave her a small, sealed package, and escorted her out. "I hope to see you again soon, MacKenzie," she said. "By the way, is that your proper name?"

"It's my last name. I don't like my first name, so everybody calls me MacKenzie. See you soon."

*   *   *

"How did it go with the dragon lady?" Hanna asked over a burger in the dorm cafeteria. Hanna and MacKenzie usually met there for lunch, and almost always for dinner.

MacKenzie laughed. "That's a good description of her, I think. She's formidable, has strange, unknown powers," she said this in an eerie voice, like a magician casting a spell, "and a very large and obvious weak spot."

"So where's she vulnerable?" Hanna asked, straining to get her mouth around the over-sized sandwich.

"An ego like this," MacKenzie replied, holding her hands out as far she could reach. "But I found out something really important." She paused until she had Hanna's full attention. "She knows Duncan."

Hanna's jaw dropped open, and then she giggled at herself for having such a stereotyped reaction. MacKenzie shook her head. "Do you think that's how she knew all those creepy things about Jeremy?" Hanna asked. "Do you think Duncan has been feeding her stuff?"

MacKenzie shrugged. "It's the best guess we've got so far. If not, it sure is a remarkable coincidence." MacKenzie didn't believe in coincidences, and Hanna knew it.

"I spoke with Jeremy today," Hanna said. "It looks like his new job, whatever it is, is going to keep him pretty busy for a while."

MacKenzie nodded. "I hope he's okay. Personally, I think he's in over his head."

"So are we," Hanna said. "I'm still wondering if I'm going to get kidnapped again. But you look as if you've got something else on your mind. What else is there?"

"I borrowed an implant from Dr. Berry," she said. "So far, all my computer work has been on the simulators at the lab, but I'm beginning to think that the simulators don't tell the whole story. This is starting to get too creepy, Hanna."

*   *   *

Whatever the agenda had been for Jeremy's 10:00 meeting with Peter, it had been torn up and discarded. From the moment he came back to the office Jeremy noticed a frightened calm among the other staff. He didn't know that this was the telltale sign that the boss was in a lather about something. Jeremy found out as soon as he walked into his office.

"Do you have any idea how much we paid to set up this office?" Peter asked Jeremy. "It's supposed to be a secret. Your training has already covered that -- several times, I believe. Maybe you haven't picked this up yet, but this is a secret operation, and right now you're one of our biggest secrets. So what do you do? Your first week on the job you run off on a private mission and bring two of your girlfriends into the office to impress them."

There were a lot of things Jeremy could have said, but he kept them in. He didn't think it was wise to argue with an angry person, much less an angry boss.

"And then this morning you go and visit Lenzke. I don't know what you're thinking, mister, but we don't let on who works for the agency. The network would just love to follow a few of us around and find out who all our contacts and co-workers are." Peter paced around the room.

"From now on, Mr. Mitchell," he said, turning to face him, "you're on a tight leash. The only reason I'm not getting rid of you," Jeremy thought that was an intentionally ambiguous choice of words, "is because that stupid stunt you pulled at the Chocolate Bar actually gave us some good information." Jeremy searched for any signs of a smile, or an "atta boy," but it didn't show.

And because nobody else can see the net spies, Jeremy thought, but it didn't do any good to argue.

"I know you're a young man, and this is all new to you, and you want to impress your girlfriends. But you need to grow up and get over it. This is serious business. The agency's work isn't for show and tell. Got it? We're dealing with a conspiracy that threatens the communications technology of the whole planet. There's no time for adolescent stunts."

Jeremy stood silent, waiting for the tirade to finish. Peter looked him over with something like approval.

"We want our agents to be risk takers. You've got that on your side, anyway. And I'm glad you can stand up to a good dressing down. But your training has only begun. You have no idea what you've gotten into."

"I'm transferring you to another office. Maybe you have what it takes to do field work, and maybe you don't. We'll find out. I'm sending you where you can be useful to me, and get some more training as well. The network has been trying to find our central operations center for a long time, and you're our only way to detect these spies they have. You leave immediately. There's a hovercar waiting for you outside."

Dismissed, Jeremy thought Peter should have said as he headed for the door.

*   *   *

"Amazing," MacKenzie muttered to herself for about the hundredth time as she continued to monitor the differences between the computer simulations of the implant's function and what the implant actually did.

"Hey, brain child," one of the other students said. The dull ones regarded that as an insult, but MacKenzie thought it fitting that even when they were being rude they recognized who really knew what was going on. "If you're not going to tell us what you're working on, can you at least keep the ejaculations to yourself?" MacKenzie didn't even hear him. She was so involved in her work that a fire might have singed her clothes before she noticed the heat.

She was running a series of comparisons between the implant she borrowed from Dr. Berry and the computer-generated model. They performed precisely the same on all the standard diagnostic tests. It wasn't until MacKenzie started to simulate input from an optic nerve that the computer model and the actual hardware started to give different results. Whenever she entered any of the type of input the implant would use to adjust itself to its host, the computer model simply displayed an internal calibration routine. As far as the computer model was concerned, that information never made it onto the hole. The implant itself performed completely differently.

MacKenzie pushed her workstation to the limits of its remarkable abilities to find out what was going on. The artificial intelligence routines were searching everything ever written on the optic nerve and creating a database of its known, probable and even speculative functions. MacKenzie fed all of this into the computer model and, through an interface she designed herself, into the implant. The computer model's reaction was predictable: it didn't react at all, or it displayed the internal calibration routine. The implant, on the other hand, processed every type of input MacKenzie could throw at it and sent a corresponding signal into its communications relay.

The really disturbing thing was that all the normal functions -- all the things the implant and the computer model had in common -- corresponded to standard communications output. But whenever she fed simulated input from a human optic nerve into the implant, the resulting communications output had a completely different signature. MacKenzie could only think of one reason to give this output a different signature -- hiding it. Someone had designed the implant to feed visual information onto the hole with a carrier signature that every textbook on communications science said was not used or useful. Not only that, but the standard computer simulations of the implants were designed to cover over this feature.

The conspiracy was getting more and more complicated. MacKenzie called up the records on who designed the implant's communications routines, but the only record said "National Institute of Standards." The computer simulation, likewise, had been written by NIS. *So what is it? Did Duncan infiltrate them or something?* she wondered.

After coming to a logical break in her studies, she stored all her research for the day in her private file, encrypted it and recited her magic incantation, "My eyes alone or turn to stone." It was a silly thing she had picked up from a cheap novel, and it embarrassed her to say it, but it had become a habit, and a superstition. Besides that, invoking the cosmic forces against evildoers was the signal to her mind and body that crunch time was over and bed time near.

On the way back to her dorm she checked her in box, having, as usual, turned off her message indicator while she was working. Everything seemed pro forma except one anonymous message from a public terminal, which grabbed her attention.

From Public Terminal 21352, it read. *Congratulations. You've figured out the technological side of the conspiracy. But at what price? Do you think Dr. Berry gave you one of the regular implants, or maybe a special one? Is the conspiracy so dumb that they let communications hole specialists find out their secrets, or do they want something from you in return? Are you going to join them when they make you an offer you can't refuse? You'd better hope they don't catch you.*

She had once told Jeremy simply to shut his eyes and ignore the ghostly images of the net spies. Now she realized how hard that would be, and how much harder it was to realize that someone might be watching her, and she had no way to know it.

*   *   *

One of the conditions of Jeremy's employment with Peter was his agreement to spend at least five hours a day in the training center, which was a restricted address on the hole that contained a series of workbooks and interactive films. His scores on the first few lessons were impressive. They covered secrecy, surveillance techniques and, of course, procedure. Every once in a while Jeremy peeked into the intermediate lessons, which provided an introduction to martial arts and weapons training, but he was still a long way from graduating to those.

The number of rules in Peter's organization simply astonished him, and he had to have them all memorized within a week.

It seemed that every conceivable contingency had been anticipated and bludgeoned to death by lawyers. The underlying principle of it all seemed fairly simple -- learn how to break the law without getting caught, and, more importantly, without implicating the agency. The agency's operations were sanctioned at the highest levels of government, they said, but the government retained plausible deniability if an agent was caught in a transgression. But they couldn't say it that way. Sometimes it seemed incomprehensibly vague, while at other times the procedures were mind-numbingly restrictive and precise.

It was while he was trying to memorize one of these that his hovercar came to a stop and the door hissed open.

"Mr. Mitchell," a voice said. A man in a smart uniform, almost like a hotel concierge's, was waiting outside the door. "Peter told us to expect you. Can I get you anything?"

This benefit of agency life was worth getting used to. The staff treated him like a first-class guest at an expensive hotel, with 24-hour service. Peter was very demanding of his workers, but he also provided some phenomenal perks. Jeremy had left the main office with nothing but his clothes, and he didn't even need them. With a word he could have gotten a replacement.

"Some coffee, I suppose," he said as he stepped out of the hovercar into the reception area of a very nice office complex. He looked around, curious how the hovercar made it in. There didn't appear to be a door large enough.

"This way, please," the man said, pointing Jeremy down a hallway.

"How did the car ..." Jeremy began, but the man corrected him.

"'To take full advantage of useful memory, focus your attention on things that relate to the mission,'" the man recited. Jeremy remembered it as one of the rules he was supposed to memorize, shrugged, and followed down the hall.

Chapter 13 – Choosing Sides

"Shut up," Hanna yelled at the alarm clock the next morning. At first she didn't understand why the bed felt so strange, then she remembered her guest and, somewhat reluctantly, dragged herself out of bed and walked down the hall to get two cups of coffee. MacKenzie, frightened by the anonymous message the day before, stayed the night with Hanna for moral support. The idea that someone invisible was watching her -- someone who wasn't even there -- seemed at least tolerable in the company of her best friend.

Hanna sympathized with her feelings, even though she thought they were somewhat irrational. Why would anyone want to spy on her while she slept? And if they did, they would probably know enough about her to check Hanna's room, too. She didn't let any of this on to MacKenzie when she showed up last night, looking as if she'd seen a ghost. But under the morning sun they'd have to talk it through -- a little more objectively.

MacKenzie offered to sleep in the chair again, or on the floor, but Hanna insisted they share the bed. Now she wasn't sure that was the right choice. Her neck had a nasty kink and her body was stiff.

Hanna enjoyed the opportunity to watch MacKenzie's conditioned response to the smell of coffee. Years of waking up to her aromatic alarm clock had far more impact on her than the caffeine ever could. Hanna entered with two steaming cups and watched as they quickly did their work. MacKenzie immediately sat up, took her cup, and yawned through several slurps.

Hanna sat on the chair, sipping thoughtfully as the morning light shone through her window onto the deep blue carpet. Dorm rooms at the Capitol University were small, consisting of a bed, a desk, a bathroom and the usual appliances, but they were very nice, and the cleaning robots kept them spotless.

MacKenzie sat up on the bed, looking embarrassed.

"Sorry," she said, somewhat sheepishly.

"For what?" Hanna asked. "Don't be silly. You were scared."

MacKenzie smiled. "It just seems so stupid now."

Hanna shrugged. "Life's been strange recently. Sometimes it gets to you."

They sat in silence, sipping their coffee and feeling refreshed by the sunshine. Invisible spies seemed far-fetched in the peaceful room.

MacKenzie adjusted the ventilator to let some fresh air in. After a few minutes, Hanna got up to take a shower. "Conference time in ten minutes, okay? We've got to go through this thing and figure out what to do."

"Okay," MacKenzie said. "I need to go turn off my coffee pot. I'll take a shower and meet you back here."

Hanna shook her head. "Meet me in the lobby. Let's take a walk."

*   *   *

"Whoever sent that message wanted to make it sound like he's not part of the conspiracy," Hanna said as they made their third trip around the block. "Read it to me again," she said. MacKenzie did.

"So he's saying there's a conspiracy," Hanna said, breaking it down into discreet parts, "that it's pretty deep, that you've uncovered part of it -- the technological part -- that he's not part of it, and that they're a dangerous bunch. That's what it says. It also implies, or at least hints, at a few things; that Dr. Berry gave you a doctored implant -- that she *wanted* you to find this stuff out -- and that she's part of the conspiracy and will make you an offer at some point."

"Also," MacKenzie said, "the very fact that he sent the message implies that somebody was spying on my work. Somebody knows what I'm doing, and the only people who fit the bill right now are Jeremy, Duncan and Dr. Berry."

Hanna slowed her pace and stared absently at the sidewalk, then abruptly decided to change course and head across the street to one of the many small parks in the District of Columbia.

"We can't discount the people who kidnapped me, either," she said as they made it to an unoccupied bench. "If they got everything they could out of me, they would know that you've been on to something."

"Yeah," MacKenzie said. "But they could just be working for, or with, any of the three people I mentioned. You know," she continued, "I don't have any reason for it, but I've always assumed that those goons who captured you were connected with Duncan somehow. I don't know who else to suspect."

"Yes you do," Hanna replied, looking at her seriously.

"Dr. Berry?" she suggested, but Hanna's expression said no. "Jeremy?" MacKenzie asked, incredulous.

"We know he's connected to these 'net spies,' but we don't know how. He knows you have some ideas about how they operate -- or at least how they work. And it's pretty obvious that he's in way over his head in some kind of cloak and dagger thing. It's very possible that somebody is using him."

MacKenzie knew that Hanna liked Jeremy, so she was somewhat surprised that Hanna could make such an objective assessment of him. A thought suddenly occurred to her.

"Wait a minute," she said. "Duncan knows who Jeremy is, right? Remember what he said at the Chocolate Bar? 'Is *he* here,' as if he were afraid of him. So maybe Duncan and Jeremy are on opposite sides." She paused to think about that for a second. "So let's just assume that one of them is in on this conspiracy and the other one is a good guy. In that case, which one is more likely to be the good guy?"

Hanna's eyes raced back and forth, assembling a mental list of pros and cons for each position. MacKenzie could compose programs as easily as falling out of bed, but Hanna had the same facility with arguments.

"Okay," she said. "Let's assume the images are on the wrong side.

Jeremy was plagued by them, which implies he is on the good side, in addition to everything else we know about him. Duncan was asking about your methods, which could imply that he was on the good side -- trying to find out what the bad guys were doing -- or on the bad side -- trying to cover his tracks.

"However," she continued, "we haven't heard much from Jeremy since he's been in this little club of his." She said it with a little sarcasm. "It could be that he's been recruited by the conspiracy. Maybe they've convinced him of their goals, or maybe he's been bought out, or just plain duped. He is a little naïve about how things work in Society, and besides, we really don't know much about his character, after all," she said it with a frown, and MacKenzie knew Hanna had been wondering about that for some time. "So we shouldn't assume that Jeremy is on the right side."

"But we also have to consider the message," Hanna continued. "Who would be more likely to send it, Jeremy or Duncan?"

"I guess Duncan. I don't know why Jeremy would want to spook me," MacKenzie said.

"I agree. It seems to me that only the good guys would want to contact you. The bad guys might want to kill you," she blurted this out before she had a chance to think about it, and then regretted it, "but I can't see why they'd want to arouse your interest."

MacKenzie tried to ignore the comment about getting killed, but it stuck with her.

"Unless, as the message implies, they're going to try to recruit me," she said. "Still, it would be an odd way to approach it." She thought about that for a minute. "So what you're telling me, bottom line, is that we just don't know anything." MacKenzie finally said, exasperated.

Hanna grinned. That wasn't her conclusion, but she didn't want to say anything more until she had thought it out further. "No, what I'm saying is that I think we need to meet Duncan again. Let's ask him what he's up to."

"But what ..." MacKenzie began, and then changed her mind. She looked down at the pavement and frowned. "I guess it doesn't really matter. It's not as if we can hide from the net spies." But then something else occurred to her. "But what about Duncan's connection with Dr. Berry?"

"I've wondered about that, too. We'll just have to ask him."

* * *

It was the eye again, twitching nervously. Jeremy hated that eye. He wanted to carve it out with the hunting knife in his right hand, but the images changed too quickly, just as they always did. His mind flashed back and forth from Amy's dead body, to the eye, to the bloody knife, to the Community council, to the tears of his mother as he bid her a final farewell, to the knife, to the eye, and on and on. These same events continued to haunt his sleep. Sometimes other images would be added -- Dr. Berry warning him of implant psychosis, Hanna smiling at him, Dr. Elizah telling him that there was no name written on Amy's arm, his father, his face torn between anger and admiration for his son's rash actions, the path he and Amy liked to walk on Sunday afternoons, but which led to the field where she was murdered. But the knife, the eye, the body, the council; they were always there.

He awoke with a start, sweaty and wide-eyed, his heart pounding in his chest. He looked around the room to get his bearings, and then remembered. He reached for the pad of paper he had left on the table next to the couch in his office and tried to write something about the dream, but nothing came out. The images faded before his conscious mind was clear of the animal fear that filled him during his haunted sleep. All he managed to write was "bloody knife, eye, body, council."

* * *

It struck Hanna as uncomfortably coincidental that the only reason they were able to contact Duncan was that Dr. Berry had given his full name to MacKenzie. She didn't believe in coincidences, so she decided there were two options: Providence was guiding them to Duncan, or they were being led by the nose into a trap. "Either way, I'm game," she said with a fatalistic smile. "I can't stand just waiting around while those invisible things might be spying on us."

Hanna wondered if Dr. Berry wanted to find Duncan, and she was using MacKenzie to lead her to him. That led her into a series of ideas about who's on which side, and what everyone is trying to do, but she realized it was still all speculation. She needed more facts.

MacKenzie sent Duncan a message with a copy to Hanna.

To Duncan Douglas. Hanna and I would like to meet with you. Alone, this time – for both of us. We suspect we might be followed, so take precautions.

"After what you pulled last time," Hanna said, not in an accusing voice, "he might not want to see us at all."

*　　*　　*

Jeremy wasn't at all sure what his mission was in the new office. Under Peter's orders he had spent 15 of the last 30 hours in the training center. Not that he minded. In fact, it was fun. But his schedule was so tight he didn't have any extended time alone, and he was beginning to miss it. In the Community, company was something you craved. If you met someone along the road, you talked for a while because you'd been busy with your own thoughts for the last few hours. His life in the agency was the polar opposite. He'd never experienced such an overload of activity, and it was starting to wear on him.

He was frequently interrupted in his training sessions and taken to meet someone, to be tested on his studies, or to get a hands-on lesson with some new gadget. It seemed that every time he went anywhere, his guide would take him on a long, winding trip through the facility, making frequent stops in side offices or computer rooms. He began to wonder if all the "training" wasn't just a farce and the only reason they wanted him there was to keep an eye open for net spies.

*　　*　　*

Hanna and MacKenzie headed to the top floor of the Graham Memorial Library on the Capitol University campus. Duncan had agreed to meet them in one of the private study rooms. It seemed like a safe location, but Hanna wasn't convinced they were going to be able to get a room.

"They're almost always packed this time of day," she said as they stepped off the elevator, and sure enough, every room had the 'occupied' light on. As they looked at each other, not knowing what to do, a young woman approached them. The pupil of her left eye looked odd -- slightly large, and off center -- and it gave her a sinister look.

"Are you looking for Duncan?" she asked. They nodded, and she pointed them to one of the rooms. "Go in there. He'll be with you shortly."

They opened the door to the study room and saw three people sitting around the central desk. A chalk board on the wall had a series of equations and a few drawings scribbled all over it. They looked up at Hanna and MacKenzie, who suddenly had an awkward feeling. Each of them had the same odd left eye, just like the woman. When they saw Hanna and MacKenzie, they immediately wrapped up their conversation and left. One of them intentionally left a large paper envelope on the desk. It seemed that Duncan had arranged for someone to reserve this room to ensure that it would be available at the proper time. MacKenzie thought the secrecy was a little overdone, but considering what she suspected was going on, she couldn't complain.

Hanna opened the envelope, which contained two black eye patches and a note that instructed them to put them on their left eyes. Hanna looked quizzically at MacKenzie, but nodded knowingly and immediately put the patch on. Hanna followed her example. They sat in silence until Duncan showed up. Duncan's left pupil had the same, eerie look.

"I take it you understand what this is about," he said, pointing to his left eye. MacKenzie nodded, but Hanna didn't respond, so he explained.

"As your friend here has discovered, our implants feed what we see onto the net," he said. "They're not supposed to -- or, at least it's not supposed to be known that they do. But they do. If we wear these," he said, and Hanna realized the enlarged pupils were just dark contact lenses, "it blocks the transmission -- what we see doesn't get onto the net, so nobody can spy on us."

"Unless they bugged the room," Hanna suggested.

"I had it scanned," Duncan said nonchalantly, "and I have people stationed around us watching for any kind of surveillance. We are completely secure. Getting out might be a problem," he said with a wry grin.

Duncan sat quietly for a moment, allowing the seriousness of the situation to impress itself upon Hanna and MacKenzie. This wasn't a college prank, or a neat computer project, but they already knew that. Hanna's kidnapping had already raised the stakes beyond the mundane, and as she considered the danger and seriousness of the situation, she wondered why she was here at all. MacKenzie was the computer genius. Hanna's only involvement was that she knew Jeremy and MacKenzie. It was somewhat unsettling that that was enough.

"So what did you want to talk about?" Duncan asked.

"The conspiracy," MacKenzie said, intentionally using the word from the anonymous message. Duncan just stared at her for a moment, trying to read her face.

"And what do you want to know about the conspiracy?" he asked, nodding his head slightly as if to say "yes, it was me."

"First, which side are you on?"

Duncan laughed. "What's the point of the question? Do you expect me to say I'm a bad guy? But I suppose you have to ask," he conceded. "First, however, I want you to know how fortunate you have been. You've fallen into the middle of the crime of century, and, so far, you've stayed alive. That's something. This game gets rough from time to time," his eye strayed ever-so-slightly toward Hanna, "but we're the good guys." MacKenzie wondered if he was responsible for kidnapping Hanna. "If the conspiracy had any idea how close you are to figuring them out, your life wouldn't be worth a cat's whisker. The only thing that has saved you so far is that we managed to distract Dr. Berry while you were working in your lab."

MacKenzie tried to think it through. If Duncan had sent her the message, then he had to have information from the net spies. That was the only way he could have known what she had been doing. So does that mean the net spies are working against the conspiracy? If so, what worse thing is the conspiracy doing? Duncan began to smile. He seemed to guess what she was thinking.

"It's far more complicated than you imagine," he said.

Hanna and MacKenzie each had several competing theories that tried to tie together the isolated pieces. They peppered Duncan with questions, trying to make sense of it all. After an hour of conversation that seemed to stray from one topic to another, never bringing them any nearer to a conclusion, Duncan convinced Hanna and MacKenzie that the best way for him to explain what he was up to, and why, was to take them to his central office.

When they agreed, Duncan gave an order and several of the students who were waiting outside began to move. Duncan poked his head out of the study room and gestured for Hanna and MacKenzie to follow. Each step of the way -- from the room to the elevator, from the elevator through a back hallway, and out the freight entrance to a waiting hovercar -- black-eyed students were guarding the way, motioning for them to continue, or keeping them back if anyone ventured too near.

Just as Hanna began to wonder if, after all this secrecy, Duncan was going to let them know where his office was, he flipped the privacy switch in the hovercar and the windows went dark. The on-board computer system had been pre-programmed for their destination, so

Duncan merely told the car to go and they took off.

When the doors opened ten minutes later they found themselves inside a small garage. The outside door had already closed behind them and Duncan led them through another door -- a security door, MacKenzie noted -- into a large warehouse. It was only half full, and the collection of machines, offices and computer stations gave the place a disorganized, eclectic feel.

Hanna noticed five large virtual reality tanks against the side wall. She had never actually seen one because she had no interest in what they were typically used for. In fact, it made her uncomfortable to see them here. She knew what they were from the unavoidable and somewhat garish advertisements that hyped all the fun things you could do in a virtual reality tank. She didn't care for that sort of thing. Real life seemed more interesting to her than fantasy adventures in a computer simulation.

But she knew how they operated. The tanks were about 10 feet high and were filled with a solution that could be adjusted to make a human body neutrally buoyant. The person in the tank, called a "rider," wore an elastic, waterproof, skin-tight suit that monitored every bodily movement and fed that information into the tank's program, which provided real-time responses. The suit not only monitored what the body did, but provided appropriate stimulation to the skin, depending on the program. Someone in a virtual reality suit could go skiing, practice karate, climb Mt. Everest or swim in a coral reef -- all without leaving the VR tank. The suit would provide the appropriate visual, tactile, auditory and olfactory stimulation. They were still working on a virtual sense of taste.

MacKenzie didn't notice the tanks. She only had eyes for the computer hardware. Because of the nature of the communications links between the hole and the implants, computer functions done through an implant interface were limited, despite the fact that the implants were connected to the most powerful computers in the world. Normal implant use didn't even approach the limits of implant computing, but for the serious computer user, like MacKenzie, it was necessary to work at a terminal where high speed interfaces allowed the user to pull out all the stops and run elaborate computations.

One wall of the warehouse was packed with terminals and state-of-the-art processors. Holographic bubble displays floated in front of the programmers, displaying complicated mathematical processes in three dimensions. To Hanna they just looked like computer-generated art, but MacKenzie saw several familiar patterns. Duncan's lab was at least three times the size of the lab at the university, which was a good-sized computer lab in its own right. MacKenzie was mesmerized.

Duncan removed his black contact lens and told his guests they could remove their patches. "We've managed to protect this area," he said, and then noticed that MacKenzie wasn't hearing him. "You're never going to figure out what's going on until you look over there," he told her, pointing to the tanks, "and notice this," he said, indicating the high-speed connection between the tanks and the wall of computer hardware.

MacKenzie looked, but she was too impressed with the hardware to see the big picture. Hanna picked it up first.

"That's how you spy on people," she said, pointing to the tanks. "You monitor everybody's visual information from the hole with those things," she pointed to the processors, "and they generate a virtual reality simulation of the world, which gets fed into the tanks. So somebody in one of those tanks can 'go' anywhere -- inside a virtual image of the world -- without really going anywhere. They're there, but they're not there, just like the net spies."

Duncan smiled and MacKenzie looked at Hanna in surprise, then she went into hard-core genius mode, as Hanna would call it, dropping her mouth half open and getting that characteristic look on her face; the one that looked to Hanna like someone who was recovering from a stroke. She was taking Hanna's layman's explanation and putting it through all the changes.

"Of course," she said after a minute of near paralysis. "The best way to interpret all that visual information from everybody's implant is to render it in 3-D, and the best way to do that is in a tank. That's why you need all that hardware," she said, looking again at the bank of processors. "At first I thought it was overkill on the computing power, but now I have a hard time believing it's enough. Processing all that data should take twice what you've got here."

Duncan smirked. "We've come up with a few short-cuts, but we really need someone like you to help us find new ones."

Chapter 14 – On Watch

Jeremy had no doubt of it, now. The only reason he was being paraded around the office several times a day was to keep an eye out for net spies. He resented that they didn't have the decency to tell him this -- as if he couldn't figure it out on his own -- so he decided to see the boss about it.

What is it with these people? he wondered as he walked down the main corridor to the corner office. Jeremy imagined a disturbing trend in agency actions: they had a habit of using people and not caring how they felt about it.

He paused in the hall, realizing that he didn't know who the agent-in-charge of this particular office was. That was easy to solve, he realized, and called up the roster, which was updated continuously as Peter deployed his resources into new positions. He noted with satisfaction that he was assigned to this office as a "special agent."

"Oh, that's just great," he said aloud when he noticed who the AIC was.

"What's just great, Mr. Mitchell?" a familiar voice said from just ahead of him in the hall. The AIC himself had come out of his office.

"I just found out that you're in charge here," Jeremy said, realizing he was now right outside the man's office.

"And do you have a problem with that?" Lenzke asked. The question could have been the prelude to a fight coming from another man's lips. Lenzke said it more like someone performing a psychological diagnosis of a patient.

"Nothing I can't manage," he wanted to say, but his better judgment prevailed.

"I have a question about my assignment here," Jeremy said. "Can I have a minute of your time?"

"Certainly," Lenzke said, walking past Jeremy back into his office.

As he passed, Jeremy smelled something very faintly. He remembered it from somewhere -- something very recent -- but he couldn't place it. Jeremy followed Lenzke into the office, and, remembering his procedures, waited until the door was shut to speak.

"It's fairly obvious why I've been assigned to this facility. Why hasn't anyone explained my mission? Why all this nonsense about meeting people on the other side of the building?"

Lenzke looked confused, and then laughed. "You're right, it's obvious why you're here. You're supposed to be smart enough to figure out obvious things, Mr. Mitchell. Do you think all the training we've been giving you is so we can hand-hold you through every assignment?"

Jeremy hadn't thought of it that way, and he felt stupid. He couldn't have expected them to tell the hired hands to take him around the office so he could look for invisible spies. That was need-to-know information, and the work staff didn't need to know. He also realized that he had been thinking of his work with the agency as a kind of master-slave relationship. But he wasn't merely a hired hand. He was supposed to think for himself and take initiative, provided he kept within the lines.

"You're right," he admitted.

"Then you know what to do," Lenzke said. "But there is one thing I want to clarify. You are not to leave the facility, and you're on-call until further notice."

*   *   *

"The only way I can prove myself to you is to take you for a ride," Duncan said. Hanna didn't make the connection -- hadn't they just taken a ride in a hovercar? -- until MacKenzie looked over at the virtual reality tanks.

"Let's suit up," Duncan said. MacKenzie nodded.

Hanna had to convince herself that there was nothing inherently wrong with the tanks. *Just because people use them for creepy stuff doesn't mean they're inherently creepy*, she told herself as she followed Duncan and MacKenzie to a bank of doors that looked like dressing rooms. She glanced at MacKenzie before she went in, seeking some assurance. MacKenzie gave her the thumbs up and they both went in.

The dressing room was small, and there were no directions. Hanna wasn't quite sure what to do.

To MacKenzie. Chat mode requested.

Accepted.

What do we do?

In my room there are shelves on the left side. Do you have any?

Hanna looked around. *Yes, on the back wall,* she said.

The lowest drawer is the smallest suit -- child size. You'll probably wear the suit in the fourth one up.

Hanna opened the drawer and pulled out the suit. It was a thin, black material, similar to something she had seen in MacKenzie's computer lab. The fabric was a complicated web of fibers that provided the computer interface with dual interactivity. Every time the person wearing the suit moved, the fibers registered the change and sent the appropriate signals through the interface. Similarly, the virtual reality program could send a signal to the suit that would simulate a punch to the midsection, or the feeling of water against the skin, or a kiss.

Once the suit was on, Hanna was somewhat surprised at how loose it was. How could it measure her movements if it sagged so much? She walked out of the dressing room looking like someone who had lost 100 pounds in two months.

"No, silly," MacKenzie said, and Hanna noticed that MacKenzie's suit was skin tight. "You look like an elephant. You've got to turn it on." She reached up to the side of Hanna's goggles and pressed a button. Hanna's suit immediately tightened up over her whole body. The sensation was almost like diving into water.

"There," MacKenzie said. "Hey, you look good in that," she said, looking her over. Hanna struck a model's pose and smiled.

"If you two are ready, we can go in now," Duncan said, business-like, as usual. Hanna tried very hard not to notice how the suit accommodated Duncan's anatomy below the waist.

The three of them looked like scuba divers in their tight black suits as they walked up the steep stairway to the top of the VR tanks. Three were open, revealing the clean solution they were about to plunge into. If the water had been cloudy, as it was in some of the seedier VR shops, Hanna could have seen the crisscrossing laser beams that continuously monitored the rider's position in the tank.

"Okay," Duncan instructed. "After you jump in, throw this switch on your goggles." He indicated which one, and Hanna reached up to touch hers. "That will shut off all outside light and enable you to see the VR images. You might be disoriented for a second or two. Don't worry about it. We're all going to the same location, so just look for me and follow."

"How do we follow you?" Hanna asked. "I've never done this before."

"You can just walk around, like you would in real life, but we're going to be moving a little faster than that. When you want to move, tap the button on your right wrist and point in the direction you want to go. The longer you point the more you'll accelerate. You stop by making a fist. Don't worry, you'll catch on." Without waiting for a reply he jumped into his tank. MacKenzie followed immediately, and Hanna, still telling herself it was okay, went last.

* * *

When Hanna opened her eyes she was standing in the middle of the warehouse, facing in the direction of the virtual reality tanks. But she knew her body wasn't actually there. For a moment she wasn't certain if she was really in Duncan's warehouse, but as she looked around at the physical features of the room, it was clearly the same building. The three windows were on the east wall, where they should have been. The support beams were all in the right places. The southeast corner had that peculiar corner wall she had noticed, but the contents of the room were all wrong. Instead of computers, workers, VR tanks, offices and empty pizza boxes, there were wooden crates.

Then she noticed workers milling about, checking the crates, moving them from place to place, opening one and closing another. As she studied the things in the room she noticed that some things looked very real, while others had a computer-generated look. Even some of the faces had it. One man who was working by himself seemed to be almost completely an animation. There was something about the texture of his clothes that wasn't right. It looked too perfect to be real. But the thing that disturbed Hanna the most was when she saw the man's desktop floating in front of him. She was too far away to make out what he was doing, but she was sure that she would be able to read it if she got closer. It gave her a guilty feeling, as if she was trespassing, or a peeping Tom. But she knew that none of these people were really in the warehouse. It had to be some kind of computer-generated illusion.

MacKenzie moved next to her, or, rather, the virtual image of MacKenzie moved next to the virtual image of Hanna.

This is weird, Hanna sent, remembering that they were still in chat mode.

"We can talk, you know," MacKenzie's image said aloud. "Nobody can hear us unless they're in the same program, which for us just means Duncan. You can do just about anything in here that you can do in real life -- that's the idea, remember?"

Hanna reached over and touched MacKenzie's shoulder. It felt like she was really touching her shoulder, but she knew that both their bodies were actually suspended in tanks of liquid about 15 feet from one another. And they were wearing those black VR suits, but MacKenzie's image was wearing blue overalls, a red turtle-neck and a pair of walking shoes. They had to be virtual clothes, because MacKenzie didn't own a pair of overalls. Hanna was suddenly concerned about what she was wearing and looked down at herself. She was dressed exactly the same, only her shirt was blue. MacKenzie laughed.

"Don't worry," she said, "I took care of it for you. I didn't think you wanted to go for a walk with Duncan while you were buck naked. Virtually, that is."

"Thanks," Hanna said, and giggled. "But what is this place? It's not Duncan's warehouse, but it looks the same."

"I suspect he's figured a way to put a false signal on the hole so nobody can spy on his operations."

Duncan came out of the bathroom a moment later.

"I forgot to go before," he said. Hanna didn't even want to think about how that worked. "But let's get going." He pointed to a control panel on his wrist that had four buttons. Hanna noticed that she and MacKenzie had one too. Duncan pointed to the lower left button so Hanna could see what he was doing, then he pressed it and pointed straight up with his right index finger. His body began to accelerate toward the ceiling.

"If I can touch you," Hanna said to MacKenzie, "doesn't that mean that he'll smash into the ceiling?"

MacKenzie reached out and put her arm right through Hanna. "Once you touch this button, everything becomes transolid. Let's go," she said.

As soon as Hanna pushed the button she could no longer feel her body weight pressing her feet against the floor, although she was still standing in the same place. She looked, pointed up and watched as the ceiling got closer and closer. She winced as her head came in contact with the virtual ceiling, but in an instant she was through. It was an amazing sight. She was looking at the roof of the warehouse, but as she continued to ascend her field of vision grew wider, taking in the surrounding parking lot and a moment later several city blocks.

*   *   *

Jeremy realized that the rest of the workers at his new assignment had no idea what he was up to and, now self-conscious of his mission, he tried to forestall any unwanted questions. He had to come up with a reasonable excuse for his wanderings.

He was taking a walk now, somewhat more comfortable with the lay of the facility, and he glanced down one of the hallways to see a bank of terminals. The facility was crammed full of electronic devices of all kinds. He knew that some electronic devices interfered with implant communications, and he suspected the workers would blame them for any random noise, since humans naturally look for patterns in events. He decided to pretend that he was doing a study on the implant communications glitches the workers experienced while they were in the office. He would make his rounds every day, ask everyone on duty whether or not they had had any problems with their implants, and, if necessary, he would imply that there was some suspicion of interference from the electronic equipment.

The story was a phenomenal success from his very first attempt. Everyone was thrilled that the agency was paying attention to the problem, which they had suspected anyway. Furthermore, he learned a great deal from some of the more technically minded workers about how implant communications really worked. Signal distortion was a common and regularly occurring problem with everyone, whether they worked in an area with lots of electronics or not, but whether the machinery was really causing more glitches than would be expected in another environment or whether the workers simply paid more attention to the glitches at the office, Jeremy never found out. All that mattered to him was that everyone was happy to see him and report their latest problems and pet theories.

The other advantage of his imaginary assignment was that he had free rein of the entire facility. He also took the opportunity to make friends with the support staff.

While he was in the administrative wing, questioning some of Lenzke's administrative assistants, the AIC himself came into the room and listened as Jeremy questioned a Mr. Edwards.

"Is there something you need, sir?" Edwards asked Lenzke as he came in the room.

"No," Lenzke said. "I'm just waiting for a reply from Peter, and I thought I'd watch Mr. Mitchell at work. Have you found anything out yet, Jeremy?" he asked.

He's quick, Jeremy thought. He hadn't told Lenzke what he was doing.

"It's too early to say, but it seems that the biggest problems are concentrated near the central computer area," Jeremy said. It was a bald lie, but he had to make up something for the sake of the people listening in. Lenzke came closer and spoke to Edwards. Jeremy picked up that distinctive smell again. It was very faint, but he was sure he had smelled it before; he just couldn't figure out what it was.

"What do you think of Mr. Mitchell's study, Edwards?" he asked.

"It's about time somebody did it," he said. "I think we've all been wondering about this for a long time."

Lenzke nodded and went back to his office. Jeremy looked at Edwards with a smile and sniffed, visibly and obviously. Edwards smiled back, then looked to be sure Lenzke was gone.

"So you've smelled her, eh?" he said. "We keep telling him to run his clothes through the launderer after he sees her, but he doesn't listen."

Jeremy smiled, but his heart almost stopped. He realized where he had smelled that perfume before -- on Dr. Berry.

*　　*　　*

Duncan, Hanna and MacKenzie were moving along at an incredible speed over a virtual image of the streets and buildings of

Washington, D.C. Duncan would have liked to go faster, but it was making Hanna dizzy. He decided to use the time for a lecture on the mission of his organization.

"After the riots, you see, everyone was desperate for some peaceful resolution to the crisis," he said in a quick, but deliberate tone. "So when the government offered to hand over the encryption technology for the net, nobody doubted that they had. The fools! They thought that the government had learned its lesson and was going to play nice. To be fair, most of the government did. But several agencies -- or at least people in the agencies -- kept the key to the encryption routines, and they've been monitoring the hole for decades."

"Why?" Hanna asked. "What have they done with all that information?"

"A lot. More than I know, I'm sure, although we've figured out some of it. Do you remember when Miller disappeared?"

Oh no, not another Miller story, Hanna thought. Clayton Miller had run an eccentric campaign for president in 2036, claiming that the hole had been compromised, that the government was stealing from people, that innocent citizens had been arrested and all records of their existence erased -- every good conspiracy theory had to involve Clayton Miller. He had gathered a small but devoted following and threatened to renew violence against the government, but then he suddenly disappeared.

"Well, the truth of the matter is that Miller was on to something. He was a nut, don't get me wrong," Duncan clarified -- nobody with any sense allowed himself to be associated with Miller, "but he was also a computer genius, and he'd been developing a pretty strong case for some of his anti-government theories."

As Hanna wondered how all this fit into her developing perception of Duncan and his work, she watched the Potomac River slip underneath them. Far ahead she could just make out the edges of the Appalachian mountains. MacKenzie also enjoyed the view, but she decided to break into the conversation.

"How do you know all this about Miller?" she asked. She hated conspiracy theories, and she didn't want to have anything to do with Duncan if he was a Millerite.

Duncan didn't answer for a moment, and Hanna and MacKenzie wondered what else was going to come out of all this.

"I hate to tell you this, and I wish it weren't so, but our organization has some of Miller's former operatives. They're nuts, and they're hard to control, but they're useful nuts, and I need them." He paused and shook his head. "They're useful most of the time, anyway. Sometimes their methods are too severe for my tastes." He glanced quickly at Hanna, and MacKenzie noticed.

"So it was your group that had Hanna kidnapped?" she asked. Hanna looked over quickly, starting to put the pieces together. She took the news of Duncan's involvement in her capture dispassionately, which surprised her. Perhaps the affairs of the world had less of a hold on the mind while the body soared ten thousand feet above the earth.

Duncan pointed down and started to descend toward a series of office buildings. As they got closer to the ground they began to intersect hovercar traffic, which was quite unnerving for Hanna, even though she realized that she was still "transolid" -- the virtual hovercars would go right through her.

"Yes," Duncan said to MacKenzie, "in a way it was my group, and I'm sorry about that. We have to use scoundrels from time to time, and we can't always keep them on a leash. I didn't authorize the kidnapping, but the people who did it were connected with us."

MacKenzie stopped right where she was, about 300 feet off the ground, above something that looked like an old-fashioned power station, and refused to budge. She waited until Duncan and Hanna circled, and nodded with her head back towards Washington.

Hanna clumsily maneuvered herself next to MacKenzie, set a hand on her shoulder and smiled.

"King David had the same problem," she said. "Let's hear the whole story before we make a decision, okay?" Duncan nodded appreciatively, but MacKenzie glared at her with a look of incomprehension. After a minute, Hanna prevailed on her and she gestured to Duncan to lead on.

They continued to descend in silence. Duncan pointed to a narrow alley between two of the high rises and they all went in, leveling out at ground level.

*　　*　　*

After a particularly long session with an engineer in one of the labs, Jeremy had found it particularly hard not to yawn. He hadn't slept well for the last two nights and wanted to take a nap. At first his work ethic resisted the idea, but then he realized that he was going to be on 24-hour call for the foreseeable future. Besides, the building had no windows and was fully staffed around the clock, so sleeping at night was a convention he didn't feel any need to follow. Added to everything else, the couch in his office doubled as a bed.

On his walk back to his office he tried to make sense of the perfume. What did Lenzke have to do with Dr. Berry? Was it just a coincidence -- did Lenzke's girlfriend use the same perfume? No, that was too much to believe. "Don't trust coincidences," he had learned in his training. The perfume was probably Dr. Berry's.

On a wild hunch he checked the agency roster to make sure she didn't work for Peter. It seemed ridiculous -- Peter had identified her as a target of some of his investigations -- but he had to be sure. She wasn't there.

Feints within feints, he remembered from one of his favorite books. The real question was who was using whom. Was Dr. Berry infiltrating the agency through Lenzke, or was Lenzke keeping an eye on Dr. Berry? Then he remembered that it was Lenzke who had sent him to Berry in the first place. Why would he do that?

He tried to work it through, but his eyes were getting heavy.

Maybe I'll work it out in my dreams, he thought, and was sound asleep moments after his head hit the pillow.

*　　*　　*

"Here's where the program gets a little tricky," Duncan explained to Hanna and MacKenzie as they stood in front of an alley door. "This is a real office building and there are people walking around in it. Our computers are monitoring what they see, which means that what we're seeing in this simulation is what's actually happening, in real time, in Virginia. If we go around opening doors or moving things, it uses up processor resources, because we're forcing the virtual representation of the building out of sync with reality -- that is, with the data the system is getting from all those people's implants." He pointed inside. "It slows down the system, and we don't want to do that. So, the easiest way to reconnoiter this building is to reconfigure the program to make some structures solid and others transolid. So you can walk through walls and doors -- and the people -- but the floors will hold you up. It'll take some getting used to, but you'll catch on."

He looked at Hanna and MacKenzie to make sure they understood. "This is important. The government has its own intruders." Hanna hadn't heard that term before, but she assumed that was what Duncan's group called the net spies. "If we see any, we abort, immediately. All you have to do is hit the power button twice -- it's on the side of your goggles, Hanna -- and you'll be back floating in the tank at the warehouse."

That's where I really am anyway, Hanna told herself, but she understood that there had to be some ambiguity in language when switching back and forth between reality and virtual reality.

"How can we tell another ... intruder, from a regular person?" Hanna asked. "You both look real to me."

"And how could we see them anyway?" MacKenzie asked. "They'd have to be in a different set of tanks connected to a different virtual reality program. Where would your computers get the data to make them visible to us?"

Duncan shook his head. "We're not exactly sure how, MacKenzie, but for some reason we can see each other sometimes. It's just one aspect of this business that we haven't figured out yet. But to answer Hanna's question, intruders aren't as clear and well-defined as everybody else. You'll know what I mean if you see one."

From MacKenzie. At least his confidence includes us.

To MacKenzie. I wish I was so sure.

Duncan motioned them forward and they walked through the security door into the well-lit hallway of the office building.

*   *   *

Jeremy just couldn't bring himself to sleep during regular work hours. He awoke again after only a half-hour nap, surprisingly refreshed, ran his clothes through the launderer, ordered a cup of coffee from the concierge and started another jaunt around the facility.

He hadn't figured out what was going on with Lenzke and Dr. Berry, but he decided he'd better talk to Peter about it. Procedures required all agents to report any incident that might involve a breach of security.

*   *   *

After entering through the back door, Hanna felt as if she was burgling the place. The first time she saw someone, she felt an urge to dart behind a door and hide. It took a minute to get used to the idea that no one could see her except MacKenzie and Duncan.

Hanna and MacKenzie walked around obstacles and tried to avoid touching anyone, but Duncan went where he wanted to go, heedless of people or things. Sometimes he walked right through a plant, a desk, a wall, or even a person, and one time he actually stood with his feet on the feet of a security guard and read his implant desktop.

"This way," he said after he had found what he wanted, and started walking. He headed off, through walls, furniture and people, paying no attention to the layout of the office, but when he saw that Hanna and MacKenzie weren't used to being so reckless, he decided to take a more conventional route.

"I brought you here for two reasons," Duncan said. Hanna tried to imagine what his real mouth, back in the VR tank, was really doing, while this virtual image of his mouth spoke. The head gear for the VR suit fit the face as well as the body. Where did the air go? Did he blow bubbles in the solution in the tank? And then she remembered that she was in a suit, in a tank, just a few yards away from him, several miles from where she thought she was. She tried blowing out to see how it felt. Duncan saw her, and his disapproving look brought snapped her back to attention.

"First, I wanted to show you how the intruder technology works," he said. "Second, and more importantly, I want to show you that the government has been using this technology to spy on everyone. We're heading to the central computer station. I'm confident you'll see enough to persuade you to join up with me."

Hanna and MacKenzie looked at each other in stunned surprise and apprehension. They knew that Duncan wasn't showing them all of these things out of the goodness of his heart, or merely to satisfy their curiosity. He wanted something out of them, and now, for the first time, that something was explicit. He was going to try to recruit them into his organization.

In a few minutes they were standing in the middle of a large, wedge-shaped room with more than 50 manned workstations. Most of them had flat, 2-dimensional screens, but a few had the more expensive, holoprojector bubble screens. At the apex of the room sat an elevated chair manned by a supervisor who watched all the workers. Hanna stood near the apex, behind one man's chair, and looked over his shoulder at the display on his workstation. The image on the display was eerily reminiscent of what she had just been doing. It seemed to be a 2D view from a camera that was moving through a building, passing through walls, stopping from time to time to look at someone's implant desktop, but it was clear to Hanna that what she was seeing was an image generated from something or someone -- another intruder, probably -- on an intelligence gathering mission in another office complex. The image wasn't very good, and she instantly saw the advantage of doing such work in the VR tanks. Even the holoscreens didn't allow you to get inside the image, like she could.

The man at the station seemed to be monitoring the work of one of the government's intruders in the field.

She still worried that the people in the room could see or hear her. Her mind told her that she was miles away, but the reality of the simulation was compelling -- except for sound. The VR programs tried to mimic the sounds of the office, but they were inexact. She could ask the computer to simulate voices, based on the movement of a person's mouth, but that was iffy. The programs only received up-to-date data if someone with an implant was watching the speaker, thereby feeding real-time information on the movement of his lips back over the hole and into the VR routines.

She knew they couldn't hear her, but it was with some initial trepidation that she called aloud to Duncan, across the crowded room. "So, is someone back at your warehouse monitoring what we see?"

"No," Duncan said, turning to look at her. "We don't have this technology yet. They have a head start on us." He turned back and scanned four or five workstations, looking for something interesting.

Hanna continued to watch the monitor, wondering why a net spy -- or intruder, or ghost, or whatever the right word was -- was sent on this particular assignment. Then she recognized a face in a crowd on the monitor's screen. Hanna couldn't remember where she had seen that face before, but she knew he was an important man. Maybe he was the president of some company, or a legislator.

But then she turned and caught a glimpse of a familiar face, not on a workstation, and her adrenaline pumped.

"Abort," she yelled. "Duncan, abort now."

Greg Krehbiel

Chapter 15 – Lenzke

Jeremy had finished surveying the first floor staff except for the technicians stationed in the central computer area. He feared this group, suspecting some of them might see through his concocted cover story about interference from the electronic equipment.

The computer area constituted the heart of the Agency's operations. Fifty workstations hummed round the clock as hotshot programmers put them through the paces. He didn't know exactly what they all were doing, but he'd gleaned from stray comments here and there that this was Peter's pride and joy.

The room itself reminded Jeremy of old movies of NASA's mission control center in Houston, except that the workstations were arranged in arcs rather than in rows, and some of them had 3-D displays. The supervisor sat in a raised swivel chair, overlooking every station. His chair was equipped with a magnifying screen that allowed him to read the fine print on a monitor 20 yards away.

The etiquette of the room prohibited Jeremy from simply talking to one of the workers, as he did everywhere else. He had to get permission from the supervisor first. Jeremy stood next to his chair, waiting to attract the man's attention and talk with him. He didn't seem to be busy, but he didn't show any sign of attending to Jeremy, either. Jeremy wondered if this was an act -- a kind of passive assertion of dominance -- but he didn't get much of a chance to think about it.

While he was waiting on the supervisor, he had nothing to do but survey the room. Just beyond the first arc of workstations he saw a man who seemed to be standing in the middle of the second arc. Jeremy assumed there was a gap in the workstations, hidden from his view, but then he noticed something odd. He closed his left eye to be sure.

When Jeremy opened his eye again the man turned enough for Jeremy to see his face. It was the same man Hanna and MacKenzie had met at the Chocolate Bar that night; the man he had spied on for MacKenzie.

Almost as soon as Jeremy recognized him he looked up -- not at Jeremy, but in another direction. He appeared to be startled. Jeremy turned to see what he was looking at and thought he caught a glimpse of another net spy, a woman, but she vanished before he could be sure. His peripheral vision told him that the man was gone as well.

"Shut down these terminals and clear this room immediately," he said to the supervisor in a commanding voice. The supervisor looked at him in angry surprise. Jeremy didn't have time to get into a contest of wills.

To Lenzke. Urgent. Net spies seen in central computer area. Recommend immediate evacuation.

He made a quick visual sweep of the room as he sent the message, then systematically searched every square foot.

"Everybody out," the supervisor called a moment later. "Move it. Move it," he yelled to his astonished staff.

* * *

After Jeremy was convinced the area was free of net spies he left the main computer room and reported to Lenzke. The formerly quiet and well-ordered halls were now abuzz with activity. Workers were tearing the place down, almost recklessly. In a matter of minutes it seemed that hundreds of technicians were packing up the electronic equipment. Movers were dismantling desks. Cleaners were vacuuming and picking up discarded paraphernalia. Men in white suits followed with sophisticated scanning equipment, ensuring that not the smallest particle was left behind. When Jeremy arrived at Lenzke's office, the two of them were standing alone in a bare room. Only the carpet was left.

Lenzke questioned him carefully and at length about the event. Jeremy took offense at his brusque and somewhat prosecutorial manner, but when Lenzke was done with his questions he smiled and assured Jeremy that he had done the right thing.

"The bad news is that this will set us back a couple days at the least," Lenzke said, "and we've got some important operations going on." Jeremy could hardly believe the time estimate. Could they really move an entire office in a couple days?

"But the good news, for you at least, is that you're at liberty until further notice. There'll be no office for you to watch for a little while, so go have some fun." Lenzke smiled at him -- an odd smile, Jeremy thought. He was trying to be friendly, but the strain between them showed.

Then the words sunk in. A couple days off? He hadn't expected that, but he shrugged his shoulders and headed for the door, beginning to like the idea that he could pick up and go anywhere he wanted without worrying about luggage, money or advance plans. And, despite his best efforts, he was almost beginning to like Lenzke.

*   *   *

It was about 6:00 when Jeremy arrived at the Capitol University campus. Hanna and MacKenzie liked to eat dinner together in the dorm cafeteria, and, although he wasn't thrilled at the prospect of dormitory food after the gourmet meals he'd eaten for the last week, he really wanted to see them.

Getting into the cafeteria turned out to be easier than he thought. It was a woman's dorm, but the cafeteria was open to the public and there were quite a few men there. He didn't see Hanna or MacKenzie, but he needed to eat anyway. He ordered a plate of food, picked up a self-service cup of coffee, and took a seat.

After a couple minutes -- far shorter time than he expected for a chicken pot pie -- he received the signal that his meal was done and he started toward the food dispensers. As he reached for his plate he felt someone brush against his shoulder, and then heard a sharp hiss. Before he had time to wonder about it, he began to feel dizzy. He turned to see what was going on and noticed a nurse beside him with a concerned expression. "Are you feeling okay, Mr. Mitchell," she said, and then he blacked out.

* * *

Jeremy awoke, and before he even opened his eyes he realized he had a splitting headache. He groaned as he sat up and looked around the room. He was in an office, sitting in a comfortable, padded chair, and Hanna and MacKenzie were sitting opposite him on the other side of a large desk. They were both wearing eye patches. And then he noticed that he was as well.

"Hanna?" he said, and then grabbed his head and groaned again.

"Drink this." She offered him a small cup of bluish liquid. "It'll help your head." He took it and swallowed it in one gulp. "I'm sorry they had to do this to you, but we had to be safe. Listen to me, Jeremy, and trust me, okay? Don't send any messages to anyone for a little while. Not until you've heard what we have to say. Promise?"

Jeremy nodded and tried to sit up straight. Whatever she had just given him was sickeningly sweet and made him very thirsty. "Can I have some water?" he asked.

MacKenzie poured him a glass from a pitcher that was behind her on an inexpensive lamp stand. Jeremy realized that the headache and the thirst were an aftereffect of whatever his kidnappers had used to knock him out in the cafeteria. What was harder to understand was how Hanna and MacKenzie were involved.

"I'm really sorry, Jeremy," Hanna said again.

"So what's the deal?" he asked, trying to reconcile himself to the fact that his life was going to be complicated from now on. And perhaps that was fitting, he thought -- that trouble should pursue a man fleeing from justice.

Hanna shook her head. "It's a long story, but the bottom line is that you've fallen in with the bad guys."

Hanna and MacKenzie took it in turns to explain the VR tanks, the suits, and their trip with Duncan to the agency office. They were convinced now that Duncan was telling the truth: the hole had never been safe. The government had been using it to keep an eye on everybody, sometimes using the information their intruders discovered to manipulate public opinion, sometimes for the crass political goals of those in power, but most of their effort was directed toward keeping an eye on anyone who might be on to them, or who might try to disrupt the political situation.

Hanna told him about the incident in the control room, and she told him what she saw. One of the terminals was monitoring Daniel McMillan, a U.S. Congressman from the state of Illinois. He was the most likely man to run against the powerful senator from Illinois, Wanda Powell. Powell's ratings were dropping, but McMillan was a rising star. Powell was also the chairwoman of the Senate Armed Services Committee, and she was hawkish towards China.

Jeremy vaguely recalled reading something about China. There had been growing tension with the United States, and many analysts believed that stability in the domestic political landscape was the best way to mollify the fears of some of the more radical Chinese factions. If Powell had her way, there would probably be a trade war with China, if not a shooting war, within months.

"So what does this have to do with anything?" Jeremy asked, still a little disoriented from the drugs.

"McMillan died of a stroke about an hour ago," she said.

"And you think the ...," he was about to say "the agency," but he caught himself. "You think the people in that room had something to do with it?"

"It would be a pretty fantastic coincidence otherwise, don't you think?" MacKenzie asked.

Jeremy was beginning to doubt coincidences.

Hanna explained that after they left the computer area, Duncan took them on a VR tour of some of his previous trips, which had been stored electronically to be used as evidence against the government.

What they saw was horrifying. Nearly all of the 23 people murdered in the District of Columbia over the last two years had been under surveillance. Duncan suspected that some of them were members of other underground organizations like the Millerites. Scores of other people had met untimely deaths from sudden heart attacks or strokes.

Jeremy hoped he would be offended at the suggestion, but he found such cold-blooded and ruthless tactics all too easy to believe, not only from his lessons at the agency, which spoke casually about neutralizing targets and eliminating security risks, but because it was what he had been raised to believe about Society anyway.

"So why don't you just go public with all of this?" he asked. "Broadcast it on the hole."

Hanna shook her head. "Duncan says that's the last resort. He's actually quite sensible about this thing. At first I thought he was a nut, but I'm growing to respect him a lot." Jeremy felt a flush of jealousy, but tried to suppress it.

"He says most people are being left alone," Hanna continued. "It's not as if things are that bad. We don't want to start a riot or anything. It's just that the government has assumed the role of the invisible hand, manipulating things -- by coercion, murder, whatever it takes -- to keep order."

"And now it seems that they're manipulating pretty serious stuff. If they want to keep Powell in power, that's not good news," MacKenzie added. After a few rocky decades of experimentation in the early parts of the century, with radical growth followed by equally radical contraction and isolation, China had finally found its own path to prosperity and had begun to assert itself throughout the western Pacific Rim and eastern Europe. There was some fear that Australia might be in jeopardy, and India was showing signs of sympathy with China's goals. The United States wasn't directly threatened, but U.S.

interests in central Europe, the Middle East and Northern Africa could be at stake.

"If Duncan were to go public with what he knows," Hanna continued, "there would be Pandemonium. Duncan thinks that would be a greater evil, and he's not willing to do it. Not yet, at least."

Jeremy brooded in silence. His headache made thinking painful, and he resented this guy Duncan's interference in Hanna's life. But he also had a keen sense of responsibility. He knew there were bigger issues involved. Like it or not, he was in the middle of it now, and he would have to do what was necessary.

"I'm not completely convinced," he said at last. "I'm not saying I doubt you," he continued, looking up and giving them both a serious look, "but I can't jump to conclusions about this. I've been wrong too many times in the last few weeks to make any hasty conclusions. I'm willing to keep an eye on things," he continued, "and I might even let you know what I find out, but don't count on it."

"That would be good," MacKenzie said. "Would it be too much to ask you to look the other way if you see us again?"

Jeremy nodded. "Until I've got a better handle on things, yes, it would be too much to ask. But if I find anything, or make up my mind, how should I contact you? If the hole is compromised, it's likely they're watching me as well: if not out of suspicion, just as a general security procedure." In fact, he knew that they were, but he didn't feel the need to disclose that.

"Write letters," Hanna said. "We still have a postal service, you know."

"Just remember to keep your left eye closed when you write, or turn off your implant," MacKenzie added. "They can only monitor what somebody with an implant sees. Understand?"

"Yeah, I think so," Jeremy said, and then noticed something else on Hanna's face. "Is there anything else I need to know."

"Dr. Berry's involved with this somehow," she said. "Duncan's been keeping an eye on her. It seems incredible, after what she put you through, but he thinks she might be working for you -- I mean, for the group you're in."

Jeremy tried not to show his reaction to that comment.

"Yeah, we know," MacKenzie said. "You can't say anything. She's not directly involved with the intruders at all. Or that's the way it seems. Duncan does computer work for her, and he's been snooping through her files. He can't find anything to link her to the intruders. She's involved somehow, but he's not sure how. Keep an eye out for her."

"I have a question," Jeremy said. "Why did Duncan want to kidnap me at the hospital?" he asked. "Was he trying to recruit me?"

"It wasn't Duncan who did that," Hanna said quickly, and somewhat defensively. "But it was someone ... connected with him." She looked up apologetically. "I can't tell you everything."

Jeremy studied her face in silence. "I've got to think about that some more," he said, "but right now I'm starving. You had your goons interrupt my dinner, you know." Hanna smiled.

"Okay, let's eat. But don't forget this," MacKenzie said, holding out a small, metallic box.

"What is it?" Jeremy asked.

"This is a dark box. It blocks communications to the bug you were wearing when we caught you, which is inside."

Jeremy didn't understand, but it was clear that Hanna and MacKenzie were watching his face carefully to see how he would react.

"Oh, I see," he said after a minute. "You weren't sure if I knew I was wearing that thing?"

"Did you?" Hanna asked.

"No. Or, ... I suppose I should have guessed," he said. It was standard procedure for the agency to monitor its agents in the field. "Certainly you don't believe I came here to spy on you," he protested.

"I was trying to meet you in the cafeteria."

Hanna shook her head. "No, Jeremy, we don't. But you have to remember that you're on the other side now. We have to be cautious. And so do you."

"Yeah," MacKenzie added. "They're sure to notice that your bug went black. You'd better have a good cover story for them."

"Once you're out of here," Hanna added, "you'll need to put it back. We found it under your collar, right here." She indicated the spot on the back of his neck where the bug had been located, and Jeremy realized that Lenzke wasn't just giving him a fatherly pat when he let him go that afternoon.

* * *

"So did it work?" Duncan asked. "I took a big risk letting you girls try this." MacKenzie bristled slightly at being called a girl, but it was better than "lasses."

"I think so," MacKenzie answered. "But relax, Duncan. We didn't tell him anything the agency doesn't know already. Even if he talks, we haven't lost anything."

"Not true. If he talks, it's likely that I'll lose a promising young computer scientist." He smiled at MacKenzie, but she didn't like the idea of anybody owning her.

As Duncan was speaking, his administrative assistant, Levi, came into the room and whispered something to him. Duncan's usually stern demeanor turned positively grave. He nodded to Levi, who immediately left the room. Duncan remained silent for a minute.

"It seems my computer work for the doctor has been a little too comprehensive," he said, looking up. "We keep an eye on your friend Dr. Berry from time to time, to make sure our cover is safe," he explained. "She and her staff have been re-evaluating all the data on Jeremy ever since he disappeared. It looks as if she's beginning to suspect what's really going on." He shook his head. "She's not stupid, you know," he said with a wry grin. "In fact, she's a very good scientist.

And her assistant, Dr. Jenkins -- he's even better. He's almost at your level, MacKenzie."

Duncan shook his head again. "This really messes up my time-table."

*   *   *

Half way through dinner, Jeremy got a call from the agency and had to excuse himself. Hanna and MacKenzie ate in silence, then had a de-briefing session with Duncan. He expressed concern about Jeremy. Could they trust him to keep quiet? Did their security hold up, or might he have learned things they couldn't afford to let out?

He seemed even more nervous when Hanna and MacKenzie said they had to go back to their dorm room and take care of odds and ends at the university.

"Duncan, you're getting paranoid. We're not spies, but we do have clothes and things we need to get, and we have classes, and all that."

He tried to smile, but the stress on his face turned it into a grin.

"Of course. And I won't keep you here. You have to make up your own minds. Go ahead, and borrow one of my hovercars if you like."

When they left, none of them were sure they'd see each other again.

*   *   *

Did they hide the thing to keep it from me, or so that I couldn't reveal where it was to anyone who captured me, Jeremy wondered as he took the pin-sized listening device from the "black box" and stuck it back in his collar. At the same time he realized that this kind of suspicion was a part of agency work. You never knew who to trust, or whether you were really serving the purpose you thought you were. Agents were cards in Peter's hand, and the cards didn't know what part they were playing.

Jeremy checked the readout on the hovercar's status board. He would arrive at the address Lenzke had given him in ten minutes. He used that time to perfect his alibi for the last few hours. He also wondered if he wanted to tell Peter what Hanna and MacKenzie had told him. But that was a big decision. He had to think it through.

The hovercar made its final approach to the pre-programmed coordinates as Jeremy did a few breathing exercises to relax. He was under orders to come with the windows darkened, so he had no idea what to expect when the doors opened. When they did, his initial reaction was confusion. He seemed to be in exactly the same reception area of the agency office that had been torn down just several hours before. The same man in the same concierge-like uniform greeted him and asked if he needed anything, in almost the same voice.

"Nothing, thanks," he said, just to be certain that something was different.

"This way, sir," the man replied. Jeremy followed him out of the reception area and saw the first hints that this was actually a new location. Teams of workers scrambled down the unfinished hallways, pulling optical cable, touching up the paint or arranging the flowers on a walnut desk. Jeremy glanced through open doors on the right and left and saw workers spraying carpet on concrete slab floors. This office was being put together as quickly as the other had been taken apart.

"This way, sir," his guide instructed him. They slipped behind a wall of plastic sheeting and the noise and dust of construction was gone. Everything was immaculate on this side of the barrier, but there was a faint hum. The ventilation system was running at full strength to get rid of the smell of paint, wood stain, carpet, and wall-paper glue.

"Come in, Mr. Mitchell," Lenzke said as soon as they arrived at the door. The hallway, the door, and, Jeremy saw when he went inside, the office itself, were almost exactly the way they were in the other office.

"It's SOP, Mr. Mitchell," Lenzke said. He saw that Jeremy was still looking around, comparing what he saw with how he remembered things. "We have regional offices all over the globe. It makes no sense to have to learn a new office layout each time you move, or each time we have to move an office. This way, every worker always knows where his office is and what it's going to look like."

Jeremy nodded, and then noticed that there were two technicians in the room with Lenzke. Both of them had "sweepers," which is what the technicians called their all-purpose scanning devices. A sweeper consisted of a series of broad-range, powerful transceivers that could detect and locate any communications device.

The technicians scanned Jeremy, quickly discovered the bug, removed it and placed it in a small, silver box, similar to the "dark box" MacKenzie had used.

"One M23 bug, sir," one of them reported to Lenzke. He waved them off and they left. Jeremy had anticipated this.

"A bug?" he asked. "Do you know anything about this?"

"Don't worry, son," Lenzke said. "You didn't do anything wrong. It's ours. It's one of our ways of protecting you when you're out, but we lost contact with you for a while. Where were you?"

"I'm afraid I disobeyed orders, sir," he said. "You told me to have fun. I went looking for two girls I know, but I couldn't find them. I was a little tired, so I took a nap." *At least that will explain why my eyes were closed,* he thought.

"Two girls?" Lenzke laughed. "You can tell me about it later. Right now, we want a sweep of this whole complex. Look it over as carefully as you can, round-the-clock, until further notice. And by the way, Mr. Mitchell, that ploy you used last time to explain your wanderings was good thinking. Figure out some kind of follow-up on that."

"Yes, sir. Thank-you."

"And Mitchell," Lenzke said as Jeremy was turning to leave. "Where did you sleep?"

"I ate at the Capitol University cafeteria and then went to a grassy spot just outside. There were lots of college kids resting there, and I lay down on the grass and just dozed off. "

"Did you happen to catch the name of the building you were next to?" Lenzke persisted.

"No," Jeremy said. "But it was the only one I saw that had painted, white walls." MacKenzie had told him that the computer lab sometimes interferes with communications. Since the bug operated on very low power, sitting on that side of the building, where the park was, could easily explain the black-out.

"Okay," Lenzke said. "There's one last thing. Later this week we're going to put you through a series of tests to find out why you can see the net spies," Lenzke continued. "It's nothing invasive or painful, just some neurological tests. If you have any questions about it, you can contact the chief physician. She knows all about your case."

Jeremy nodded and left.

Greg Krehbiel

Chapter 16 – The Underground

Attached to the back of Duncan's warehouse was a series of dilapidated row houses that, from the outside, looked as if they were uninhabited. Duncan had converted the houses into living quarters for his staff and had made a passageway from the back of his warehouse into the row houses. From the inside, they were quite nice, but they had no windows. Because of the possibility that the agency would try to take some action against Hanna and MacKenzie, Duncan had insisted that they stay in the living quarters until they decided either to join up with him, or to take their chances some other way.

"I feel so silly wearing this thing," Hanna said. MacKenzie glowered at her. They were supposed to be quiet until MacKenzie was done checking the room for bugs. They had both put on their eye patches as soon as they entered the living quarters. The security protocols that Duncan used to protect the warehouse from intruders were down temporarily for maintenance, so they had to wear their patches. MacKenzie took out the gadget Duncan had given her to search for bugs and got to work, meticulously sweeping every inch of the room.

"All clear," she said after three minutes of searching. "I know it's a pain, Hanna, but we've got to check, and we've got to wear the patches while the protocols are down. As long as we're wearing them, they can't see what we're doing: with these patches on, an intruder could sit right here in the room with us and not know we're here because we're depriving it of updated visual input."

Hanna thought about that for a minute. "So what would they see? Nothing?" Hanna asked.

"No. The computer stores the most recent visual information it has on the room. So let's say you left this drawer open," MacKenzie said, opening the top left drawer of the dresser, which they had agreed would be Hanna's, "and then looked away," she turned her head to face

Hanna, "and then closed it without looking back." She closed the drawer, still looking at Hanna. "If we were to get in one of those VR tanks and come here, we'd see your desk drawer open, because that's the last visual input the computer has."

Hanna nodded.

MacKenzie sighed and looked at Hanna seriously. "So what am I going to do, Hanna? Duncan wants me to take the rest of the semester off and work with him. He says he has enough pull with the department that I won't even lose my credits."

Hanna shook her head sadly. "Credits seem like an odd thing to be worried about. Duncan says our lives might be in danger."

"I've been trying to forget about that part," MacKenzie said impulsively. "I am a little scared," she admitted, "but if you're concerned about safety, we should just leave -- get away from here."

"No we can't, MacKenzie. Something's got to be done, and Providence has dropped us in the middle of it. We'd be cowards, or worse, to back out." She stopped and stared into nowhere -- an expression MacKenzie recognized as Hanna's thoughtful pose. "There's something else, too. I haven't told you everything I saw in that computer lab before Jeremy showed up.

"I couldn't be positive," she continued, "but it looked like they were monitoring some of the presidential candidates." She looked up with a worried look. "These people are getting their hands into everything. Somebody's got to stop it, and you've got the ability to make a real difference. You have to help Duncan."

MacKenzie turned away and looked up at the wall for a minute. "We don't both have to stay with Duncan," she finally said, as if she was speaking with difficulty. She turned toward Hanna with a pale, frightened look. "It's likely to be dangerous. I don't imagine the conspiracy will play nice if they find us out."

"'Wherever you go, I go.'" Hanna said, to MacKenzie's great relief. "Besides," she said in a lighter tone, "I'm already involved. If they get to you, they're sure to get to me sooner or later."

MacKenzie nodded. "You're probably right." They were both silent for a minute as they realized the seriousness of their predicament. The conspiracy was trying to control the country, if not the world, and from what Duncan had shown them, they had already directly murdered hundreds of people. They wouldn't think twice about snuffing out two young women who got in the way.

"I don't see why we just can't go public with this," MacKenzie said, exasperated. "I mean, aside from the fact that we promised not to."

"No," Hanna said. "I think Duncan's right. We have to find a way to shut them down. You could never predict how the public would react if they were told. Duncan thinks the markets would collapse and we'd all get blown back to the 19th century in about two weeks. He also thinks that if we had some kind of national catastrophe like that, China would take advantage of it and do something stupid."

She thought for a moment, slowly shaking her head. "I think Duncan's right that we shouldn't go public, but I don't agree with his end-game scenario. I'd be willing to wager that the conspiracy has a contingency plan in place, in case someone exposes them. If we went public, we'd play our only card and they'd beat us. And then there'd be nothing to stop them."

"But what could they say?" MacKenzie asked. "If Duncan showed the world what he showed us? How could they make people think it's a good thing to have government goons staring over their shoulders all the time?"

"Who knows?" Hanna asked, throwing her hands in the air. "People are sheep, you know. If you pull the right strings, you can make them think what you want."

MacKenzie didn't look convinced, so Hanna tried to explain.

"I'm sure there would be a negative reaction at first, but people would start to settle back into their routines. Life goes on, after all. And then they'd start to realize that it didn't really matter. They hadn't been bothered by it when they didn't know about it, so why should they be now? 'And,' they might think, 'if this is how the government keeps the peace, so be it. It doesn't hurt me.' So, in a way, going public *might* play into their hands. They might be able to get popular sentiment behind them, and then there'd be no chance at all of stopping them."

"But Duncan can document that they've had innocent people thrown in prison," MacKenzie protested, "that they've murdered people who were politically troublesome, that they've ..."

"And who do you think the public will believe?" Hanna interrupted. "A sour Scot with a crazy story? Duncan will make his case, and then the conspiracy will come back with everything they've got -- all their spit and polish. And don't forget Miller. Duncan says he was mostly right, but now everybody thinks he was a fruitcake. They've rewritten history, MacKenzie. What's to stop them from doing it again?"

MacKenzie wasn't entirely convinced, but she knew Hanna's prediction was plausible. She was certainly right about Miller. Everybody thought he was a nut. Was that just the power of the conspiracy's public relations? Could they make black white and white black?

She shook her head and stared at the carpet. Hanna sensed her discouragement.

"Which makes it all the more important that we find a way to stop them now -- on our terms."

"Do you think we can? Really?"

"I don't know. Do you think David could kill Goliath with a sling and a stone?"

MacKenzie grimaced. "If our chances are that bad ...."

"Okay, okay," Hanna interrupted. "All I mean is that it's hard to predict the future. And what does it mean to have a 'chance,' anyway? If we win, then our odds were 100 percent, and if we lose, they were zero."

"You and that brain," MacKenzie said, resigning herself to the task. "So what do we do?"

"You, my dear computer genius, are going to figure out how to throw a wrench in their machinery, and I'm going to keep you out of trouble."

*   *   *

Jeremy spent the next 10 hours on his feet, walking the halls, talking to workers and looking for net spies. He actually liked the work. He liked meeting and interacting with such a diverse group of people, and he learned a lot about the culture he'd adopted. It was truly world-wide -- except for the communities, of course, and some hold-outs in Australia.

He also discovered that there was quite a lot more tension among the staff than he had realized. It was inevitable, he knew, that cliques would form in any large organization, but the tension seemed to go beyond that. It wasn't security personnel against support staff, or technicians against the lawyers -- there seemed to be distrust within each group.

On one of his trips he found the office supply closet. He hadn't spoken to the office manager yet, so he took the opportunity to go in and talk. He also slipped a plain envelope and a piece of paper in his pocket while the office manager wasn't looking.

"What do we use the paper for?" Jeremy asked the man, whose name was Henry.

"Not much," he chuckled. "Some countries have pretty bad links to the net, so old-fashioned mail is still the best way to go. And, of course, there's Australia."

"I wouldn't even know how to mail something if I wanted to," Jeremy confided.

Henry seemed to guess more than Jeremy intended. He grabbed a plain envelope and ran it through some kind of imprinting device, then handed it to Jeremy. The upper right hand corner had a miniature hologram of an eagle with the words, "U.S. Post Office, First-Class Postage" written in an arc over its head.

Henry put his finger to his lips, signaling Jeremy to keep it quiet.

"I've heard about you," he said. "People like you around here. When you want to mail it, just give it to me."

Jeremy nodded his thanks and started his battery of questions about trouble with implant communications. Henry, like most everyone else in the office, seemed to believe that the allegedly random glitches in hole communications were caused by "all this electronic gadgetry." Jeremy took everything down carefully on the notepad in his implant, but after finishing his survey he paused before leaving.

"Is there something else I can help you with?" Henry asked.

"Maybe," Jeremy said, "as long as it's off the record." Henry's head nodded, slightly, and Jeremy continued. "Sometimes I get the sense that I'm in the middle of a feud around here. Is there something going on in this office that I ought to know about?"

Henry looked down at the floor for a minute, then looked up again, with a serious expression. "Boy, there's always something going on around here. Nobody's called it a 'feud,' but that's not far from the mark."

Jeremy shook his head. "I don't even know what the sides are, or whose side I'm on."

"And that's probably why you're popular right now," Henry chuckled. "Aside from your natural charm, and all, I mean," he added with a grin.

"Is there somebody I ought to talk to?" he asked.

"You're talking to him," Henry said. "I'm not taking any sides, and I suggest you do the same."

"So who's Lenzke's girlfriend?" Jeremy asked suddenly.

Henry's smiling face became dead serious. "Ever read the Book of Revelation, boy?" Jeremy shook his head. "Read chapter 17," Henry said, and turned back to his work. The interview was over.

While Henry wasn't looking, Jeremy returned the blank envelope he had stolen and slipped back out into the corridor.

As he continued along to his next stop, he wondered if he would ever use that envelope -- did he really want to betray the agency to Hanna and MacKenzie? He also wondered what the Apocalypse had to do with anything. Was Henry just a nut, or was there some figurative message there? He'd have to check it out later.

But what about Hanna and MacKenzie -- and Duncan? They wanted information about the agency's work, and Jeremy wasn't sure which side he wanted to be on.

The government *was* spying on people. Hanna had convinced him of that fact. But so what? He had always assumed that to be the case anyway. He came into Society expecting government snoops looking over his shoulder. He also expected that Society's keepers were feeding the population a bunch of lies. For a short time, a few weeks ago, it looked as if that might not be true, and the promise of genuine liberty had exhilarated him, but now that he found that the liberty was restricted, why should he go on a crusade to correct it? By some twist of fate, he had made himself a comfortable living in Society -- the agency needed his talents, for the time being -- and as long as they weren't doing anything dreadful, why should he bother about it? After all, governments need to protect themselves. And it wasn't as if the population was suffering under cruel tyranny. The standard of living was high, crime was almost non-existent, the nation was at peace and people were generally happy. If a few of them were being watched in secret, so what?

That left Jeremy in an uncomfortable position. If he really believed in what the agency was doing, he should report what he knew about the opposition. In fact, if what the agency was doing was really in the best interests of the country, that made Hanna and MacKenzie dangerous rebels. He should turn them in.

*   *   *

MacKenzie was in her element, now. Duncan had assigned her one of the most powerful workstations in the office, and she was pushing it to its limits. It had been a few days since she had the opportunity to work on any of her ideas about how to restore privacy to the hole. Her private theories had been floating around in the back of her mind in a disorganized way all that time. Somehow, that always helped her to work.

But now she had a double advantage. Not only had she been subconsciously working on the problem for days, but Duncan had brought her up-to-date on his work. She had spent the last two hours refining and re-tooling her ideas, eliminating false trails Duncan had already followed.

The sun was just coming up, now. Hanna crawled out of her bed and started looking for the coffee maker. She came through the passage from the row houses into the staff living quarters, which were in the back of Duncan's warehouse, but she couldn't find any evidence of coffee, except for a slight whiff, from time to time. It led her about like a will-o-wisp, but she couldn't find the source, and almost everyone was asleep. She was starting to get nervous.

She saw MacKenzie standing like a statue in front of her workstation. MacKenzie had that look on her face -- that far-away expression that Hanna called "genius mode." Hanna knew better than to disturb her when she was like this, but then she noticed the mug at MacKenzie's elbow. *The alarm clock*. Hanna suddenly remembered that MacKenzie had brought it along. Two minutes later she was standing beside MacKenzie with a large mug of her own, comfortably waiting for her best friend to drop back into the real world.

Hanna wasn't a third of the way through her pint of coffee when, just as if someone had thrown a light switch, MacKenzie leaned over and started keying in new commands.

"Good morning," Hanna said, knowing it was safe to talk now.

"Hey," MacKenzie replied. "I'm on to something."

*   *   *

He took a deep breath to fight the effect of adrenaline as he saw the tall, blonde-haired man approach on the narrow forest path. He wanted to reach for his knife, just to be sure it was still there, but he didn't want to scare his prey. Weatherstone didn't make eye contact. He had seen Jeremy coming, but he looked down at his feet as they approached each other.

"Jeremy," he said, lifting his head as they came within five feet. He still didn't make eye contact. "I'm so sorry about what happened to Amy," he said. Then the eye flickered and the images took their usual course: the knife flashed, his mother cried, the gavel came down in the council courtroom. Images and sensations filled his head: the knife, the bloody body of Weatherstone, the sticky, warm feeling on his hand, the sound of air rushing into a punctured lung, Dr. Berry's face, his mother, the twitching eye, the knife as he wiped it clean on Weatherstone's pants, a woman's eye, twitching, his mother, Amy, the knife.

He sat up suddenly in his bed and immediately reached for his pad of paper. It was getting easier now. The more he tried to remember his dreams, the more details he could recall when he awoke. "Weatherstone had an implant," he wrote.

*   *   *

"Well, Mr. Mitchell, we need you to do your first field assignment," Peter said the moment Jeremy entered his office. Two men were already there, standing behind Peter's desk. One was a technician -- Jeremy thought his name was Gary -- and the other man Jeremy hadn't seen before.

"There's one thing we haven't told you yet," Peter said. "But you need to know it for this mission. Not all the net spies are on the other side. We have some of our own."

Jeremy decided not to fake surprise. "I guessed that," he lied. Peter raised her eyebrows. Gary smiled, but the other man had no reaction at all.

"Very well," Peter continued. "You'll be working with two of our own and a few field operatives to sweep a city block. We want to make sure it's clear of any other net spies. And Mr. Mitchell," he said seriously, "our enemies don't always play nice, so we can't afford to either. Do you understand?"

Jeremy nodded. "I understand."

"This is Taylor," Peter said, gesturing to the man Jeremy didn't know. "He'll be the AIC on this mission, and he'll brief you on your orders. Do you have any questions?"

"No," Jeremy said. "But I'd like to talk with you privately."

Peter nodded and the two other men left the office.

"I don't like being a rat," he began when the door was closed, "but I'm supposed to report any information that might be relevant to a security leak." The procedures also stipulated that this information should go to his immediate supervisor, who was Lenzke. Jeremy expected Peter to remind him of this fact, but he was too smart not to catch the obvious implication.

"Go on," he said.

"I smelled Dr. Berry's perfume on Mr. Lenzke," he said, deciding to avoid reporting anything but the facts. "It's very distinctive, so I doubt it's a coincidence. Other staff seemed to indicate that they often smelled it on him."

Peter stared at him for a full minute without moving or changing his expression at all. Jeremy wasn't sure if he was going to catch hell for poking his nose where it didn't belong, if Peter was shocked by the news, or if he hadn't even heard what Jeremy said.

"Abort the mission," he finally said, "but keep it secret. I'll cover for you if you get in trouble."

"I'm not sure I understand," Jeremy said. "Do you want me to cancel it?"

"No. Do everything exactly by the book, but I want you to report that you see a net spy five minutes before the objective is reached. Do you understand?"

"Yes," Jeremy said. His voice showed that he was confused, but the directions were clear enough.

"I want you to report to me when you return, but not immediately. De-brief with Lenzke, go about your normal business for a few hours, and then see me."

Dismissed, Jeremy thought.

Chapter 17 – Hijacked

"Hanna, where are you going?" Duncan asked. Hanna suddenly stopped and looked up. Duncan was looking at her with an expression that was somewhere between curiosity and suspicion. Hanna felt as if she had been daydreaming. She looked around, somewhat surprised that she was standing at all, and shocked that she was in Duncan's office. Duncan could read the surprise on her face.

"Are you okay?" he asked, quickly changing from suspicion to concern, and offering her a chair. She ignored him and remained standing. "Have you been getting enough sleep?" he continued.

Hanna shook her head. "It's not that," she said. "I wasn't sleeping. I don't know what I was doing." She looked around, as if there might be a clue lying on the floor, then she grabbed her head with one hand and the edge of the desk with the other. Duncan immediately stepped closer, ready to catch her if she fell. She changed her mind and sat down in the chair.

"What's amiss, lassie?" Duncan said with genuine compassion, inadvertently reverting to his natural accent. Hanna sat in silence. Duncan gave a meaningful head-signal to Levi, who had come to the door. He rushed off.

"I ... I don't know what I was doing here, Duncan. I wasn't trying to ...."

"Now, now, don't worry about that," he shook his head. "How are you feeling?"

"Strange," was all she said, and continued to stare blankly ahead. Duncan stayed by her side until Levi returned with MacKenzie and another of Duncan's staff, who immediately knelt down in front of Hanna, took her pulse with one hand and examined her eyes with the other.

"Did she faint?" he asked.

"No. At least she didn't swoon," Duncan said. He turned to MacKenzie and whispered his suspicions. MacKenzie knelt down next to Hanna and took her hand.

"I didn't think of it before, Hanna, but we never did test your implant programming after you were kidnapped. Will you let me look things over?" Hanna just squeezed MacKenzie's hand and smiled. In a matter of minutes it was MacKenzie who looked as if she needed the nurse. She was in genius mode, searching every nook and cranny of Hanna's implant protocols.

"Somebody has done a serious job on her implant," MacKenzie said after a few minutes. "I can't even begin to figure out what it all did, but I've saved it for reference and set everything back the way it's supposed to be."

Hanna looked up at MacKenzie with disgust and concern. "So what do you think happened?"

"I can't say, but it looks as if somebody's reconfigured your implant to receive some kind of signal -- one I've never seen before. But don't worry now, I've fixed it." She turned quickly to Duncan. "I thought these people who kidnapped Hanna were friends of yours."

Duncan drew a deep breath. "Not friends," he said sadly, "just useful acquaintances. But we've had somewhat of a falling out recently. I can't vouch for what they do." He stared long and hard at MacKenzie before continuing. "I assume we can monitor the frequency they were using, in case they try to send anything else to Hanna."

"Yes," MacKenzie said. "I'll be watching it."

*   *   *

Compared to field work, wandering around the agency office looking for net spies was positively exciting. Jeremy's preconceptions about the glamour of "real spy work" crumbled under a suffocating load of boredom. It was even worse that he knew he was supposed to sabotage the mission before they really did anything.

Most of the day was spent sitting and waiting. The "contact area," as Taylor called the one-bedroom apartment that was the center of their surveillance, was on the corner of a sleepy intersection in Northeast Washington. It was sleepy now, anyway. Early in the morning it was full of business traffic, but for the last four hours there had been almost no activity.

Jeremy's day had started well before dawn. He arrived at the apartment in a hovercar and made a preliminary sweep of the building. Getting in was easier than he had expected -- no one asked him for identification, whether or not he lived in the building or who he was visiting. He had walked all the hallways and stairs of the small, three-level complex accompanied by two of the agency's net spies.

That was a strange experience -- walking along next to the invisible net spies, and actually to work with them. He was accustomed to thinking of them as the enemy. It was even more jarring when they contacted him over the hole. Taylor told them all to remain in continuous chat mode while the operation was going on. It was eerie to be "speaking" with a person that you could see, but who wasn't really there.

Jeremy had to do one more sweep of the apartment later in the day, and then he took up his station. The apartment was on the narrow end of a triangular city block. Jeremy sat in a hovercar parked close to the apex. From there he could watch the entrances on both streets as well as the roof. Jeremy reminded Taylor that a net spy could approach the block from the base of the triangle and enter the corner house through the walls. Jeremy would never see him if he came that way. Taylor admitted the possibility, but it didn't seem to bother him.

"Risk is part of the job," was all he had said.

Jeremy thought all the preliminary work was a bit overdone, especially for an operation that was supposed to take no more than fifteen seconds. A net spy could show up at any time, of course, and the fact that one wasn't there at 10:00 didn't mean one wouldn't come by at 3:30. Of course there might be high-traffic areas, so the surveillance might do some good, but no amount of surveillance could prevent a net spy from coming at just the wrong time.

Taylor just wanted to be confident that this location wasn't on a major route, or near an area the other side liked to patrol. Then he could be more confident the operation wouldn't be interrupted, and that was enough.

After hours of watching and waiting, the target finally arrived. A hovercar taxi pulled up and a man got out. Jeremy thought he recognized him, but he wasn't able to see his face. Once the man was inside, Taylor contacted the team.

It's show time. All clear?

Clear, Jeremy replied, looking around again. He knew he had to abort the operation soon, but he wanted to wait to see if he got any more clues about what the "operation" was. As in most field missions, he only knew what he had to know to do his part of the job.

The other stations reported clear as well. Jeremy wasn't sure what to expect now, but he had a good idea. They weren't going after property, but the person who had just entered the building.

One of the windows on the left side of the apartment building brightened as someone inside turned on a light. Jeremy noticed that the light was reflected in the window of a large delivery vehicle. By chance, the reflected light gave Jeremy a clear view of the man's face. It was Dr. Jenkins.

They're going to kill Jenkins, he thought, and he was suddenly afraid he might have waited too long. The light in the window went dark.

Abort, Jeremy sent. *I see two net spies entering the building from the North side.*

Taylor responded immediately.

Scatter. Chat mode off.

"Scatter" was an agency word for beating a hasty retreat. Jeremy mechanically performed the procedures -- he darkened the windows of his hovercar, discarded chat mode on his implant and ran the pre-programmed escape route on the hovercar's navigational system. But his mind was elsewhere. Had he acted in time, or was Dr. Jenkins lying dead in his apartment, killed as a consequence of Jeremy's curiosity?

He knew the "operation" was going to be rough, but this was different. He almost knew Dr. Jenkins, and now, except for a curious twist of fate, he would have been an accomplice to his murder. What had the man done to deserve this? Jeremy would probably never know, he realized. Certainly Lenzke wasn't going to tell him.

There had been no trial, just an execution for reasons deemed sufficient by the agency, in its sole, unfettered discretion. Jeremy had flattered himself with the notion that the agency simply kept order in Society. But was this the price of order?

Order, he thought. *That's Lenzke's problem. He wants to impose his version of order on everything he touches.*

For a moment he was angry that the agency thought he would participate in such a thing. But then he realized that he might have had no choice. Jeremy was no saint. He had killed a man, and Lenzke knew all about it. Could that be held against him here, in Society? Or maybe Lenzke thought Jeremy's conscience had been dulled by the experience.

But I had cause, he thought. *The man raped and murdered my wife.*

And we had cause, Lenzke's voice replied in Jeremy's thoughts, and Jeremy knew that Lenzke would have some excuse; some justification for killing Dr. Jenkins, just as Jeremy had justified his murder of Samuel Weatherstone. Both acts were illegal, and Jeremy had fled the Community rather than face the charges. But were they moral?

Mine was. Jeremy had convinced himself of that fact over and over again. Weatherstone was going to go free for his crimes because there had been a mistake gathering the evidence. But he deserved to die. He needed to die.

But what about Jenkins? Was murdering him justifiable? The problem was that he would never know. But as he thought about it he realized the key difference between killing Weatherstone and killing Jenkins. There had been consequences to his actions. Jeremy knew he was going to have to face the criminal justice system for what he had done. The Community had permitted him to choose banishment instead of facing trial, but there had been consequences: he had renounced the jurisdiction of the Community and fled the only life he had ever known. But the agency, and Lenzke in particular, answered to no court.

Jeremy remembered a line from his history lessons. "Power corrupts, and absolute power corrupts absolutely." An earthly power that answers to no higher tribunal is bound to be corrupt.

Jeremy's mind was made up. He closed his left eye, took a piece of paper from his pocket and wrote a short note as the hovercar continued on its journey.

*   *   *

Jeremy followed standard procedures to be certain he hadn't been followed from the scene of the operation back to the agency office. He found it odd that he should go through such a routine when he had every intention of betraying the agency to its enemies as soon as he returned, but a breach of procedure would only call attention to himself.

After his de-briefing with Taylor and Lenzke -- who was hopping mad they hadn't pulled off the mission and wanted immediate plans drawn for a follow-up -- he went straight to the supply room to see Henry.

"I'd like to take you up on your offer," Jeremy said. "Can you make sure this gets out?"

Henry smiled the satisfied smile of a man who wanted and expected to be taken up on his offer. "You got it."

"And ..." Jeremy began, but Henry cut him off.

"That's understood," Henry replied. "Have you looked into the Harlot yet?"

Jeremy was confused for a moment. "Do you mean from the Apocalypse? Yeah. Are you saying that's the kind of woman Lenzke's hanging out with?" Jeremy was hoping Henry didn't think Dr. Berry *was* the woman of Rev. 17.

"Two peas in a pod," Henry said.

Jeremy nodded, thoughtfully. He gave Henry a look that said "thanks." Henry nodded.

*   *   *

"Look what I got today," Hanna said to MacKenzie. She was holding a plain, business-sized envelope with no return address. "I picked it up at the post office." She had set up a post office box to receive letters from Jeremy, just in case. She was sure the conspiracy would be keeping an eye on her dorm room for a little while, so she didn't want anything from him going there. It wouldn't do to have one of their intruders see the envelope.

"Should we show it to Duncan first?" MacKenzie asked.

"It's addressed to me," Hanna said with a mischievous smile.

Dear Hanna and MacKenzie,

It's been a long time. I'd like to get together. Since, as I explained before, there's no way you can visit me, I hope to drop by soon. I should be free on Saturday. There's a nice restaurant three miles due west of where we met last time. Please meet me there for dinner.

Jeremy

"I don't get it," MacKenzie said. "Is this some kind of code? And are we being set up, or does he want to help us?"

"I don't know. My first thought is to look at a map and see if there's a restaurant three miles west of here," Hanna said.

Duncan devoted one corner of the office -- next to the VR tanks -- to a detailed, holographic map of the D.C. area. It reminded all his intruders that they needed to know the area like the backs of their hands to be effective. Hanna and MacKenzie studied it carefully. There were several buildings three miles west. They selected these with the laser pointer and read the details on the pop-up view screen. It gave the name of the building's address, any other public information about it, like its hole address, and any notes Duncan's intruders thought to enter.

None of them was a restaurant.

"We're going at this all wrong," Hanna said. "Jeremy didn't know where he met us. At least we hope he didn't. So he can't mean three miles west of *here*."

They looked back and forth at each other, at the letter and at the map, trying to figure out what was going on.

"Hey, wait a minute," Hanna said. "Look at this." She pointed to an Italian restaurant farther to the left.

"But that's way farther than three miles west of here," MacKenzie objected. But then she saw it too. "I see. It's three miles west of the campus cafeteria. But we didn't meet him there."

"Exactly," Hanna said, and rushed off to Duncan's office. MacKenzie followed, glancing back at the map and trying to figure out what Hanna was up to.

Hanna showed Duncan the note from Jeremy. He read it quickly and then looked up at her and MacKenzie. "I don't get it," his expression said. Hanna took Duncan and MacKenzie back across the warehouse to the holomap.

"Look at this," she said. "There's no restaurant three miles west of here, which is where we really met with Jeremy." She indicated the warehouse with the laser pointer. "But there is a restaurant three miles west of the cafeteria."

"And that means?" Duncan asked.

"I think he's spooked," Hanna explained. "He's afraid that someone might intercept his letter, so he's written it so that even if somebody in the conspiracy did get a hold of it, it'll just look like he's trying to set up a date. But he's really giving us the location of the new office."

MacKenzie shook her head, confused, but Duncan looked on with interest. Hanna traced her finger down to the bottom of the map. "This is where their office was set up before," she said. "To the west there isn't much -- just houses -- until you get here, three miles away." She pointed to a small cluster of office buildings.

Duncan smiled at her. "Their new location. Very good. We'll check it out later."

*　　*　　*

Despite his misgivings, Jeremy enjoyed being back at the agency office. He was growing to dislike and distrust the agency itself, but he enjoyed interacting with the people. He was back on patrol now, walking the halls, continuing his somewhat pointless questioning about implant interference. But he enjoyed it more than field work.

He knew he had to meet with Peter, but he had told him to wait a little while. As Jeremy walked the hallways he noticed that the office construction was finished. All signs of remodeling were gone. If he had slept through the evacuation of the old office and been placed in this new one, he would never have known that the agency had moved. It was identical, as far as he could tell.

After several hours of wandering the halls he decided it was time for a break. Returning to his office, he thought he saw something in one of the hallways and stopped for a better look.

"Is something the matter, Mr. Mitchell?" one of the support staff asked.

There was. Jeremy could clearly see four net spies at the other end of the hall, apparently talking amongst themselves. He couldn't make out faces very well, but he was certain that one of them was Hanna.

"No," he said. "Nothing's the matter."

"Will you be needing anything then, sir?"

"Yes, actually, thank you. Would you bring a bowl of onion soup to my office?"

"Certainly, sir," the man said, and headed off towards the kitchen.

A few minutes later, Jeremy was picking through the cheese on the top of his French onion soup and using his implant to search for news of the death of Dr. Jenkins. He knew that as he relaxed in his office, at least four net spies were roaming the building.

Chapter 18 – Global Trouble

Jeremy awoke from sleep on the couch in his office to the sound of light tapping on the door. He put on a pair of pants and checked his implant. It was 1:10 a.m. *Who could that be?* he wondered.

"Open," he said. The door mechanism hissed as the pneumatic pistons filled with air. His room was dark, and he expected the bright light of the hallway to pour in and blind his eyes. Instead, he saw the silhouette of a medium-sized man framed in dim light from the hall. He didn't wait to be invited, but came in quickly, pressing the manual close switch.

"Dr. Jenkins is alive, it seems," Peter's voice said.

"Lights," Jeremy said, sitting up and reaching for his shirt. The automated lights instantly came up to their day-time brightness.

"Yes. I aborted the mission in time. I was concerned that I might have waited too long."

"So you knew it was Dr. Jenkins?" he asked. "You weren't supposed to know that."

Jeremy explained what had happened, and how the reflection in the truck window just happened to give him a view of Dr. Jenkins' apartment. Peter shook his head.

"You can't plan everything. No matter how hard you try, something like that can always ruin an operation. We didn't want you to know that it was Dr. Jenkins because we knew you might have met him at Dr. Berry's office. I suppose you're having second thoughts about the agency right now." His voice was unemotional and unapologetic.

"Yes," Jeremy said. He let it hang in the air for a few moments, then continued. "Why did you approve a sanction against him?"

Peter shook his head, sadly, and now with a hint of apology. "I've given Lenzke far too much slack with the net spy project. He had intelligence reports that said Jenkins was about to blow our entire hole operation. Secretly, I wished he did, and had. But I have a commission from the president of the United States, Jeremy, and that commission is to be performed, even at the cost of human life. If Dr. Jenkins gets in the way, I'm authorized to take him out of the way. That's rough, I know," he said, looking him in the eye, "but that's life."

Jeremy had never seen Peter so morose, or so personal. He almost seemed human. He sat down next to Jeremy on the couch.

"But we've got a bigger problem on our hands," he said, assuming a more business-like demeanor. "Lenzke hasn't filed anything about his meetings with Dr. Berry. That's a serious breach of procedure. That he would do such a thing implies things I'd rather not consider."

Jeremy was still shaking off the effects of his sleep. He was new to this spy game, and he couldn't decide what Peter was talking about. What did it imply?

"I don't follow you," he said.

Peter shook his head. "For Lenzke to be seeing one of our field contacts like this implies one of two things. Either he has a callous disregard for procedures, or he is involved in something that goes above -- or through -- me. Unfortunately, Lenzke is a stickler for procedures."

"So you think he's threatening you?"

"That's a possibility I have to consider, but I can't wait around to find out," Peter said, suddenly standing, with a look of cold determination and hidden energy. "We need to talk to Dr. Jenkins -- you and I. I've arranged things. We're leaving in 10 minutes. Get yourself ready."

*　　*　　*

Duncan's office didn't have any of the standard group-display equipment MacKenzie had access to at school. Her computer science professors always insisted that part of writing a brilliant program was making a brilliant presentation to a group -- otherwise you'd never get the project out of development and into commercial practice -- so they required all the students to make monthly presentations on their work to a mixed crowd of students and professors. MacKenzie hated those presentations. She wasn't much of a public speaker, and frequently asked Hanna to come along and give her pointers. But she was glad of the experience now.

MacKenzie had made a major breakthrough on tracking the intruders, and Duncan wanted her to explain it to the entire staff of his organization. She and Hanna woke up before dawn, and they spent hours trying to rig a projector that would be something like the one MacKenzie used at school. A normal broadcast, using the implants, was out of the question, and MacKenzie didn't like the interface with the holoprojectors.

As they worked, Hanna interjected several pointers on making the presentation and was pleasantly surprised at how willingly MacKenzie took them to heart.

While MacKenzie put the finishing touches on the make-shift projector, Hanna gathered bed sheets to make a suitable projection screen. It was crude, low-tech, and looked remarkably out of place next to the sophisticated computers against the east wall of the warehouse, but it would do.

Gathering a crowd for the presentation was the easiest part. The "in-house" staff -- those who lived on the premises -- were naturally curious and somewhat amused by the display of low-tech theatrics, and it was difficult to keep them away. As the rest of the morning shift arrived by hovercar, they gladly joined in the carnival atmosphere. Someone happened to bring in several dozen donuts, and the morning's work was largely shot. Duncan disapproved of the waste of time, but he decided to make the best of it and joined the rest of his staff.

MacKenzie stepped in front of the "projection screen," donut in hand, and waited for everyone to calm down.

"Sorry about the low-budget props," she said, gesturing towards the bed sheets, "and I assure you that Hanna will re-make all the beds she raided." There were a few chuckles, and Hanna smiled. MacKenzie rarely came out of her shell in a group.

"Okay, to business. Most of you have been working on how to block the intruders from using the hole for their dirty deeds," she began. "I've seen most of that work, and I think we're close to a solution. Since you all seem to have that part of the problem well in hand, I've been working with Duncan on a different issue, namely, why can our intruders see their intruders sometimes and not others? Here's what I've figured out.

"The fact that we can see them at all implies certain things. Most importantly, it implies that their virtual location is available on the net, somewhere. You all know that -- I've seen it in your work. But how do we access that information? That's been the problem, because, as you all know, the VR program doesn't do all the work itself -- it interfaces with the VR goggles to determine virtual location, and we don't know how their goggles work. We only know two things for sure: they don't work the way ours do, and they don't work the way the ones on the open market do. If they did, we could locate their intruders easily.

"Several of you have gone through every line of the VR program code, trying to figure out how it knows where the enemy intruders are. I began to wonder if a solution could be found by looking at the implant locator," she said. The 'locator' was the term for the implant utility that allows a hole user to determine his precise location anywhere on the planet. "But let me ask you a question. How many of you use your locator?" No one raised a hand. "Why not?"

One of the technicians spoke up. "Because when you use your locator you're basically broadcasting your location to all the hackers out there," he said. "There's a black-market utility that lets you get a fix on anyone who uses the locator. I don't want people to know where I am."

"Right," MacKenzie said, "and it just so happens that I stumbled across a copy of that utility. But don't tell anyone," she said with a conspiratorial smile. "I took the thing apart line by line, looking for clues on how the VR program knows where the other intruders are. I didn't find anything, but I found a few subroutines that looked suspicious, and I began to tinker with them. I tried redefining variables, adding a line or two here and there, but nothing worked until I fed that black-market utility into our VR program." She heard a sharp intake of breath from someone in the crowd and quickly added, "A copy, of course. I didn't chance corrupting the working code.

"This is what I found," she said, and Hanna tossed another switch on the projector. The map of the United States suddenly showed about 20 pin-point lights. There were about seven of them in the Washington area, three in New York City, four in California, two in Denver and the rest scattered along the east coast.

"I'm not sure, but I think this means that we can see the other intruders when someone is running this nasty illegal program," she said. "But the bigger issue is that we can track them now. Each of these points of light represents an intruder. Duncan and I suited up and did a spot check last night."

There was an awed silence for a few minutes as every eye gazed at the map. This was a major breakthrough, and they all knew it.

"What are those lights over there?" Duncan asked. He was pointing to a section of wall to the left of the bed-sheet screen that had a cluster of several points of light. Hanna turned the projector to the right so the lights would fall on the screen. She got to Hawaii, but that wasn't far enough. She adjusted a few settings on the projector and went further east. In a moment she was displaying 16 points of light scattered around China.

"What cities are they?" Hanna asked.

"They're not cities," Duncan said. "They're military bases."

*　　*　　*

Jeremy had become accustomed to riding in darkened hovercars, not knowing where he was going or when he was going to get there. But riding with Peter was difficult. He managed to make Jeremy feel uncomfortable, despite his uncharacteristic friendliness and his obvious concern about Lenzke. Jeremy tried to sit quietly and review the briefing Peter had provided an hour before.

Lenzke had always been worried about funding for the agency, he had said. He wanted to develop an independent source of income so the agency's work wouldn't be threatened by changes in funding. Peter had refused his recommendations again and again. "We serve the government. If they cut our funding, we have no mission and we get other jobs." Lenzke always protested that the work of the agency was too important to be subject to the whim of politicians.

Peter was concerned that Lenzke was trying to pull something off behind his back to "fix" this funding problem, but Jeremy suspected there was a lot more to it than that. He recalled his talk with Henry about tensions in the office. Henry didn't act as if this was just an argument over money, or a political thing. That wouldn't justify his description of Dr. Berry. Jeremy remembered the language from the Apocalypse: "The great whore with whom the kings of the earth have committed fornication." "Kings of the earth" had an ominous sound to it. No, this was no intramural dispute about whose plan the agency was going to follow. This was much bigger.

The hovercar came to a stop. Peter gave Jeremy a serious nod before the doors opened. They stepped out of the car and into the night. Jeremy immediately recognized the place. They were walking up the steps to Dr. Jenkins' apartment.

"You must be Peter. Come in," Dr. Jenkins' cheerful, but somewhat sleep-deprived voice said after he opened the door. "Jeremy!" he continued, recognizing him. "Where have you been? And how are you feeling? Have you seen Dr. Berry recently?"

"No, I haven't, and in case you were thinking about it, please don't let her know that I'm here," Jeremy said quickly. "I don't know what she's told you, but I'm just fine, okay? I hope it'll all be clear to you before the night's over."

Dr. Jenkins gave him a concerned look, but he nodded and smiled. This made Jeremy feel even more guilty about his near-involvement in the man's murder. *I've got to see this crisis through,* he thought, *but no matter how it turns out, I'm quitting the agency. This work stinks.*

Dr. Jenkins ushered them into the living room and closed the door. He made apologies for the mess and cleared off a place for them to sit on the couch. Medical books, journals and other assorted papers had been stacked on every available surface. He picked up a heap of papers from the couch and wandered around for a minute looking for a place to put them. The entire room, except the floor, was terribly cluttered, but not dirty. Dr. Jenkins seemed to have an aversion to putting anything on the floor, for, after finding nowhere to deposit his arm full of papers, he went into a back room.

Jeremy glanced around and thought for a moment about his wife. She had been a miserable house-cleaner, but, fortunately for Jeremy, they never owned enough for their house to get quite this disorganized. But then he noticed that something was different about the mess in Dr. Jenkins' house. Amy, his wife, always left cups and dishes around the room. Sometimes even clothes. It had always bugged Jeremy. There was nothing like that here. It was disorganized, but it was clean.

Dr. Jenkins returned with a carafe of coffee and three cups, which he set on top of a few large books on the coffee table. Jeremy realized how odd it was that Dr. Jenkins had any books or papers at all. Dr. Jenkins noticed his confusion.

"You wouldn't believe how much implant work a doctor has to do in the course of a day," he said. "You're always checking patients' records, looking up the literature on something, or checking the specs on a new drug. Back when I was on staff at St. Michael's, I just couldn't bear to look at my implant for another second after I got off work, so I developed the habit of reading real books." He thumped his hand on a few. "But you didn't come here for chit-chat and coffee," he said, looking at Peter. "What can I do for you?"

"Have you ever seen this man?" he asked, and handed him a pocket-sized work pad with a picture of Lenzke.

"Yes, I've seen him. I hope he's not your sister's husband."

"No. Let me remind you, this is official government business," Peter said, handing Dr. Jenkins a holographic identification card. "Do you know his name, and where have you seen him?"

"I suppose you know already," Dr. Jenkins said, losing even more of his good natured smile. "His name is Carl Lenzke, and he's been seeing my associate, Dr. Berry."

"Seeing her? Are they romantically involved, or are they business associates?" Peter asked.

Dr. Jenkins snorted a laugh. "You don't know Dr. Berry. I guess I'd have to say both."

"I want to remind you, as we discussed earlier, this conversation never happened," Peter said. Dr. Jenkins nodded. "Very well," he continued. "We have reason to suspect that Dr. Berry and Mr. Lenzke are involved in illegal hole traffic. Have you seen anything that would make you suspect that something like that was going on?"

Dr. Jenkins' face suddenly turned pale. He looked away, stared blankly at a wall to gather his thoughts, then turned back, his face composed.

"I was hoping I was wrong," he said. "I hoped I was misreading things, but yes," he looked up, "I've seen a few things that I've wondered about." Peter's look said, "such as?" so Dr. Jenkins continued.

"Dr. Berry and I do a lot of research on the implants, so we have some pretty impressive computers in the office. One day I was working late, and I don't think Dr. Berry knew I was there. I heard Carl's voice -- Mr. Lenzke, that is -- and I noticed they were both at one of the workstations. I overheard something they said. Something about 'our man in Taipei,' and something else -- I can't think of the words right now, but somehow it made me suspicious. Something came up, and they went into Dr. Berry's office. I slipped in and peeked at the workstation.

"What I saw on the screen looked like an automated search, at first -- just like the ones Dr. Berry and I do sometimes. But then I noticed the background. I could see the back of a hovercar seat *behind* the workstation desktop, and then I realized what I was seeing. The workstation was displaying the image of what someone with an implant would see through their left eye if they were working on a project, sitting in a hovercar. I was impressed with the graphics, but I thought it was just a computer model to simulate what a person *might* see. I didn't even suspect that anyone was *actually* seeing it until about a week later.

"I was in early that day, and Dr. Berry and Mr. Lenzke were at the same workstation. I overheard her say, 'And this is what he's seeing right now?'

"I'll tell you, it put me in a cold sweat. I've been trying to convince myself since then that it didn't mean anything, but now here you come asking me about it."

So is that how she knew what was going on with me? Jeremy thought. *Was Lenzke feeding her information from the net spies that followed me in the park that night?*

"Dr. Jenkins," Jeremy said, "do you remember the night Dr. Berry ordered me committed to the hospital?"

"Yes," he said.

"Was she with Lenzke that night?"

"I'm sorry, I can't be sure. I left the office early that day and didn't hear about the order until the next morning."

Jeremy shook his head. *How am I ever supposed to sort all this out?*

"So you think Dr. Berry and Mr. Lenzke are spying on what people can see with their implants?" Dr. Jenkins asked Peter.

"It's far worse than that," Peter said, "but I'm afraid I'm going to have to contradict what Mr. Mitchell said earlier. We can't explain it all to you right now. I hope we can later." Jeremy knew that was a lie. "But did either of them say anything else that might indicate what they're up to? Anything at all?"

"Yes, as a matter of fact," Jenkins said. "Just yesterday I heard them say something about 'making their move.' I have no idea what that meant, but that's what they said."

"Okay. Can you think of anything else?" Peter persisted. "Any detail, even if it seems trivial."

He thought for a minute and sipped at his coffee. "No, I'm sorry," he said, "but I can try to keep my eyes open for you, if you like."

"That's very tempting. We could use some inside information, but I can't ask you to do that," Peter said. "In fact, I'd like you to leave the country at once. Your life is in grave danger." Dr. Jenkins looked at him with a curious expression. "You may not know this," Peter continued, "but just yesterday an assassin tried to kill you. Mr. Mitchell was able to prevent him from getting to you."

Dr. Jenkins started to laugh, and then caught himself, realizing that Peter was serious. "You know," he said, "there was a strange man who tried to push into my room last night. He reached in and turned off the lights, and then just ran away. I thought he was some kind of nut." He looked at Jeremy and Peter seriously for a minute. "I'm not sure if I'm supposed to believe you," he said, "but thanks, Jeremy." Jeremy felt ashamed of himself, but he smiled.

Dr. Jenkins looked aside for a moment as he opened a hole message from Peter.

"London?" he asked. "You're sending me to London?"

"The flight is prepaid. It's not bad this time of year," Peter said. "And I think you ought to go. Now. I'll reimburse you for any out-of-pocket expenses. And in fact, we should be leaving as well, unless you can remember anything else from Dr. Berry or Mr. Lenzke."

"No," he said, still glancing at the message on his desktop, "I'm afraid not. If I come up with anything, where can I reach you?" Peter showed him his I.D. card again, and he copied the address into his mail utility. He took a last swallow of coffee, and then rose to leave. Jeremy and Dr. Jenkins followed.

"Oh, there is one other thing," he said. "I'm not sure if it's relevant, but I heard Dr. Berry and Mr. Lenzke say something about selling short on Cheung Kong. I don't know what that means, but that's what they said."

"Thank you very much, Dr. Jenkins. If you think of anything else, please send me word. Right now, you've got a plane to catch."

As Peter and Jeremy walked back out of the apartment and down the brick walk, Jeremy asked Peter if he'd learned anything important.

"Absolutely," he said. "I don't have an agent in Taipei. It's sounding more and more as if Lenzke's running a rogue operation inside my agency. If he's been running the net spy program behind my back, there's no telling what assets he's got out there."

"And what's the significance of Cheung Kong?" Jeremy asked.

"It's a major Chinese stock. You sell short when you expect it to go down."

Chapter 19 – In the Wilderness

Jeremy and Peter stood in silence on a street corner, waiting for the hovercar to come back. Jeremy was beginning to wonder whether the enemy was really the agency, or maybe just Lenzke. Peter was tough, but he wasn't convinced he was heartless or cruel, and he wasn't at all sure, now, that he was responsible for the things MacKenzie and Hanna had told him about. From a calculated, operational standpoint, he was wrong to give Dr. Jenkins those plane tickets -- it exposed the agency to more risk of detection by Lenzke and Berry. Furthermore, whatever risk there was to Jenkins' life was worth the additional information he might be able to feed to them.

After all, he thought, *he just signed the guy's death warrant yesterday.*

But that was yesterday. Something was fundamentally different today. Something had clicked in Peter's mind, it seemed to Jeremy. Yesterday, Lenzke was a trusted subordinate. Today, he's the loose cannon who's doing God knows what. If Lenzke had been running a secret operation, maybe it was Lenzke that Duncan was after, and not Peter at all. Maybe, in fact, Peter and Duncan were allies in this fight, or at least co-belligerents.

Peter believed in order and procedures, but he submitted that order to appropriate authority. So Jeremy reckoned. Lenzke, on the other hand, seemed to believe in procedures only because they suited him. What he really believed in was power. The Community was his practice run, and now he's trying for the world. To Lenzke, his ideals, his plans, were more important than such abstract concepts as right and wrong. What would that kind of man do with power, Jeremy wondered. He was the type who would manipulate people -- even governments -- to do his will.

The more he thought about it, the more Lenzke's fingerprints seemed to be all over the evils that Duncan wanted to stop.

"You're going to have to fire me, you know," Jeremy said aloud.

"I haven't filed all my contact reports either. I've had contact with some people in the network."

"I know," Peter said coldly. "Tonight was your last chance to come clean. I'm glad you chose to trust me, Jeremy." The hovercar pulled to a stop at the curb. Something approaching a smile crossed his face. "For the first time, we're really working together."

*   *   *

Peter gave a voice command to the hovercar to take them to Boise. Jeremy didn't bother to ask what was in Boise, or why they were going there at 2:00 in the morning, but the two-hour journey would give him time to tell his story, including everything he knew about Hanna, MacKenzie and Duncan. Taking Lenzke down was the number one priority now, and Jeremy suspected that Duncan knew more about Lenzke's operation than Peter did. Besides, he had a growing suspicion that Peter wasn't the bad guy.

When Jeremy finished telling Peter all about his contacts with Hanna and MacKenzie, and everything he knew or suspected about their operation, Peter sat back in the hovercar and stared blankly into space. He remained that way for so long that Jeremy thought he had fallen asleep with his eyes open, or was in some kind of trance. But he suddenly turned and looked at him.

"What is your analysis of our situation?"

Jeremy shook his head. "I think we're toast. I'm not exactly sure what Lenzke's up to, but the conspiracy sounds so carefully planned, I doubt he's failed to protect himself against a straight-forward attack from you."

"Agreed," Peter said. "He would have anticipated that, and he would have someone in place to take me out of the way if I came in and tried to shut him down." Jeremy was amazed at how matter-of-factly he referred to his own death.

"And another thing," Jeremy said, "if he has agents in the field, and if he's ready to make his move soon, we've got very little time to stop him, if that's possible at all. I think we have no choice but to go outside the agency for help."

"Agreed," Peter said in that dry, analytical tone. "And the only logical choice is your friend Duncan. None of the other intelligence agencies are likely to have as much information on him. We need to contact him right away."

*   *   *

Hanna curled up around her body-length pillow, covered with a quilt her grandmother made for her on the day she was born. She had the top bunk. MacKenzie, on the bottom, felt more comfortable with the latest high-tech sleepwear -- a computer-generated and maintained bubble of air, warmed to her specifications, and slightly scented.

Hanna jolted awake.

EMERGENCY Message from Jeremy. cc MacKenzie. Chat mode requested.

She sat up in bed, unsure what had just happened. She was in the habit of turning off her mail routines before she slept, but the settings she selected allowed "emergency" messages to get through. She had never been awakened by her implant before, and she was very confused. *Was that Jeremy's voice?* she thought, and then wondered if it was just part of her dream.

EMERGENCY Message from Jeremy. cc MacKenzie. Chat mode requested, the implant repeated.

Accepted, she sent immediately, and nearly jumped out of her bed to wake MacKenzie. She tried to shake her awake, and then, realizing that it was futile, turned savagely on the alarm clock.

"Brew, you stupid thing," she yelled. Much to her surprise, the unorthodox voice command worked. She could hear the daily dose of beans rattle into the grinder: the engine began to hum like an old jet plane, and she saw the "hot water" light turn on.

Hi Hanna. Sorry to wake you. Something big is happening soon, and we need to work together. Are you anywhere near Duncan? Can you wake him?

Work together? Hanna sent. *What do you mean?* Had he forgotten that they were on opposite sides?

I'm sitting in a hovercar with the director of the agency. He's not the problem, Hanna, I promise you. We're dealing with a rogue agent. He's been running the net spy operation and he's got some plot he's hatched with Doctor Berry. We need your help to stop him.

Just a minute, Hanna sent. MacKenzie was just getting up as the water began to pour through the freshly ground beans and the delicious smell filled the room. Hanna tried to explain the situation to her as quickly as she could, but MacKenzie just shook her head and said, "Give me access to your mail account." Hanna agreed and MacKenzie quickly read the chat dialog between Hanna and Jeremy. In a moment she was pouring herself a mug of coffee and monitoring as Jeremy and Hanna resumed their conversation.

Jeremy, I hate to ask this of you, but we need some sign that this isn't a set up. Some sign of good faith.

MacKenzie gave Hanna the thumbs up. There was an awkward silence for a moment as they waited for a reply. On the other end, Jeremy was talking it over with Peter.

We believe the agent's operation has something to do with China. I can't tell you more right now.

Hanna's heart skipped a beat. "Wake up Duncan," Hanna said to MacKenzie. "Hurry."

*　　*　　*

"Boise?" Duncan said. "Boise? What in the world is in Boise?"

"Peter and Jeremy, as far as I know," Hanna explained. MacKenzie had brought him, wrapped in a robe, straight from his bed into their apartment. "Look, Duncan, things are coming to a head. There's no time to be cautious, now. It's too much of a coincidence that MacKenzie discovered that the intruders are in China, and then

Jeremy tells us something big is about to happen over there."

"Yeah, that's just the point," Duncan said. "It's too much of a coincidence. I feel like I'm being set up. This 'Peter' person would love to hang my hide on his office wall, I'm sure."

Hanna didn't know if this approach was going to work with Duncan -- she hadn't had any meaningful talks with him, so she had no idea where he stood on such matters -- but she couldn't hold it in any more. "Yes, you are being set up, Duncan, but not by Peter or Jeremy. If you believe they're clever enough to contrive coincidences like that, then I say it's time to surrender -- there's no fighting against people like that."

"So who?" Duncan said. "Who's setting me up? Dr. Berry?"

Hanna shook her head in amazement. *This is what St. Paul meant about suppressing the truth,* she thought.

"No," she said. "Providence. God. Ever heard of Him?"

Duncan stood impassive against Hanna's fit of temper. Then he frowned for a solid minute. Hanna didn't know what to think. She just waited.

"You don't believe in coincidences, do you?" Duncan asked.

"'God foreordains whatsoever comes to pass,'" she recited, "but I don't believe we can understand the purpose behind every seeming coincidence. There comes a point, though, where you have to recognize that God is doing something -- or letting something be done, anyway. Some things we just have to chalk up to 'chance,' but at a certain point, the odds get a little too iffy. Somebody's behind this, and I don't think it's the good doctor."

Duncan stared past Hanna into the nothing beyond. He turned to MacKenzie and looked at her for several seconds.

"And what do you think?" he said. "Can you think of a reasonable technological explanation for this? Is there any way Jeremy, or Peter, or somebody associated with them could have monitored your work this morning? Could they have known we suspected something in China?"

MacKenzie glanced at Hanna, and then gave Duncan a long look. "A month ago I'd have said no way. I took every precaution I could think of to keep my work secret. But I can't be absolutely certain. You have a pretty good mechanism in place to guard the warehouse against intruders, but who knows if they've been able to beat it? And there's always the possibility that they have some other technology we don't know about. It's an odd coincidence -- and I don't believe in coincidences either -- but I'm not as certain as Hanna that you can rule out human involvement. Somebody staged this coincidence, it seems, but I can't say who."

"Okay, technology isn't going to give us a firm answer, so let's turn to the softer sciences. What about Jeremy?" Duncan asked. "Do you know him well enough to say whether he'd lead us into a trap?"

Hanna and MacKenzie shared a troubled look. *I wish I did,* Hanna thought. Duncan could read her expression.

"Then we need something else," he said. "I have a feeling that we have to move on this one. No, Hanna, I haven't forgotten about Providence," he said, "but I've put a few more miles on my religion than you have, and I tend to doubt things that aren't as sure as sure. Maybe God arranged this, or maybe He allowed it to be arranged. He lets some suspicious characters into His counsel, from time to time." Hanna picked up the veiled biblical reference, and smiled. "So let's proceed, but let's be careful. We'll meet with Jeremy, but we'll propose another meeting place -- one that's a little safer."

*   *   *

"I know my geography lessons were based on old data, but isn't Boise a city?" Jeremy asked. When he and Peter stepped out of their hovercar at 4:00, he expected to be in a building, or on a street, or in a parking lot. Instead, he found himself in a small clearing in a wooded area. It was a moonless night, and somewhat cloudy. He couldn't see the stars well enough to get any bearing at all.

Peter laughed, and his laughter was a welcome relief from the tension of the last few hours. They had been going over their situation again and again, trying to figure out every conceivable interpretation of the data. Their best theory was that they were in serious trouble: Lenzke had consolidated a power base inside the agency, had rogue agents, and net spies, in the field under his sole control, had outside help, and was about to pull off a major operation that could have serious international implications. Furthermore, if he pulled it off, he would probably make a killing in the stock market and be able to fulfill his dream of running a truly independent agency.

They were past discouragement or depression. They were in that stage of passionless abandon where everything that could be done had been done, and the rest was up to the Fates.

"We're a few miles outside of Boise," Peter explained. "I like to come here from time to time to get away. There's a path just up that hill," he said, pointing off to his left. "I'd take you if there was enough light to see." Jeremy looked to his left, but he couldn't see the path. They sat in silence for a minute on the hood of the hovercar.

As Jeremy's eye grew accustomed to the dark, he began to get the feel of the landscape.

"You know," he said, "this place reminds me of a park I used to visit back home."

"In the Community?" Peter asked.

"Yeah. I went there with my wife on Sunday afternoons."

Peter ordered a cup of hot tea from the hovercar's mini-bar and sat down on the grass.

"Tell me about her."

Jeremy hung his head for a minute and collected his thoughts. "We were married for about a year before she died," he began, "but I knew her a lot longer than that. She was my best friend. We did everything together." Jeremy leaned back against the hood of the hovercar and looked at the sky, lost for a moment in the memory.

"Wait just a second, Jeremy," Peter said. For a second he almost sounded like a friend, but that phantom had passed. The head of the agency was speaking again, and Jeremy quickly sat up and looked at him, expectantly. "Was your wife's name Amy Mitchell?"

"Yes," Jeremy said. "Of course. But if you recognize the name, you must be thinking of someone else. Amy lived her whole life in the Community."

Peter held out his hand, signaling Jeremy to be quiet for a minute. He turned away, and then stiffened.

"You killed the man who murdered your wife, right?" Peter asked.

"How did you know that?" he asked, wondering if Lenzke had told his story.

"I didn't, but I remembered something from a report Lenzke filed a few months ago. He was working on a secret project -- advanced implant technology."

Peter slammed his hand against the roof of the hovercar with a curse. "I really shouldn't tell you about this, but I have to. We were working on a direct link to the human brain -- an advancement on the net spy technology. It was a very scary thing, let me tell you. Instead of sending verbal messages, it implanted the message straight into the subconscious mind. We could literally put thoughts into people's heads, but we had to abandon the project after an agent was killed. Give me another minute," he said, now obviously scanning something on his implant.

"Yes, here it is. Listen to this: 'Communication with agent Stormwater's implant has not been perfected. As a test of the brain feed, we directed him to perform surveillance on Sue Anderson. Stormwater's brain misinterpreted the signal and killed Anderson. Stormwater himself was killed by Anderson's husband.'"

The similarities were too striking to ignore. Weatherstone had become Stormwater. Amy, a three-letter woman's name, became Sue. Mitchell, a common surname, became Anderson. This was obviously an unartful re-write of Jeremy's experience.

Jeremy's hot blood was rising again.

"How did you make the connection with Amy's name?" he asked. "The report doesn't mention her."

"An earlier version of the report had her proper name. Lenzke corrected it, but somehow I remembered the original. I think he wasn't as careful about the names because the players were all in the Community. No one would have suspected that."

So Weatherstone wasn't truly responsible for his crime, it seemed. His brain misinterpreted a directive that Lenzke had fed him through his implant. But the thought that he had killed the wrong man didn't lead Jeremy to remorse. Weatherstone had been one of Lenzke's pawns. *And that's what happens to pawns,* he thought as his mind descended into dark thoughts of revenge.

Greg Krehbiel

Chapter 20 – Alliances

"They're willing to meet," Jeremy said as the sunlight began to give color to the cold countryside around the hovercar.

"Read it to me," Peter said.

"To Jeremy from Hanna," he said, reading the message out of his inbox. "The three of us, Duncan, MacKenzie and I, want to meet with you and Peter, but we want to meet you virtually, as net spies. That way there can't be any tricks. You pick the location, and we'll meet you there at 9:00."

"Clever," Peter said. "It's a good suggestion, but it exposes us to some risk." Jeremy looked confused, so he explained. "All the VR tanks are in the Washington office, and that means we might run into Lenzke, or one of his cronies." Jeremy's expression said that he would love to meet Lenzke this morning, but Peter read his thoughts and shook his head.

"This isn't the right time for that. There are more pressing concerns, Mr. Mitchell, than your private dispute with Lenzke. Is that clear?"

"Yes, sir," he said coldly, but he noted with satisfaction that he didn't rule out the possibility that another time would come.

"Good," he said. "Go ahead and agree to their terms. Just make sure you pick a private place -- the inside of a water tower, maybe. I don't want to take any chances. Who knows what other tricks Lenzke's got."

*　　*　　*

Duncan laughed when Hanna passed on Peter's suggestion of an underwater meeting, and the inside of a water tower seemed about as private as he could imagine.

MacKenzie spent her time before the 9:00 meeting on the intruder project, and she poured herself into it. Hanna, on the other hand, had nothing to do, and was getting nervous. This wasn't helped by the fact that she had started drinking coffee just after 2:00 in the morning. She had to do something to relax, and she realized that she hadn't checked the news for several days. She called up her favorite news site on the hole -- it was updated continuously by *The New York Times* and usually had some entertaining graphics.

The lead story made her heart stop. There had been a coup in China. The old government hadn't exactly been pro-American, but the new regime, based on preliminary reports, was positively bristling for a fight. Australia and India had gone on full military alert. China's first official act was to announce an immediate cessation of all trade with the United States until the U.S. government made certain concessions. The *Times* analysis piece that accompanied the report said it would be a cold day in Hell before the United States acceded to their demands, and that a serious trade war was inevitable.

A link to a series of graphics showed the impact the coup had on the financial markets. The average price of all shares had taken a hit on news of the coup, but the Chinese stock market had dropped through the floor. Investors were losing billions of dollars.

It's started, she thought. *We're too late.*

To Jeremy. Check the Chinese stock market this morning, she sent, and then ran to Duncan's office. She noticed that he had the stock figures up on his workstation, and he looked as if he had seen a ghost. When Hanna entered he looked at her, then theatrically made the sign of the cross and folded his hands in prayer.

*   *   *

The five figures would have been quite a sight if anyone could see them as they sat on the inside bottom of the Greenbelt, Maryland, water tower. They couldn't even see each other, since no one had thought to put a light on the inside of the reservoir. MacKenzie, who had missed the story about the market crash and didn't know how serious things were getting, had decided to be a wise-acre and programmed her VR suit to dress her in a hot pink scuba outfit. She looked quite fetching, Hanna had said as soon as they "left" the warehouse for the meeting sight, but Duncan was too wrapped up in his thoughts to notice, and Peter and Jeremy couldn't see her in the dark.

"Are you here yet?" Duncan asked as soon as the threesome arrived.

"We're here," Jeremy answered. "Peter is with me."

They settled themselves on the floor of the water reservoir.

"I assumed when you suggested that we meet virtually that you'd found a way to ensure that we'd see and hear each other," Peter said. "Congratulations, although it doesn't help us much here. That's something our computer specialists haven't figured out yet."

"Have you seen the market?" Duncan asked in a gruff voice. He wasn't in the mood for chit-chat.

"Yes. We may be too late," Peter said.

"Hanna said that we might have a common enemy; that one of your subordinates might be running your intruder network. Do you have any idea how large your intruder force is?" Duncan asked.

"I'm not sure ..." Peter began, but Duncan cut him off.

"There's no more time for secrecy, Peter," he said in an icy tone. "It's really hit the fan, now, and if we can't work together to stop this maniac, we might be facing a war. Tell me: How many intruders can you field at any one time?"

"Ten," he said, and then added in a humbled voice, "to my knowledge."

"Wrong," Duncan said. "You have 45 in the field right now. Would you like me to tell you where they are?"

There was a painful silence for a moment, and then Peter spoke. "Yes, I'd like to know."

"One is assigned to each of the incumbent President's potential rivals in the primaries. A few are monitoring Senators, or their political enemies. A few are watching businessmen in New York. We're not sure yet what they're up to. All the rest, more than 20, are in China, mostly at military installations. Now who is this lunatic who's doing this, and how do we stop him?"

"His name is Carl Maria Lenzke," Jeremy said, "and he's mine."

"Killing him isn't going to stop the damage, Jeremy," Peter said. "He's got other people working with him ...."

"Berry?" Duncan asked.

"Yes," Peter continued, "and lots more, but I don't have many names. What we need to do is find a way to block his use of the hole. Have you made any progress on that?"

There was silence in the dark tank for a full minute. Finally, Duncan spoke. "Let's go for broke, MacKenzie. Tell him what you've got."

MacKenzie tried to speak and realized she had a scuba regulator in her mouth. She spat it out, simultaneously reconfiguring her VR program to dress her more conventionally.

"Obviously I've found a way to locate intruders," she said. "Now that I can do that, we could broadcast their location to everyone. We could even attach a visual to the message, which would almost allow people to see the intruders, like Jeremy can. But that's a very temporary measure. What we really need to do is block out that bandwidth on the repeaters. If the visual information isn't broadcast to the net, the intruder technology is worthless."

"I'm not up on all the technical details, but I think I follow what you're saying," Peter said. "The implants are in contact with signal repeaters that send our individual datastream into hole traffic. The net spy protocols use that datastream to construct a VR image of the real world. But if we changed the repeaters so they didn't transmit the visual information, then the net spy programming wouldn't have any data to work with. Is there any way we can do that without replacing all the hardware? Can we just reprogram the repeaters remotely?"

"I don't think so," Duncan said. "We've protected our headquarters from your intruders by physically altering all the repeaters within signal range. It's not a simple operation. If it was, we'd have re-wired the District already. We have five workstations dedicated to monitoring what those three repeaters pick up and re-transmit, and sometimes it makes for spotty communications even at that. Our solution isn't feasible on a large scale."

"I'm afraid the news only gets worse," Peter said. "The intruders are only part of the problem. I have reason to believe that Lenzke has revived an experiment we ditched a few months ago. It allows us to send unmediated brain signals through the hole."

"What does that mean, 'unmediated brain signals'?" Duncan asked.

"It means the recipient doesn't even know he's received a message. It just goes straight into the brain. We officially abandoned the project a month ago because it was too risky, but I suspect Lenzke has been using it. It's hard to imagine that he could contrive the fall of the Chinese government just by spying on people. I've got to assume he's been controlling some people, and I know he has some operatives over there."

Duncan slammed his hand against the wall of the tank. "I thought we were closing in, but this sets us back, and we don't have time for it. What do you think, MacKenzie? Can we do anything about Lenzke's puppets?"

"I have no idea," she said. "I'd have to see how the thing works. But, before we move too far along here, I do have a possible solution to the intruder problem that I haven't discussed. Instead of altering the repeaters, we could just send a lot of noise over the bandwidths the VR programs use, which would completely mess up the visual signal."

"That sounds good," Jeremy said. 'Would it work?"

"What about this brain-link you've got, Peter," Duncan said. "Can you give any information on that to MacKenzie? She's a wiz with this stuff. If anybody can throw a wrench in it, she can."

There was an uncomfortable silence for some time. It was difficult enough carrying on a conversation in the dark, seemingly underwater. The VR suite made them all feel as if they were underwater, except when they spoke, which was a curious sensation. It was like trying to speak underwater, except that there were no bubbles, and the water never came into your mouth. But the silences were truly disconcerting.

Jeremy got impatient with Peter's delay. "Peter," he said, "are you still with us?" There was still no response. He reached over to where he had been sitting to shake him, but he couldn't find him. The rest of the underwater party began to suspect something was wrong and began to call out. Things were getting confusing.

Suddenly, Jeremy's received a message.

From MacKenzie. He must have turned off his suit. You'd better turn yours off and go see if everything's okay.

* * *

The VR suit was a new sensation for Jeremy, but leaving the dark, virtual water tank only to find himself blind, and floating in a real VR tank put him completely out of sorts. At first, he didn't know what to do, but then he remembered to throw the switch on his goggles. Suddenly, his eyes were adjusting to the light of the tank's targeting lasers, which made a pattern on his dark suit and on the inside walls of the narrow tank. Peter should be in the tank next door, and he'd have to get out to check on him. He depressed a switch on the back of his goggles which overrode the buoyancy control and made him float to the surface.

The lid to the tank automatically opened. The first thing he saw was a pair of women's ankles in high-heeled shoes. As the lid opened he saw the bottom of a skirt, and then more and more of Dr. Berry.

"And here's the other one," she said as Jeremy began to pull himself out of the tank. She lowered a steel-finished pistol and aimed it at his head. Jeremy was no gun expert, but the bore of the pistol barrel staring into his face seemed uncommonly large. "Just stay right there, Jeremy," she said. Lenzke was standing next to her with a shotgun. It was aimed straight at Peter, who was still floating in his VR tank.

"You haven't missed much, Mr. Mitchell," Lenzke said. "I was just explaining to Peter that he's a day late and a dollar short. My clever investment strategy has ensured the solvency of the agency for years, and with Peter dead, I'll be able to consolidate my hold on the agency staff. The only small thing standing in the way is that rag-a-muffin crew you've been hanging out with. Did you really think we hadn't tracked you to their headquarters? Did you really think I bought that story about taking a nap on the university lawn? Ha," he laughed. "Taylor and ten agents are ready to storm the facility this afternoon."

"And don't bother trying to warn them with your implant," Dr. Berry added. "We've cut off your hole communication."

"Yes. You'll find that Dr. Berry thinks of everything." He looked at her with obvious affection.

"What are you going to do with your new puppets in China?" Peter asked.

Lenzke laughed. "Don't be a fool,' he said. "I haven't got time to waste with you. I just wanted to take care of this part of the operation myself. You're such a fool, Peter -- a blind, soft fool," he said, looking at him with scorn. "You worry so much about rules and regulations, delegations of power and procedures. The world could fall into anarchy and you wouldn't do a thing unless you had a Congressional mandate. Well, my friend, the concept of the 'invisible hand' is taking on a new meaning. These hands will keep the peace, and order," he said, taking Dr. Berry's hand in his and holding them aloft.

He lowered the shotgun with his other arm and aimed at Peter's head. Jeremy knew this was the end, but he wasn't going to go without a fight. He reached for Dr. Berry's legs and tried to pull himself up. He was going to grab her gun -- probably too late -- but at least he would try. She offered no resistance, which surprised him, but as he leaped out of the tank, imitating a swim team move, he heard a series of shots. He was too late.

As he stood erect on the short deck that encircled the tops of the agency's VR tanks, Dr. Berry tossed her gun onto the deck and put her hands up in surrender. Jeremy was taken completely by surprise, and then he heard a voice laughing. He didn't know what to do until he saw Lenzke's body lying dead on the deck, four bloody holes in the back of his white shirt.

Chapter 21 – Endings

"I don't get it," Jeremy said.

"Dr. Berry was working for me, Jeremy," Peter said as he pulled himself out of the VR tank, dripping wet. He pushed Lenzke's body aside and looked down at it with contempt. "We had to play it out to the end to find out where all his assets were located, and we needed you to establish contact with Duncan and his group."

"So why didn't you move sooner, so you could have prevented the coup in China?"

"Don't worry about the Chinese," Dr. Berry said. "We manipulated the news reporting on the hole in the D.C. area," she continued, looking at the amazement on Jeremy's face. "Nothing has happened in China. You didn't think we were going to let the country come to the brink of a war, did you?"

"So you were a good guy all along?" he said, shaking his head.

"I'm beyond good," Dr. Berry replied. Peter smiled wickedly, but he put a consoling arm on Jeremy's shoulder. "I'm sorry we put you through so much, Jeremy. Once you understand it all, I think you'll see that it was necessary."

"I just want to know one thing," he said, looking down at Lenzke's dead body. "If you planned all this, why couldn't I have been the one to shoot him?"

*   *   *

"So what are they doing in there?" MacKenzie asked. She, Hanna and Jeremy were sitting, listless and silent, next to MacKenzie's workstation at Duncan's warehouse. Jeremy's head had been nodding slightly. He jerked up and looked around, his eyes wide. Hanna laughed at him.

"They've got a lot to work through," Hanna said. "They've thought they were enemies for months, and now it turns out they were on the same side. And so were we, it seems," she said, elbowing Jeremy in the ribs.

"I suppose," Jeremy said, preoccupied.

"You're not feeling guilty about working with Lenzke, are you?" MacKenzie asked.

Jeremy snorted his disdain for the thought. "I came here -- to Society -- to escape," he said, "but trouble just followed me. And then I had a glimmer of hope that I could get some vengeance for Amy's death." He had told them all about Amy and Weatherstone the night before. "But that didn't work out either. Now, I'm just tired. I feel as if I haven't had a good night's sleep for weeks."

Hanna reached out and took his hand.

Duncan's door opened a moment later and he, Levi, Peter and Dr. Berry came out, all smiles. They walked straight over to where the three friends were sitting.

"It's only fitting that you three should be the first to know," Duncan said, "considering all you've been through. We've been comparing notes from our operations, and we've got a pretty complete picture of what's been going on, and what to do about it."

"We should be able to keep the hole secure, and nobody will ever have to know what almost happened," Peter said, "except for a few of the good people of Washington, who'll need to know how the news got messed up this morning. We weren't able to control the transmission as well as we'd hoped."

"So what are you going to do now, Duncan?" MacKenzie asked. She had fallen in love with his computer lab, and she didn't want to lose her position with him.

"Peter needs to weed out everyone in the agency who's sided with Lenzke, and I need to find a new mission for my staff. We decided that makes a pretty good fit."

"And a pretty good reason for a party," Dr. Berry added.

*   *   *

That night, a chartered cruise ship worked its way up the Potomac towards the national monuments. Jeremy and Peter were standing at the railing on the port side, watching the reflection of the moon in the swirling water.

"I'm sorry I couldn't save Amy, Jeremy," Peter said, putting his arm on his shoulder. "I didn't even begin to suspect what Lenzke was up to until Weatherstone killed her. At least I managed to let you in on settling the score."

He shook his head. The victory seemed empty.

"So why can I see the intruders?" he asked.

"You have a special implant," Peter explained. "Dr. Berry knew what Lenzke was up to. She and Dr. Jenkins designed an implant that would read the visual information used by the net spy protocols. That's the one she put in you."

"And what about implant psychosis?" he asked.

"It's a terrible disease," Peter said. "Be thankful you don't have it."

He looked back into the water and thought.

"What were you doing messing with my Community, anyway?"

"Lenzke was in charge of picking the agent for the brain-link test. For security purposes, nobody knew where the agent was located, or who he was, except Lenzke. That was a big mistake on my part. Anyway, it turns out he had been doing some practice runs on the Community to get ready for the big operation. I didn't know about that. He began to control things and manipulate the politics of the Community. He was using you as guinea pigs."

"Humph," Jeremy said. "Arrogance. That was his downfall."

"Yeah," Peter said. "Power corrupts, but it can turn around and bite you, too."

"So what now? What are you going to do about the net spy

protocols?"

"We're going to dismantle them, and I'm going to work with Duncan, MacKenzie and Dr. Berry to make sure it can't happen again. I'll have to file a report with the President, and he might want my head on the White House gate, but if he doesn't, Jeremy, and if you're still willing, I'd love to have you work with me. We brought you into this because we hoped you could help us understand what Lenzke was up to. Since you were from his community," Jeremy bristled somewhat, and Peter retracted that -- "what he *thought of* as his community, I mean. Sorry. Anyway, he would have a natural feeling of ownership over you and be less suspicious that you were compromising him. Your role was somewhat different than we planned, but you turned out to be a real asset. You've got what it takes to be a good agent, Jeremy. You've still got a job, if you want it."

The cooperative, friendly Peter was back now. But Jeremy wasn't in the mood to be conciliatory. He just looked at the moon on the water.

"Think about it, okay? Can I get you anything?"

"Yeah," he said coolly. "A vodka and soda with lime."

Peter smiled and patted him on the back.

"I'll send it up to you." He went below decks as Jeremy continued to stare at the black water.

Despite Peter's offer, he didn't want to think about the future, or the past -- he just wanted to escape somewhere. He needed time to sort out what he was going to do with his life, and with whom. He wondered how things would shake out in the Community, now that Lenzke wasn't manipulating it. Did he want to go back? Society seemed terribly complicated, but right now it was hard for him to imagine going back to a simple, agrarian lifestyle.

What would he do if he stayed? Work for Peter? It was too early to think about that. There were too many other things to resolve first.

Where is my drink? he wondered, and looked back to the stairway that came from below deck, where the party was going on. Dr. Berry was standing at the head of the stairs with two drinks in her hands. She walked over to the railing and gazed out at the water.

"So, do you hate me?" she asked after a minute of sharing the view.

Jeremy looked at her again and smiled. "No. I just need some time to myself. Get away for a while. Relax. Swim. Ride a horse."

"Jeremy, I'm so sorry about all the things we had to put you through. Please believe me that it was necessary. A lot was at stake. Maybe more than you know, or ever will. Our plan might not have been the best, but it worked. And it's not as if Peter and I have had a joy ride these last few months."

Jeremy inhaled deeply and looked at the moon. He shook his head, smiled weakly, set down his drink and walked back down the stairs to the lower deck.

A 10-piece jazz band was playing "Begin the Beguine." Duncan, dressed in an expensive white tuxedo, was dancing with one of the women from the agency, and Duncan's staff was captivated at the sight, as if they'd never seen anything like it before. A few of the technicians from the agency surrounded MacKenzie, throwing questions at her in a very animated discussion. Hanna was talking to someone from Duncan's group -- he hadn't learned all their names yet -- but she noticed Jeremy coming down the stairs and kept glancing in his direction. Jeremy walked toward them, stopping to greet people along the way.

He stood beside Hanna as she continued to chat with a somewhat drunken computer specialist. He was obviously trying to find whatever piece of glory he could from the victory over Lenzke, although he didn't know who Lenzke was, or how he had been beaten in the end. Jeremy held out his hand.

"I'd like to thank you personally for your involvement in the operation," he said. "It was a tight squeeze at the end, but we wouldn't have made it without a lot of hard work from people like you." The man took his hand and shook it vigorously, smiling as if he'd just received an Olympic medal.

"I need another drink," the man said, and walked to the bar. Jeremy winked at Hanna, and they stood together in silence, enjoying each other's company.

"Look," Hanna said, "we're pulling into the dock."

"The party's supposed to go all night," Jeremy said, looking around. Several other people had joined Duncan and Peter on the dance floor. "And it doesn't show any signs of slowing down. But I was wondering if you'd be willing to go ashore with me. I feel like having a chocolate malt."

Hanna smiled. "Should I invite MacKenzie?" she asked.

Jeremy looked over in MacKenzie's direction. Dr. Berry had joined the throng of computer experts and was quizzing MacKenzie about something. MacKenzie, red-faced and laughing, nearly spilled her drink on Dr. Berry's dress.

"I think she's doing okay," Jeremy said.

"Well, I really ought to tell her we're leaving," Hanna persisted, and turned away to send MacKenzie a message. Jeremy watched MacKenzie as she straightened up a touch, and then looked toward Hanna. She raised her glass in a toast and winked at Jeremy.

"She says she's having a blast, and we should go enjoy ourselves."

They walked arm in arm down the gang plank onto the concrete quay. A row of hovercars were at their disposal, and they picked the closest one. They climbed in and told the hovercar to take its time getting to the Chocolate Bar.

END

If you enjoyed this book ...

… please give it a positive review on Amazon.com, Goodreads, Facebook, or wherever strikes your fancy, and please recommend it to (or purchase it as a gift for) family and friends.

About the Author

Greg Krehbiel is a happily married father of five wonderful children. He's had a distinguished career in professional publishing, including lengthy gigs in editorial, product development, IT and tech development, marketing, and audio and web conferencing. He has a degree in Geology and studied theology as preparation for ministry -- then thought better of it. He's a home brewer (beer, wine and mead), an occasional jogger, an avid writer, and enjoys camping and fishing.

About Crowhill Publishing

"Krehbiel" is a German name that roughly translates to English as "Crow Hill." Crowhill Publishing is the imprint for all of Greg Krehbiel's books. Find out more at http://crowhill.net.